The Shroud

By David W Moore III
based on a screenplay by
Joseph Patton Mashburn and Joseph Paul Ferina

Prologue

Italy
1046 A.D.

Abbot Thomas barely noticed the familiar echoes of the canto as he concentrated on the numbers in front of him. Winter would be upon them soon and he worried that their food stores would not be enough. Another barrel of grain had fallen prey to rats. At the very least, there were going to be some very thin monks come spring.

He put the quill down and stretched his neck. His large wooden desk was covered with reports, most with dire comments added by the Dean. *God will provide.* He had every winter before, but Abbot Thomas was of the opinion that God helped those who help themselves. Besides there wasn't much else he could do. The bishop had responded with generic sympathy to his letter requesting aid. The lack of subtlety in his retelling of the fable of the boy who cried wolf only belabored the futility of his request. Why was it that the lambs could cry hungry in the field while the shepherd could sell his post for money? With all the popes and anti-popes, it didn't surprise him that Benedict IX had abdicated to Pope Gregory VI in return for a large sum of money.

He was so deep in thought that he didn't hear Brother Stefano knocking insistently on his doorframe. After a full minute restlessly waiting to be acknowledged, Brother Stefano cleared his throat loudly, startling the abbot out of his reverie.

"Abbot..."

"Yes, Brother Stefano. What do you need this late at night that couldn't wait until morning?"

"You must come. Come at once," Brother Stefano hesitated as if struggling to find the right words. "You must see this yourself." He looked down at the floor subserviently as he finished the last statement as if he suddenly realized that he was commanding the Abbot.

Abbot Thomas studied the small man for a moment. His robes were disheveled. He realized that he had been struggling to catch his breath for the few minutes he stood before him. He might have noticed that earlier if he hadn't been so caught up in his musings. What could have this brother so agitated? He sighed.

"All right. Don't worry; Stefano, you and I have been brothers long enough for me not to take offense at mere words from you. What is this emergency that dictates my presence?"

"Come quickly. It's Brother David. He... His eyes..." Brother Stefano seemed at a loss again. "Just follow me. I've seen nothing like this before; I've only read of such things."

The abbot shut his book, stood up, and motioned Brother Stefano to lead the way. They hurried down the hall in silence. He had expected to get more of an explanation on the way, but Brother Stefano had said all that he would on the matter. The only sounds breaking the silence were the rustling of their robes and the slapping of their sandals on the cold stone floor.

As they approached Brother David's cell, the air became denser, somehow thicker. The light that came through the doorway was whiter than candlelight should have been. It was as if it were daylight beyond the threshold instead of almost midnight. *What is going on?* Still hesitating outside the door, he heard sounds of a quiet struggle inside.

Abbot Thomas steeled himself against whatever might be waiting for him on the other side and pasted a look of calm confidence on his face. Brother Stefano impatiently urged him forward. Once inside, the first thing he noticed was the two monks struggling on the cot set along the wall to his right. Brother Timothy was holding Brother David in a prone position, but not without a lot of effort. The abbot's glance darted about the rest of the cell that was significantly smaller than his. Brother Stefano waited in the hall to give them some space. Other than the cot and the two monks, there was only barely room for the small table that held a wooden bowl half-filled with water and an unlit candle. *An unlit candle? Where is the light coming from?* His eyes searched apprehensively across the room, looking for an explanation. The light seemed to emanate from nowhere and everywhere at the same time. He crossed himself quickly while muttering a prayer under his breath.

Suddenly, Brother David stiffened, ceasing his struggles. Brother Timothy kept his grip on his shoulders but looked over questioningly at the abbot. No one appeared to have the will to break the silence. What had Brother Stefano been babbling about when he had come to summon him? His eyes? Brother David's eyes had remained closed the entire time the abbot had been standing in the room, so he had no idea what was of importance with them. But there was something else beyond the inexplicable light, something subtler. Then he realized that the hairs on his arm were standing on end. The air, though stiflingly still, felt like it did just before a thunderstorm. He moved his hand to feel the outline of the cross he wore under his robe. The worn edges under the rough fabric was only slightly calming. All thoughts of grain levels and bishops and popes had fled from his mind.

Then Brother David's eyes snapped open.

The abbot's mouth flooded with the taste of copper. At the edge of his perceptions, he barely registered the pain in his hand as he gripped the cross as tightly as he could. Brother David's eyes were completely white from edge to edge. No. Not just white. All the light in the room seemed to originate from them. There were no shadows to confirm this thought, but he was absolutely certain of it. The eyes pulled and tugged his own, and gripped them tight. There was no way to tell exactly where they were looking, but he knew they were boring into him, deep into his soul. He could feel steely fingers rifling through his brain, taking inventory. He wanted nothing more than to say a prayer, but his mind was just as paralyzed as his body.

Seemingly without effort, Brother David sat up, sloughing the monk off him with supernatural ease. He turned his head directly toward Abbot Thomas, peering through unseeing eyes. The two of them sat motionless, staring at each other, one with barely contained fright in his eyes, the other with no discernible expression at all. The monk on the floor remained motionless. Abbot Thomas was worried that he might be hurt, but couldn't gather the necessary will to tear his eyes from Brother David to check.

An eternity passed and neither moved, not even to breathe. Time stood still, a captive audience, trapped by the current flowing between them. The abbot assumed that Brother Stefano was still waiting just outside the door, but that was miles away in another time. Finally, a raspy, thin sound came out of Brother David's mouth, as if he were not in the habit of speaking.

"When golems walk through firefly rain, when mankind lives in the heart of glass, playing out vitrified un-lives in formless clouds, then there shall come to pass, a great plague. It will be the longest plague to threaten this world."

Abbot Thomas could see nothing but the two pristine white, bright orbs in front of him. He could hear no sound but the rattling voice. He knew that what he was witnessing here was beyond him. *Firefly rain and hearts of glass?* Brighter minds might be able to make something out of this. But it was obvious to him that this was of extreme importance. He realized in a corner of his mind that he was being enchanted in some way, but he knew that it was not magic. This was like pure prophecy from the days of the Old Testament gripping his mind with its power. He would have to commit as much of it to memory as he could. He suspected many lives and many souls could depend on what was said here.

"Hordes of locusts will cover the land, more locusts than a thousand monks could count in their lifetimes. But they shall be as one beast, intent upon scouring the earth. They will resurrect the Tower of Babel and revel in its shadow. Blasphemy shall be the law of the land, and the righteous shall be trodden on the ground as discarded offal."

"But..." the abbot interrupted, surprising himself at his action.

Brother David continued, oblivious to the interruption. "But that is all inevitable and quite unstoppable. There is, however, a greater evil riding upon that wave. It must be stopped. It shall spring from the upside down and inverted. It will crawl onto this earth, a beggar and a thief. And men shall rejoice in it as a miracle. It will be a hollow thing and like an empty husk, it is better thrown on the compost heap. Know this: from whence it comes, shall also come the remedy. The inside out and upside down must be turned out and upright. The painted looking glass will show..."

Brother David hesitated and a pained look formed on his face.

"The painted looking glass..."

Brother David's body convulsed. He threw his head back violently as a high-pitched keening emitted from his mouth. Abbot Thomas noticed dark, almost black-lined shadows playing across the walls for the first time since he entered the room. They looked less like the shadows thrown from a candle than individual living things running about. He could somehow feel a childish glee radiating from them.

"The painted..."

A tortured scream erupted from Brother David as his body slammed back onto the wooden cot with enough force to make it jump off the floor. The shadows whirled around the room faster and faster, darting momentarily toward Brother David before jerking back to the wall. It seemed to Abbot Thomas like they were trying to gather confidence, almost as if they were actually alive. Brother David continued to lay motionless on the cot, his face contorted in pain. The abbot tried to step forward to help him but still had no control over his limbs.

All at once, the light that had flooded the room was extinguished. For a moment it was pitch black and the abbot could see nothing at all but the after-image of Brother David's body stretched taut on his cot. As his eyes began to adjust to the darkness, he realized that there was a bit of candle light flickering from the hallway. Brother Stefano was apparently still there.

"Brother Stefano," he croaked, his throat sore as if he had been screaming.

"Brother Stefano, come in at once. I need your candle."

Without uttering a word, Brother Stefano rushed in. He lit the candle on the table before placing his beside it. He looked at Abbot Thomas with fear in his eyes, but didn't say a word. Then he noticed the monk on the floor. He stooped down and put his face next to the monks face. After a minute he looked up at the abbot and nodded, the worry in his face lessening a bit.

The abbot tore his gaze away from the two monks and worked up the courage to turn back to the cot and Brother David. He was still there, lying on the cot, but now he was in the depths of shadows. What was even stranger was that it looked like some of the shadows were under his skin, not on top of it. *There! That one definitely just flowed out of his mouth and down his neck.* Now that he had noticed, he saw ripples moving under Brother David's robe like fish swimming just under the water's surface. They were becoming more frenetic with each passing moment, circling the cot and one by one leaping off the floors and walls to writhe on his body. Abbot Thomas reached inside his robe and pulled out the cross he had been gripping tightly for the last ten minutes. He held it out toward the shadow-shrouded figure, hoping to ward them off.

"Abbot?" Brother Stefano stopped, realizing he didn't know what to ask.

"Stay back, Stefano." There was still an oppressive weight

in the room. The air itself pressed down, making it hard to breathe and harder still to talk. But there was a noise, something in the background. At first it sounded like a rustling, maybe rats digging through the grain. No. Maybe it was a rattling. It was definitely in this room even though it sounded like it was far away, but approaching. As it grew in volume, he still could not identify exactly what he was hearing. He looked over at Brother Stefano. After a moment of eye contact and an unspoken question, Stefano nodded, acknowledging the shared experience. *At least I've not gone mad.* The sound was becoming clearer. Maddeningly, it remained just beyond his grasp. He noticed more movement from Brother David on the cot. The shadows had coalesced into a single sheet of black velvet, draped over his body like a blanket. There was a rhythmical rise and fall under it, too fast to be breathing. Maybe…

Laughter. It was laughter coming from Brother David. It was not a happy or joyful laughter by any means. Abbot Thomas had not heard laughter like this ever before. It had an edge of pain coloring an otherwise brutal staccato. Brother David slowly propped himself up as his laughter continued to grow louder.

"Stopped? *Stopped?* You think this can be stopped?"

Brother David's voice had taken on a deeper, more feral tone. Abbot Thomas wondered if there was anything left of the monk he knew inside. Brother David opened his eyes, eyes that moments before had been white and illuminating. Now they were obsidian windows, looking into a vast abyss that the abbot barely had the strength to keep from falling toward. He couldn't see the surface of them, just darkness like one of the shadows compressed and concentrated into a maleficent orb.

"You impudent *men.*" The last word was spit out with particular vehemence, "You can't stop this. You will bring this upon yourselves, and in so doing, cement the inevitability of your demise. Created in God's image. Ha! You don't have the slightest idea of the smallest part of your God. You make my argument for me."

The shadows began spinning maniacally, creating a dizzying effect. Abbot Thomas felt nauseous.

"You are the locusts! You are the plague. What greater plague could be thrust upon mankind than itself?" Brother David began laughing once again inter-spaced with a wet coughing that slowly wound down to an inhuman chuckle.

Abbot Thomas could not move, but he saw Brother Stefano slip out the door.

"If *I* had the power in *my* hands to command His attention..." He shook his head. "You squander it every day. You are a petty, violent, puerile *people.*"

The small part of the abbot's brain that he could still control hoped that Brother Stefano would return with help soon.

"You buy and sell your way into His presence for mere money, as if that makes any difference to Him. You fight and kill each other over who knows Him the best. It's an unending farce. And yet, He forgives *you*. He loves *you*. *I* can kill and maim. *I* too can garner His attention... Know this: as time moves forward, so does it bring you closer to the moment. Remember, you will ask for this. You will be your own downfall."

Brother David grasped the edge of the cloak of shadow and slowly lifted it off his body. It flowed like a sheet of linen, but one made up of living snakes.

"Look at me, *man of God!*"

Brother David's eyes sucked the heat out of the room. "You think you are righteous, but don't tell me you've never thought ill of another. You can't tell me you've never wanted to wring the neck of that silly bishop of yours."

The abbot stood unmoving, hearing nothing but the voice issuing from Brother David's mouth, and some distant applause. *What is that noise?* His attention focused once again as Brother David flung the cloak at him. Blackness overcame him as the shadows fought to enter his body.

"Don't fight it," he heard from a distance, as the applause seemed to be getting louder. *Applause? That can't be right.* He was fighting for his very soul and someone was clapping? There was a pressure on his chest. Something warm and slippery wound its way around his neck. He couldn't open his mouth to breathe for fear of inhaling one of the shadows. His head was pounding, but it was fading. Everything was fading. From a great distance he heard shouting. Then the shadow began shaking him. Flames danced around him throwing their flickering light onto his eyelids. The shadows lifted him back to his feet, but he refused to breathe or open his eyes.

"Abbot!"

Brother Stefano? No, you were supposed to escape.

"Breathe!"

Abbot Thomas opened his eyes. Three other monks crowded into the cell, each holding two candles. The shadows had retreated to Brother David back on the cot. The smile on his face had a sadistic tilt to it. The abbot sucked in as much air as he could to chase away the spots floating in front of his eyes. At least they seemed to be spots and not shadows.

"Saved by your *holy men*. It matters not. Now, I must leave, but I will return. I will be *asked* to return. Until then..." Brother David's laugh was more the bark of a rabid dog than laughter, but it continued on for at least a minute while the monks tried to steady their abbot. Finally Brother David fell back onto his cot and was silent. The shadows that had seemed to have a life of their own were now tethered to the flames of the candles. The chill that had come upon the room during Brother David's possession slowly receded.

Brother Stefano cautiously approached the cot and leaned over the unmoving monk. He looked up and shook his head. Abbot Thomas said a small prayer and began ushering the monks out of the cell. He had a lot to do before the sun rose tomorrow.

~~*~*

From a letter to Gregory VI from Bishop Ruiz:

Holy Father,

I thank you once again for this appointment you gave me, although I feel you may be testing me. This flock is very troubled.

I have mentioned the abbot who whines for more riches for his abbey than he truly needs. He has now gone too far. In an attempt to bring our attention upon him, he has concocted a story that is truly unbelievable. He would have us think that the prophets of old live in his community. He tries to disguise the untimely death of one of his with a fantastical story of impending doom. And when is this doom descending upon us? He doesn't know. He speaks in riddles and rhymes.

I am tempted to have him flogged for his negligence, but I will rely upon your wisdom in this matter. Please advise me on how this situation should be handled.

Yours in Christ,
Bishop Carlos San Ruiz

Chapter *1*

Italy
1987

Three shadows huddled together, moving purposefully down the cobbled street as one. No cars passed at this time of night when the silence pressed down as ominously as the dark. The three shadows were almost indistinguishable from each other, wrapped in black overcoats and topped with equally black hats. One carried a small satchel at his side, protecting it with both hands. They all stopped at the same time, looking warily in all directions.

"Are we sure this is the right thing to do?" Father Joseph asked the other two priests.

"This is but a small transgression," Father Anthony answered without hesitation. "And in this case, the end... The end is almost unimaginable. When, in the history of mankind, has anyone ever had the opportunity to do anything nearly as great as what we begin tonight?"

"Be quiet, you two. This isn't the place for this," Father Michael whispered. The youngest of the three by a visible margin, he peered nervously down the alley where they huddled. "We've had conversations about this ad nauseum, and we've all agreed that we have an opportunity here that can't be passed up. Now isn't the time for cold feet. Come on; let's go before someone sees us."

Nodding against a sudden cold breeze, the three priests continued down the alley to a small set of marble steps leading to a side entrance to the Guarini Chapel. As they stopped, Father Anthony pulled his coat tighter around his body, shivering against the cold. The domed top of the chapel loomed oppressively above, more felt than seen. He always forgot the physical presence of history in Italian architecture.

Father Anthony took the lead up the steps, looking back only to see that the others followed. When he reached the ancient looking chapel door, he stopped and knocked lightly on its burled surface. The three priests waited in the cold January air. The other two priests looked at Father Anthony expectantly.

Nothing happened.

Father Joseph fidgeted nervously. "Why isn't he here? Did we get the wrong time?"

Father Anthony knocked again, louder than before. Father Joseph's eyes searched the alley as if for looking someone to apprehend them. Both he and Father Michael looked like they might bolt at any minute.

"Calm down. This is the right time, and the right place," Father Anthony admonished. "Give him a minute or two. It is a large building."

"But he knows we are coming? I thought this was all arranged. Can we really trust someone who'd sell out their religion for a sack of money?" Father Joseph lifted the satchel he had been carrying at his side.

Before Father Anthony could respond, they heard the

muffled sound of footsteps approaching from the other side of the door. It opened just wide enough for them to get a glimpse of a dark uniform blocking the entrance.

"Avete i soldi?" the guard asked.

"What?" asked Father Joseph, jumping slightly.

"He's just asking about the money," said Father Anthony. "Show him the bag, Father Joseph, so we can get in out of the cold."

Father Joseph unzipped the satchel and opened it to show the neatly banded stacks of bills. Gunther had helped come up with the funds needed to complete his work, otherwise they would be trying to do this Mission Impossible style, and he doubted that they had that kind of ability. The guard quickly stepped back and opened the door without once taking his eyes off the bag. *One must sometimes deal with those of questionable morals to do a greater good.*

The three priests stepped into a dimly lit hallway and watched the guard re-lock the door. They stood in what appeared to be a service hallway with only a few security lights on at this time of night.

"Seguimi," the guard whispered, motioning for them to follow.

"He wants us to follow him," Of the three, Father Anthony was the only one who understood Italian.

"Yeah, I think we got that one," Father Michael whispered sarcastically, already a few steps down the hall.

They followed the guard, turning often in the labyrinthine hallway before reaching another door. The guard punched a handful of numbers on a keypad inset beside the door. Before punching the last number, he paused and turned to face the priests.

"Ora. Dammi i soldi prima di spegnere l'allarme."

"Not a very trusting guard," said Father Anthony. "He wants the money before he turns off the alarm. Father Joseph?"

Father Joseph reluctantly handed over the satchel hoping

that once paid for, he would stay paid for. The last thing they needed was to get arrested. *What would the rest of the church think, rogue priests trying to steal the shroud?*

The guard turned back and continued punching keys until they heard a high-pitched chirp and a green light flashed on the top of the screen. He stepped back, motioning the priests forward as he began to sift through the stacks of bills in the bag.

"Well, I guess that is all the permission we are going to get," Father Anthony muttered as he reached to open the door.

Even in the dim off-hours light, the sight as he opened the door was enough to freeze them all in place. The altar was set elevated on a black marble rotunda surrounded by a balustrade of gilt wood. The altar itself was constructed of the same black marble and seemed to absorb all the light in the room, and transport it into the sparse white veining. Four golden angels guarded each corner of the altar, their wings stretched out behind them, shielding it. Father Anthony barely noted the bronze friezes that adorned the altar. He had seen many churches and cathedrals, but none hummed with the power that he felt here.

"Dietro l'altere," said the guard who had entered unnoticed behind them. "Seguimi."

Father Anthony followed the guard behind the altar to a heavy looking iron grill set into the back. The guard inserted something into it and slowly swung it open. Inside, barely visible in the shadows was a silver reliquary in the shape of a small coffin. He gingerly lifted it out and set it down on the rotunda. The three priests were motionless, staring at it in awe. The guard carefully opened it and stepped away, motioning to the priests. They gathered around the case, speechless.

Father Anthony turned to Father Joseph and whispered reverently, "Do it."

Father Joseph reached into the reliquary and lifted out the ancient folded linen. He stood up and placed it on the altar. As he unfolded it, he noted the patches where molten silver had damaged the shroud centuries earlier. *Only seconds saved this cloth from total destruction in that fire. This endeavor would have been impossible. In all the millennia of earth's existence, a blink in eternity's eye and, no matter the technology, the downfall of man would have continued unchecked.*

"The Shroud of Turin," he whispered. "The sacred burial cloth that covered Jesus after he was crucified." He turned to the other priests and spoke louder. "Shouldn't we say some sort of prayer?"

Father Anthony shook his head, "Just get it over with before something happens."

Father Joseph made the sign of the cross, and then removed a small vial and scalpel from the pocket of his overcoat. He ran his fingers just above the surface of the cloth from the beard-covered face down to the hands. This close up, it was hard to decipher the sepia-toned negative image of the body, but the bloodstains were fairly obvious. "There," he said pointing to the wrist. "And there, at the head as well." He hesitated as he moved the scalpel closer to the shroud.

"Don't worry, Father. All will be forgiven when this is over." Father Anthony waved his hands at him impatiently. "Just scrape some off. You don't have to actually cut the cloth."

Father Joseph lightly scraped a few flakes into the vial, taking care not to damage the cloth. He held the vial up to the light, looking to see how much he had.

"How much do we need? I've got some here, but..." Father Joseph asked.

"He said the more the better, try a little more. It's not like we can come back for more if we don't get enough the first time, and if we steal the whole shroud, there's a chance its absence might be noticed."

Father Joseph nodded and scraped more before pocketed the vial and folding the shroud back into the reliquary. Father Michael came over to help him lift the heavy box. Together, they walked it back behind the altar, where the guard was waiting.

As they slid it back into the opening, Father Michael asked,

"What's that blinking red light? Is that part of the security system?" He pointed deep into the opening behind the reliquary.

Father Anthony translated the question for the guard. The guard immediately became agitated, shoving them aside to peer intently into the darkness. He jumped back and slammed the iron grill shut with a loudly echoing clang, eyes wild.

"Afrettatevi. È necessario partire immediatamente!" He shouted as he shooed them toward the door.

The guard shouted a long stream of Italian as he locked the grill with shaking hands.

"Go!" Father Anthony shouted, running to the door. "We need to leave now. He said it's not part of their alarm. He doesn't know who it's warning."

The three priests ran down the hallway while the guard's fingers fumbled with the alarm. They struggled to retrace their earlier path in their haste.

When they got to the street, Father Joseph stopped them.

"Here. You should take this," he said as he handed the vial to Father Michael. "You're the youngest. If it comes to a foot race, you have the better chance. But please, be careful with it. This is the Lord's blood."

Father Anthony looked about nervously, "We should split up. Meet back at the hotel only if you are sure you're not being followed."

The other priests nodded their assent. Father Anthony and Father Joseph ran off in opposite directions, their obsidian cloaks flapping like giant wings. Even in the midst of all the pandemonium, Father Michael managed a light chuckle at the picture. The image brought visions of comic book pages he'd read as a child to his mind.

Lost in thought, he almost didn't hear the footsteps coming from behind. He barely had time to dive behind some nearby shrubs before a dark figure turned the corner and raced up the street to stop at the exit from the chapel. He watched as the figure walked surreptitiously up the steps to check the door.

Father Michael held his breath as he tried to remain as still as possible. His heart beat harder than he had ever felt it. He hunched down, trying to make himself as small as possible. Fortunately the dark added to his cover. He was having his own trouble making out any features on the man standing in the open. All he could distinguish was his red hair.

Apparently, deciding that the door was locked and no one was coming out anytime soon, the man ran down the street in the direction Father Anthony had taken.

I'm not cut out for this kind of thing. Father Michael finally let out his breath. *Who was that guy? Certainly not the police. No uniform and no backup, and cops usually don't travel alone.* He shook his head. *I watch too many cop shows. But, if he wasn't with the church and he wasn't with the cops...*

Father Michael waited a few more minutes to make sure the stranger didn't return, and then crawled out from behind the bushes. He searched for signs of the stranger, then having satisfied himself that he was alone, he turned toward the direction Father Joseph had taken. He had plenty of time during the walk back to the hotel to be puzzled by the unknown man.

Two hours later, the three gathered back in their hotel room. Father Michael paced back and forth, full of nervous energy. The other two priests sat on the edge of one of the twin beds, watching as the sun began to rise.

"But who *was* that?" Father Michael asked, addressing the elephant in the room. "It wasn't the police or someone from the cathedral."

"It doesn't matter..." said Father Anthony.

"Doesn't matter?" Father Michael turned to face him. "Doesn't *matter*? Don't you think some stranger setting up an alarm on the shroud and chasing us all over town at three in the morning is important. Doesn't that concern you?"

"Keep your voice down. Yes, of course it bothers me. But look at the end result: we weren't caught. As far as we know, we weren't even seen. And as far as the larger goal, he is totally irrelevant. Why someone was watching the shroud is a mystery. Indeed, it is a somewhat troubling mystery. However, it doesn't concern us. For all we know, he might be somewhere across town right now wondering why his alarm malfunctioned. Do we know if he actually saw any of us?"

He paused. When no one said anything, he continued, "We left no visible evidence. It would take a microscopic examination of the exact spot to see what we did, and with all the testing done in the last couple years, what was found would be written off as part of that. In fact, unless the guard talks... And why would he? We gave him one thousand reasons not to." Father Anthony quickly stood up and grabbed Father Michael's shoulder, stopping him as he tried to pace past. "It's okay. We got what we needed. We weren't caught. No one else knows about the cloning except Gunther and Mary, and neither of them knows all the details. Most people don't even realize cloning is possible. Our plans are safe."

"Possible, yes, but this will be the first human cloning. Do you think Gunther can do what he promises?" Father Michael relaxed slightly as the subject changed.

"Have some faith. We are bringing about the second coming of the Lord. The little things will take care of themselves. This is meant to be."

Father Joseph added, "Anthony is right, Michael. We have what we need and can now get it to Gunther so he can start his part of this endeavor. We should be rejoicing, not fighting."

Chapter *2*

Mobile, Alabama
1988

An agonized scream sliced through the heat and humidity, as Father Michael sat nervously, looking at the posters of puppies and kittens hanging on the walls of the strip-mall veterinary clinic. Sister Mary Elizabeth stopped pacing long enough to give him a questioning look.

"Don't worry, sister. It'll be soon." Father Michael tried to sound reassuring. He stood up and walked to the door that led to the back, trying to visualize the doctors surrounding Mary.

"But will it be okay?" Sister Mary Elizabeth asked as she came up beside him, her hand resting lightly on his shoulder. "This is the first time this has been attempted."

"In more ways than one, Sister. It's the first attempt at human cloning, but in other ways, it has been done before, two thousand years ago. Immaculate conception had never been done before then, either. So, yes, I have faith. This may be a new technology, but it's just a continuation of the story we relive every Sunday. Humanity needs this now. Yes, I took some convincing, but they're right. We are living in a world of individuals who don't even know they are begging for someone to unite them."

Another scream pierced the room. Sister Mary Elizabeth reached for the knob, but hesitated.

"But why here? In this..." She waved her hand around the room. The lobby of the clinic was clean, but obviously not the height of technology.

"I wish we could have done this somewhere nicer, somewhere safer. But we have to maintain secrecy until he is ready. As a child, he will most likely be fairly defenseless. It will be up to us to raise and protect him."

"You think the devil..." Sister Mary Elizabeth's whisper trailed off to nothing.

"The devil?" Father Michael shook his head emphatically. "No. It's not that I don't believe in the physical presence of the devil, but, well, maybe I don't. I do believe in his legacy, however. Greed, jealousy, and fear can drive a man to do stupid things.

A furious banging on the glass door interrupted them. They both spun around as if a bomb had exploded. A man in his twenties waved to them with one hand while holding a wiggling mutt with the other.

We're closed, Father Michael pantomimed through the glass. *I'm sorry.*

The man waved his arms as wildly as he could while holding the dog and explaining his predicament. The door muffled his voice and made it impossible to tell exactly what he wanted, but obviously he thought it needed immediate attention. Father Michael shook his head and pointed to the clinic's hours sign etched on the side of the door. *Come back Monday,* he mouthed.

The man shrugged his shoulders, perplexed, and walked back into the parking lot. Father Michael turned back to Sister Mary Elizabeth Neither of them noticed the prolonged stare from the man before he got into his car. He put the dog down on the pavement beside him before shutting the door and driving down the street, leaving the dog behind.

~~*~*

Father Joseph felt bad as he watched Mary heaving out bucketfuls of air. Her hair hung in damp clumps from her head, testament to hours of exhausting labor. He felt sorry that she had to be on a table designed for golden retrievers, but he knew that she was in capable hands.

Gunther stood beside the only window in the room, looking nervous, as his life's work was about to come to fruition. Father Joseph was still not one hundred percent sure about that one. He had been in charge of a group of scientists conducting experiments in Germany during the war. Father Anthony had assured them that he had an attack of conscience and had found God, escaping before the Nazis had been defeated. His current expertise in cloning had its roots in discoveries he had made back then, discoveries that had been lost to the rest of the world when his research station had been bombed later in the war. He had told them that his group had not participated in any of the experiments often described in horrifying detail during the Nuremberg trials, but still, someone who could stand back and do nothing while such atrocities were perpetrated worried him. In Gunther's defense, he seemed very zealous in his furthering of God's cause now. One bonus about his past was that it had taught him the value of secrecy.

The only other question he had was the doctor delivering the baby, but he was being paid well and knew nothing about the source of the child. All he knew was that some priests were helping a poor girl deliver her baby. If he had any suspicions about the location, he had yet to voice them. The nurse, Sister Lucia, was a nun, who like Sister Mary Elizabeth, was with them. Their small group included two nuns, a handful of priests spread around the globe, and of course, Mary.

Father Joseph looked up as Doctor Richardson and Sister Lucia moved to the end of the table. Anticipation showed on their faces.

"One more big push, Mary. You're almost there."

Mary almost sat up with exertion as she screamed once more. She grabbed Sister Lucia's hand, squeezing hard enough to turn it white.

"Come on, Mary. Just a little more."

The room darkened as a cloud passed overhead. In the dim light, Father Joseph thought he could see a glow coming off Mary. Sister Lucia scrambled to turn on more lights.

"Here we go. I can see the head."

The air conditioner kicked on, adding a sudden chill to the room. Mary gave one final heave and the doctor pulled the baby the rest of the way.

Mary's panting was the only sound Father Joseph heard. Ten seconds, that seemed like an eternity passed before he got up, concerned. He ran to the table, where the doctor and Sister Lucia were huddled around the child.

"What?" Mary screamed. "What's wrong? Is he okay?"

The cloud finished passing and the room was suddenly bathed in blinding sunlight. A single shaft pierced the window and spotlighted the newborn baby. Finally, he cried. The wail echoed through the room louder than Father Joseph thought a baby could cry.

"I hear him. I hear my baby. Is he okay?"

"Yes. And it *is* a boy." The doctor held him close to Mary's face so she could see him. "We have to go clean him up, but he'll be right back."

Sister Lucia crossed herself before taking the baby from the doctor and heading to another room. He gave her a strange look as she walked away.

"Father Joseph." Doctor Richardson removed his gloves, throwing them in the trashcan. "We have a few more things to do here before Mary will be able to leave, but I would say that you can move her to her house by later this afternoon. We'll run some more tests on the child as well, but I don't see any reason that he couldn't leave then as well."

Gunther clapped Father Joseph on the back. "We did it. We actually did it."

The doctor looked at them, slightly confused.

"Yes, Gunther," Father Joseph tried to pick his words carefully. "A healthy boy for Mary. I, for one, would like to thank you for your assistance." He turned to the doctor, hoping he would forget Gunther's slip. "And yours as well."

The doctor stared at them for a few seconds before nodding his head and turning back to Mary, to ask her some questions.

"Let's share the news with Father Michael and Sister Mary Elizabeth"

Father Joseph opened the door and held it for Gunther. They nearly walked through Father Michael, who was already standing in the doorway.

"It is done. A healthy blue-eyed boy."

Both Father Michael and Sister Elizabeth visibly relaxed, then turned to each other and embraced.

"God's will be done," Father Joseph murmured.

"Will we be taking them back to the hotel now?" Sister Mary Elizabeth looked at Father Joseph expectantly. "I'd really like to get them out of this... clinic."

"Not quite yet. The doctor has a few tests he needs to run, but we should be able to wrap things up and bring them later this afternoon."

"Yes, and I have a few tests I want to run on the boy as well," Gunther interjected. "Just to make sure everything came out... normal."

Father Michael suddenly grinned ear to ear. "Well, when do we get to see them?"

Father Joseph smiled at his enthusiasm. "Sister Lucia and the doctor were cleaning things up. They should be ready by now. Come on. I think it's okay to go in."

As they walked in, Mary was sitting in a plastic chair, her legs covered by a throw blanket and holding her child. Most of the lights had been turned off, leaving the room darker than the lobby. The curtains on the single window had been drawn, but the gap between them let a single shaft of brilliantly white light shine through, bathing the child in its warmth. The two priests and Sister Mary Elizabeth dropped to their knees before them, bowing their heads reverently.

"Our Father, who art in Heaven, hallowed be thy name..." Father Michael intoned the Lord's Prayer, dwelling on the significance of each word more than he ever had before. *This is the Lord before me, in the flesh. Here and now. My whole life I've prayed to him as a disembodied entity, and now here he is. This is God.* A shiver passed through his body as he finished the prayer, watching the baby nap peacefully in his mother's arms.

"This is it, right? We're witnessing the second coming." Sister Mary Elizabeth stood slowly. "This is God." Her face was full of wonder. Father Joseph and Father Michael could only nod, their voices tied up in their hearts.

"May I hold him?" Sister Mary Elizabeth held out her arms.

Mary nodded and handed the baby to her. Sister Mary Elizabeth lit up, a smile shining on her face. She cradled the baby to her chest, but before she could say anything, her face began to turn green. Her knees wobbled slightly, as she reached her free hand to the wall to steady herself. She gripped the child tightly, not wanting to drop him.

"Are you okay?" Father Michael approached her, ready to assist.

"Just a little nauseous all of a sud..."

She pushed the baby back into Mary's arms as quickly as she could, vomiting on the floor as she finished. Mary cradled her child, losing interest in the rest of the room as she did so. Sister Mary Elizabeth's body racked with convulsions for several minutes before she could stand back up. Father Michael handed her a towel to wipe her mouth.

"I'm okay, although I'm not exactly sure what came over me." Turning to Mary, she bowed her head. "A baby should be in his mother's arms." Mary didn't look up, not noticing that she was being addressed.

Father Michael touched Sister Mary Elizabeth's shoulder sympathetically, taking the towel from her. As he watched Mary cradling her newborn, he couldn't help but wonder if the three wise men had felt the same way in the presence of Jesus. They had merely guessed at the majesty that was to come. *I know what was, then. In this world of instant communication, how much more could it be this time? The whole world will know in hours of his being revealed, that God walks among us once more. There will be no doubt. Wars will stop. Crime will disappear. It will be like Heaven on earth.* The enormity of the situation threatened to make him dizzy as well. He leaned over Mary, and placing his hand upon the child's head, he made the sign of the cross on the napping child's forehead.

"Thy will be done."

The baby's head slowly rolled toward him, as if he were falling deeper into sleep, when suddenly, his eyes snapped open, staring intently into his own. Father Michael was sure that intelligence measured him from within the small orbs. He jumped back in surprise, searching to see if anyone else had seen. Sister Mary Elizabeth met his gaze, and then dropped her eyes to the floor as she made the sign of the cross. Neither Father Joseph nor Gunther appeared to have noticed from their conversation against the far wall.

"Gunther?" Father Michael was not exactly sure what he meant to ask.

"Don't worry, Michael," Father Joseph said as he looked over at his worried face. "He will right this world again."

Father Michael decided not to correct Father Joseph's misunderstanding of his concern. As he looked down on the child again, he appeared to be napping as if nothing had happened. *Did I imagine it? Am I seeing things?* When he glanced back at Sister Mary Elizabeth, he noticed she was still muttering a prayer under her breath.

Gunther, still beaming from his success, asked, "Have you decided on a name for him yet?"

Sister Lucia stopped folding towels, and looked at him incredulously. "Jesus? Isn't his name Jesus?"

"No."

Everyone focused their attention on Mary.

"Not Jesus."

Silence hung in the air as they waited. "Christian. We should call him Christian."

"Christian," Father Joseph repeated. "That's a good name."

"A strong name," agreed Father Michael.

"Dr. Richardson, line three." The voice echoed mechanically out of the intercom, startling him.

Clearly agitated, Dr. Richardson stared at the phone. Claire knew he didn't like to take calls after three p.m.

He pressed the page button and said curtly, "Tell him I'm

gone for the day."

There was a brief pause before he heard her voice again. "This is the fifth time he's called today." He could hear her sigh even through the machine. "He won't leave a message, he keeps calling back."

"Alright, I'll take it." *But this better not make me late for my personal trainer.*

He punched the speakerphone button, not wanting to give the person on the other side of the conversation the satisfaction of the better sounding headset. "Dr. Richardson here. How can I help you?"

"Dr. Charles Richardson?" asked a heavily accented voice. Static filled the line in the voices absence.

Hmm, Italian, maybe? "Yes. Again, how can I help you?"

"Doctor, my name is... Carlo. I was wondering if we could meet somewhere. I need some... information."

"Carlo, I'm pretty tied up this afternoon. I could give you back to my secretary and she could answer your questions." Dr. Richardson glared at the door separating him from his secretary. *He needs information?*

"No, Dr. Richardson. Maybe you can answer a couple questions over the phone, then?"

"If they're brief."

Carlo hesitated as if gathering his thoughts. "Can I ask you what you were doing at the veterinary clinic on Saturday?"

"*Excuse me?*" Dr. Richardson hesitated, trying to compose himself. "Who the hell are you, and how is that any of your business?" He fidgeted nervously. What he had done had not been illegal. But it had been very irregular, and the fee given had been unusually high. He knew something had not been on the up and up, but his practice always seemed to need more capital. *What don't I know about what happened.* There had been a few things said by the priests that had seemed a bit odd.

"Carlo, I think this conversation is over. Even if I wanted to,

I can't share medical information without proper paperwork. Please don't call back unless you can fax me that paperwork."

"Wait!" Carlo shouted. "So it *was* medical?"

Crap. "Okay, look, Carlo, or whoever you are. It is a matter of public record that a baby boy was delivered. That is all I can tell you. So don't call back." *Obviously you are not official. What is your angle, and how do you even know about it?* "Actually, before you go, Carlo, what is this in reference to?"

Another pause. "But why at a veterinary clinic?"

"No, I'm not playing that game. I asked you a question, and I'd like an answer."

"Who were all the people there?"

"I'm sorry, this is going nowhere. If you have any other questions, *do not* call back." Dr. Richardson slammed his hand on the disconnect button. He immediately paged his secretary. "Claire, if that man calls back, please inform him that I can't be reached."

"Yes, doctor."

He turned around and grabbed the folder from the cabinet behind him. *Should I call them? Let them know someone is following them? Why not? They paid me well enough.* He dialed the contact number listed.

"I'm sorry, but the number you have dialed has been changed or disconnected. If you feel you have reached this message in error, please dial again."

Damn, what have I gotten myself into?

Chapter *3*

New Orleans, Louisiana
1995

Mary sat in her rocking chair on the front porch, enjoying the cool, if slightly humid March day. It would have been perfect except for the oak pollen coating everything in yellow-green caterpillar shaped sprigs. She often thought her allergies were going to be the death of her one day, but chatting with Father Mike on these lazy Saturday afternoons was a small slice of Heaven. She set her glass of iced tea down on the table beside her and looked up to see what Christian was doing.

She lived within a stone's throw of the Mississippi river on Annunciation Street. Locals referred to her style of house as a 'shotgun' double, a violent sounding name for such a cute structure. Each side of the double unit house was only one room wide. The story was that if you opened all the doors on the house, you could shoot a gun from the front door and out the back without hitting a thing. Whatever you called it, it was just big enough for her and Christian, while still being cozy.

She watched Christian throwing a ball for their dachshund in the front yard. Whenever he held it, the dog barked up a storm, bouncing up and down until he threw it again. Each time the dog fetched it, Christian would have to chase him all over the yard to get it back. *Dog training was never my strong suit.* She wasn't sure if Christian was playing fetch with the dog, or vice versa. "He's such a little angel," Mary told Father Mike for the hundredth time, smiling broadly.

"Yes, he is," Father Mike agreed. "Literally." He finished the joke they repeated every week.

The sound of Christian's laughter and the dog's barking combined to eclipse any symphony she had ever heard. *I could sit here watching him all day long.*

"Mary, you might want to call him in. It looks like it's going to rain soon." Father Mike was watching a particularly dark cloudbank approaching from the south. Mary finally took notice of that ozone smell that often precedes a good thunderstorm. Worried, she stood up and called for her son.

"Christian? Honey? You need to wrap it up. It's about to rain." Their neighbors drove up and parked their car on the street in front of the house, back from grocery shopping. Sarah and Jason made such a nice young couple. They often invited her and Christian over for their game night every other Thursday.

"Just one more? 'K, Mom?" The dog bounced incessantly on its hind legs trying to reach the ball held barely out of his reach. If he had been anything larger than a miniature dachshund, Christian would have been knocked to the ground and given a lick bath. As it was, he reeled backward from the onslaught.

Mary sighed, and then smiled wryly. "Okay, honey. Once more, but you'll have to eat *all* your vegetables tonight."

"Aw, Mom." Christian was still back-pedaling from the jumping dog. He stopped and wound up like he'd seen the baseball players do on TV.

"Go get it!" He let go of the ball a little too early and it flew in a high arc. The dog stopped jumping and began following it from the ground.

Mary's breath caught as she realized the ball was going to go over the front fence.

Sarah got out of the driver's side of the car and opened the back door to get the bags of groceries on that side. The dog's tennis ball bounced off the roof of her sedan with a loud thud. She jerked up, hitting her head on the inside of the car and dropping the bag she was lifting. A jug of milk bounced under the car while four oranges rolled into street.

"Damn it." She almost dropped the bag she held in her other arm as she tried to catch the falling groceries.

"Hold on, Sarah. I'll give you a hand." Jason shut the passenger door and put the bag he was carrying on the sidewalk, as he headed to the front of the car to help her.

Mary, engrossed in her neighbor's drama, didn't notice Christian opening the front gate to run after the ball. The guttural growl of a diesel engine jerked her attention away. Mary froze as everything began moving in slow motion. Her vision opened to a wide screen view as she finally saw her son run into the street past the front of her neighbor's car. All street sounds silenced except the pounding of her heart beating in her head. Her body was paralyzed. Even her throat was turned to stone, refusing to take a breath to issue forth the scream building inside.

The delivery truck was moving too fast for the residential street. Mary could see from her porch that even if the driver stood on his brakes, he wouldn't be able to stop before it was too late, but he was busy taking a sip from his coffee mug.

Christian picked up the ball in the middle of the street, still facing away from the oncoming vehicle. She saw him notice something on the street beside the ball and begin to play with it. He flicked with his fingers, sending whatever it was flying down the road.

Mary pressed as hard as she could with her brain to break her paralysis and scream. She felt ready to explode from the pressure, but nothing would come. Her brain, constrained from doing anything else, noticed all the insignificant details around her. The dog's forepaws were propped against the front gate while it barked as if the game continued on. Jason rounded the front of his car on his way to help his wife. Sarah knelt on the ground by the driver's side door of the car trying to reach the milk carton underneath.

Mary could hear Father Mike inside the house close the refrigerator door after refilling his drink. Her brain tried to fixate on anything other than what was playing out before her. She could even hear the clink of the whiskey bottle as he added 'just a finger full' to his soda.

The truck continued inexorably forward. It felt like hours since Christian had run into the road, but only a few seconds had passed. He straightened up, ball in hand. Mary's heart jumped. *There might still be time!* Maybe he'd see the truck and dive out of the way. She slumped when she saw him stop to wipe the ball on his shirt, not turning or noticing the truck bearing down on him.

Finally, giving up hope, her body loosened, releasing her muscles. The scream that had been reverberating through her head escaped in a rush.

"CHRISTIAN!"

She jerked into motion, heaving herself down the front steps two at a time. Christian's body froze at the sound of her scream, turning only his head to find the source. As she jumped off the last step, she waved her hands desperately at the truck driver, who finally realized what was happening and slammed on the brakes, his coffee sloshing all over the windshield. The screaming tires drowned out Mary's belated instructions for Christian to get out of the street.

The noise was enough to turn Christian's attention from his mother to the truck that was only twenty feet away from him. His eyes widened in surprise.

Jason looked from the barreling truck to his wife, slowly rising with the retrieved milk carton, to Christian, standing in the middle of the street. Sarah appeared to be out of the way, but Christian was in imminent danger of being run over.

Jason began to run toward him, but Christian's eyes grabbed his attention. They opened unnaturally wide and began to cloud over. The street seemed to ripple between them. The asphalt pulled up into a two-foot tall wave that cascaded toward the boy. It crested against Christian's knees, but instead of knocking him down it appeared to steady him, then it was absorbed into his body. A dark line traveled up his legs to his waist, draining the color from his clothes as it went. Before another second could pass, it had passed his shirt and raced up his neck.

Even from ten feet away, Jason could see the whites of Christian's eyes disappear, turning coal black, as he faced down the oncoming truck. Christian stared intently at the driver. As the truck screeched forward pulling even with the rear of the car, Christian's head snapped sharply toward Jason. Their eyes met for a second and Jason was lost. He felt himself falling out of his body and into an obsidian abyss. He scraped painfully on the razor sharp edges of a wall he couldn't see. The unbearable sound was worse yet. A jet engine roared on full throttle next to his ears, the furnace blast searing him from all sides.

Mary watched, not understanding what she was seeing when, without warning, the truck careened to the right at an impossible angle for its speed, crushing Sarah between its grill and her car. The car flipped on its side as the tires caught on the curb, rolling upside down onto the sidewalk. It came to rest pinned against the front gate. Jason's vision cleared enough to see Christian pointing at him just before he was clipped by the front end as the car crashed past. He flipped into the air and landed on the fence, hanging limply.

Father Mike knocked Mary down in his rush to get to the street, whiskey spilled over the front of his shirt. He didn't hesitate to see if she was okay as he hurdled the three-foot wrought iron fence. In seconds, he reached Christian, who was still standing in the middle of the street staring at the wreckage. He grabbed him and wrapped him up in a huge bear hug. Christian never took his eyes off the misshapen body of his neighbor folded into the twisted body of the car as Father Mike whispered nothings into his ear. His hand still clutched the yellow tennis ball.

The driver emerged from his truck, visibly dazed. He hobbled to the mangled vehicle.

"Oh my god, oh my god." He fell back into a seated position beside his truck, staring blankly at the remains of the car, mumbling to himself.

Mary wasn't sure whether to be relieved by her son's miraculous escape from death or horrified by the carnage. She brushed her hands on her pants as she stood up and approached the fence. Father Mike looked up at her and nodded. She sighed with relief. Before she could figure out a way to get to the street to be with her son, she noticed Jason impaled on the top of the fence. *Oh my God.*

His eyes seemed to follow her as she got closer. *Must be a trick of the light. He can't be...*

"The boy..." Barely a whisper, more of a croak, Mary's eyes widened in horror as Jason tried to speak. *He is. Somehow he's still alive.*

"He's okay. You just stay still while help comes."

"The boy. His eyes..." His body convulsed as he tried to talk. "It's not natural."

He stopped breathing and lay still for a minute. She feared he might have died, but he opened his eyes again, struggling to try to speak.

"Not."

"Accident." Each word came out reluctantly. He clenched his eyes in pain.

Mary scanned down the length of his body to see if there was anything she could do. Mid-way between his hip and his shoulder, two spearhead tips of the fence pierced his side, one jutting out the other side glazed in blood.

She reached for his hand to reassure him. "Shh, don't try to talk. It's going to be okay."

Jason opened his eyes and grabbed her forearm tightly.

"No. It's not." He coughed wetly and had to take a few breaths before continuing. "You. Don't. Understand." His grip on her arm tightened as the hacking continued uncontrollably. Droplets of blood splattered her sleeve.

"He is not..."

The coughing returned, tapering off to a bubbling sound. She couldn't hear his last word as he lost his grip on her arm and his eyes slowly closed, but she read his lips.

"Right."

"Mary? Is he okay?" Father Mike stood next to the fence a few feet away holding Christian so he couldn't see Jason's body. He couldn't get back into the yard with Christian in his arms. The wrecked car wedged against the gate blocked his way.

Mary shook her head.

"Did he say anything before he..." Father Mike patted Christian's head not wanting to think about what could have happened.

"No. He was babbling something, but it didn't make any sense. I don't think he knew what was happening. Thankfully so, I guess."

Mary looked back at the limp body hanging on the fence as thunder rolled in the distance. The storm was going to arrive soon. "Here, hand him to me so I can get him in before it starts to pour out here.

As Father Mike handed Christian to her over the fence, lightning flashed, sharpening the edges on everything. Christian blinked and wiped his face with his free hand.

"Wait!" Father Mike tugged on her arm to spin her back around. "Let me see something. Christian, look at me."

Christian turned his head to face Father Mike and opened his eyes. They remained completely black; there was no white, no blue.

Father Mike gasped.

"What the..."

"What's wrong? Is my baby okay?" Mary put Christian down and spun him around looking for injuries.

"His eyes. Mary, look at his eyes."

"Yes, aren't they magnificent?" Mary sighed, relieved to find nothing wrong.

"Magnificent? They're black. Completely black. Something is wrong."

Christian watched the exchange in confusion. "Father Mike, it doesn't hurt. What's wrong with my eyes?" He rubbed them with his hands.

"See, Father Mike, he's fine. We knew he'd be special. We just didn't know how it would begin to show."

Father Mike shook his head. "Jesus didn't show physical signs like this."

"No." Mary hugged Christian's head against her hip. "No one recorded anything like that, but that was two thousand years ago. I'm pretty sure not everything about him was written down. Besides, this is his second time around. If he wants to do it differently, then who are we to question?"

"I guess, but what are we going to do about it? He can't go around looking like that. Someone will wonder what's wrong."

"Christian barely missed getting crushed by a delivery truck and you're worried about eye color." She sighed. "We'll get some contacts and no one will know the difference." She turned her attention back to Christian. "Now come on, Christian let's get you in before we get soaked."

Mary led Christian up the steps as Father Mike approached the truck driver. A siren wailed from a couple blocks away.

At the top of the steps, Christian pulled Mary's shirt to stop her.

"But Momma, I wanna play again."

She surveyed the scene on the street and the clouds

overhead. "No, honey. I don't want you out in the rain."

"Do I still have to eat my vegetables?"

"Yes, Christian."

Mary turned around to go inside. Before Christian followed, he wound up and threw the ball again, watching it sail out into the street for a second time. As he turned to follow his mother, the clouds opened and drenched Father Mike and the truck driver.

Carlo sat at a small weathered desk scrolling through newsgroups. For seven years he had been trying to catch up to the trail he had lost in Mobile. That doctor had been absolutely no help. He had found no trace that priest and nun had ever lived there. He reasoned that they must have traveled from wherever their home base was, which must have been relatively close. *Priests don't have money, right?* One article after another of Gulf South happenings rolled down his computer screen.

Two Men Killed in Botched Robbery

Baton Rouge – Jonathon Reese, 21 and Corey Roberts, 19 were killed in an attempted robbery of a pawn   *READ MORE*

Fifteen Injured in Mardi Gras Collapse

New Orleans – Fifteen revelers were sent to the hospital today when a homemade stand on St. Charles   *READ MORE*

Two Killed in Delivery Truck Accident

New Orleans – The driver of a truck that killed two residents of an uptown neighborhood says he   *READ MORE*

Firefighter Injured in Warehouse Fire

Biloxi – Carl Rodriguez was treated for minor injuries sustained while trying to contain the fire at the   *READ MORE*

"What am I even looking for?" The words echoed in the sparsely outfitted room. He opened the top drawer and pulled out an old cross, standing it on the corner of the desk for inspiration.

"I found them before, I can find them again."

He decided to take a break from the computer search. He needed to clear his mind. His daily regimen of five hundred sit-ups and push-ups always helped him focus.

"I. Will. Find. You." Each word was punctuated by a sit up. "Today. Tomorrow. Someday."

He pushed well past his usual five hundred reps until his body was shaking, but nothing came to him.

Chapter *4*

New Orleans, Louisiana
2000

"Come on, Christian. We're going to be late for mass. Are you almost ready?" Mary jumped as the waffles popped up in the toaster. She put both waffles on a plate for Christian and placed the butter and syrup beside them.

"CHRISTIAN!"

"Okay, Mom. I'm coming."

She poured two glasses of apple juice and put them on the granite breakfast bar. Christian stumbled into the kitchen with his shirt half untucked and trying to buckle his belt.

"You know I hate being late to church."

"Mom, we're never late."

"I know, and I'd like to keep it that way. Now sit down and

eat your breakfast."

Christian climbed up on the stool. He was average size for a twelve year old; his feet dangled only a few inches from the floor. He reached for the butter. "Hey, Mom, leggo my... Just kidding. Aren't you eating any?"

"No, just a little juice for me." She barely suppressed a smile as he poured almost a half-cup of syrup over his waffles. It wasn't until he was gulping down his juice that she noticed his eyes.

"You forgot your contacts, honey. We can't leave the house without them. You know how crazy that makes Father Mike." She opened the back door to let the dog back in. The small yard had no privacy but was perfect for the dog.

"Oh, it's okay, Mom. Look." His eyes turned blue again. "I do have them in. I've learned how to... overpower them." They turned black as he stared at their juice glasses. "If you're not going to drink yours, can I have it?"

"Turn them back, young man." She smiled. "And you can get some more for yourself. The refrigerator is right there." She lifted her glass to her lips, wondering why he was smirking.

The second the juice hit her tongue, she realized what was wrong. Instead of apple juice, she had nearly swallowed a mouthful of apple vinegar, which instead erupted all over the counter.

"Ugh!"

Christian burst out laughing and almost dropped the juice bottle he had gotten out of the fridge. He poured another glass for his mom while she struggled to rid her mouth of the last of the vinegar. She swished the juice around her mouth, still wincing and gave him a stern look. "Just for that, you're going to help out at the church garage sale this afternoon."

"Mom!"

"And turn those eyes back this instant. We've got to leave."

Christian crammed an oversized bite of waffle in his mouth while blinking his eyes melodramatically showing the blue. He swallowed and whispered, "Whatever."

"I heard that! What am I going to do with you next year when you're a full fledged teen?"

He smiled, syrup dripping down his chin. "Love me?"

She hugged him, making sure to keep his dirty face away from her dress.

At the church, Father Mike greeted them on the wide front steps.

"Father Mike, I wanted to let you know that we have another helper for this afternoon." Christian sulked at her side.

Father Mike gave her a questioning look, but she didn't elaborate. "Well, that's great. Why don't y'all go grab a seat? I'll be in momentarily."

Out of the corner of his eye, Christian saw Phillip Mayfield and his mother coming up the sidewalk. Phillip was half a head taller than Christian and nearly twenty pounds heavier.

"Oh crap."

"*Christian!*"

"Sorry, Mom. I don't really get along too well with Phillip."

"We're going to be in church. I'm sure he won't cause any trouble here."

"He better not," Christian muttered.

Christian was hit with a blast of organ music as Mary pushed through the ten-foot tall doors. Christian glanced back to catch Phillip smirking at him as he walked up behind him. Christian's brows creased as he turned back around, until he saw the holy water. The older couple in front of them dipped their fingers in the marble bowl and crossed themselves.

Christian's smile widened in time to the swell of organ music. Mary stepped up next and wetting her fingers, made the sign of the cross and headed down the aisle. Before he followed, Christian trailed his fingers across the surface of the water. For a second, his eyes flashed black. He touched his finger to his tongue as he followed his mother down the aisle. Bitter copper flooded his mouth. He chuckled lightly.

Christian sat next to Mary, who immediately knelt on the padded kneeler and began praying. Christian knelt next to her but twisted so he could see Phillip dip his finger and make the sign of the cross. Instead of water, blood dripped down his forehead.

At first, no one noticed except Christian, who tried his hardest, but couldn't hold back the laughter entirely. Phillip's mother screamed, drowning out the strange coughing noises Christian was making. Phillip was jumping up and down, rubbing his face in a vain attempt to wipe the blood off.

Christian could no longer restrain himself and broke into hysterical laughter. He stopped short when he saw Father Mike frowning at him from the doorway.

Under his mother's watchful eyes, Christian remained on his best behavior throughout mass. Afterward, Mary dragged him straight to the parish hall.

The garage sale was being held in the large room usually reserved for gathering after the mass. Three eight-foot long tables held stacks of books, but the rest of the parish hall was littered with an unorganized circus of what could only be labeled as 'stuff'. Mary looked around at all the piles of clothing and other household goods that were strewn about haphazardly. She saw ten-year old computers stacked on top of a pile of what appeared to be a woman's work out clothes. There was what looked to be a fairly large TV buried under a rowing machine. Christian was flipping through the books on the table nearest her.

"Mom!" Christian spun around holding a black New Orleans Saints hat with the comical looking Sir Saint character on it. "Can I have it? Please?"

"We're here to help, not to buy."

"But doesn't the money go to the youth group?"

She tried to come up with another counter-argument, but failed. "Alright, but the dollar is going to come out of your allowance."

"Sweet." He tightened the snaps on the back of the cap and rolled the bill before snuggling it on his head.

"Now it looks like what we need here is a little more organization. Why don't you go take that pile of clothes and start separating them." She pointed to a mountainous pile of clothes nearby. "And fold them while you're at it."

"What?"

"You heard me. And don't act like I haven't taught you to fold your clothes."

He gave her a petulant look but picked up the shirt on top anyway. It was one of those old man, panama shirts. He rolled it over his hands in a triple roll that looked almost like a fold, and started a new pile on his right, glancing at his mom to see if she noticed. She was busy sorting cookware, trying to find the tops that matched each bottom. Next was a Nirvana t-shirt, rolled into a flattened ball and placed on his left. "Don't they have a radio in this place?"

"No, honey." Mary looked distracted. "Keep going. You're doing a great job." She looked around the room, searching for something.

"Did I bring that blender with us?"

"No, Mom. I think you left it on the counter."

"Shoot. Will you be okay here while I go get it?" She picked up her purse and rooted through it for her keys.

"Yeah, sure, Mom. No prob."

Christian waited until the door shut behind her to leave his half-sorted clothes. He wandered around until he found some toys. He picked up an unclothed Barbie and a Ken doll dressed in an old paisley jacket and nothing else.

He turned Ken to face Barbie.

"You are so beautiful, with clouds rolling through your eyes." Christian's face took on a trance-like state.

"As are you. The universe is ours. Come. Let us play." Dark smoke swirled through Christian's eyes. Barbie snapped her fingers and great white wings grew out of Ken's back.

As Christian loosened his hold on the dolls, they rose from

his hands, floating in mid-air. The dolls stretched their articulated limbs, emanating a diffused glow from within.

"In the beginning, I was. And in being, I rejoiced." Barbie spun slowly in place. "But after a time, that was not enough. I brought you forth and together, we rejoiced." Barbie tapped Ken's wings, freeing them to beat majestically.

Ken's face lit up with adoration. "And together, we were more than the sum of our parts." Barbie floated higher into the air as Ken thrashed his wings to follow. They danced an aerial waltz to a haunting, barely audible choir. Christian's hands moved slightly, directing their movements. They swooped gracefully through the air as if two parts of a whole.

Ken frowned. "And then you brought *them*. They charmed you, enthralled you." Barbie floated down to hover over a bag of green plastic army men. "They fascinated you even when they betrayed you. You were spellbound even as they warped your words."

Barbie turned her back on Ken to concentrate on the army men.

"And You *forgave* them. Do you remember that? You forgave *them!*" Ken spat out the last word scathingly as he plunged past Barbie, but she didn't notice his passing.

Ken's wings flailed with much less coordination than before, jerking him through the air as the choir settled on a minor chord. He plummeted in a free fall, his wings tucked tightly against his back, pulling out only at the last minute, inches from the tiled floor. He repeated the maneuver with abandon. Over and over, he flung himself at the floor, never quite letting himself slam into it. After a half dozen attempts, he glided out of his dive and stretched his wings to their limits. Ken smiled briefly, remembering the grand dance. He replayed their old steps, one-sided, soaring higher and higher.

"I wish your eyes would stray my way once more. Maybe if I fly higher still."

Christian waved his arm and Ken flew even higher,

watching Barbie shed a tear for the battling army men. Ken hovered just below the ceiling, directly under a halogen track light, watching Barbie shed tear after tear.

"What is that wetness on my back? Surely you weep for me as well?" Ken reached back to wipe the tears from his shoulders, but found only empty sockets where his wings had been before they melted. His fall began in slow motion.

"If my tears could flood the world, I could drown in them." His descent accelerated.

"What the *hell*?" Both dolls crashed to the floor as Christian whirled to see Phillip at the door.

"Oh my god. Your eyes... are black."

"Call not upon your god in my presence." Christian's voice echoed inhumanly. The door slammed behind Phillip.

"You. You're the one who did that earlier. You made the..." Phillip backed against the wall.

Wispy black filaments coalesced around Christian's body, swirling around it a hair's breadth from its surface. Searching tentacles reached toward Phillip.

"Made the water turn to blood? Yes, I did. In fact, take a look. I wasn't quite done."

A hand mirror flew across the room to hang in the air in front of Phillip's face. One of the threads peeled off Christian and snaked toward Phillip. It touched his forehead and blood blossomed on his skin.

"No..." Gurgling noises were coming from Phillip's throat.

"You are an abomination. You don't deserve pity, much less forgiveness." Christian's midnight eyes bored into Phillip's.

"I am an abomination." Phillip's features slackened.

"You don't deserve to live, do you?"

"I don't deserve to live," Phillip repeated.

"Go home and at least do one thing right."

The door opened and Phillip skulked through the exit

abjectly.

The undulating threads snapped back to Christian and sunk into his skin. The mirror shattered as it dropped to the floor. Christian collapsed onto a pile of baby's clothes, eyes closed in fatigue after they faded to blue.

~~*~*

Father Mike poured half a glass of Coke over three ice cubes. He opened the drawer of his desk and pulled out the Jack Daniels bottle hidden under some papers. He put it down on the desk and stared out the window at the oak-lined street. He could hear the grinding of the streetcar wheels on the metal track as it passed.

What are we going to do?

He slugged the Coke, leaving only the ice cubes before pouring the bourbon. He filled the glass past the halfway mark, before he stopped and capped the bottle. He didn't bother to put it away just yet.

Is this what we wanted?

He drank half the bourbon in the glass in one swallow without wincing and put the glass back down on the desktop. He wandered around his office looking at the pictures hanging on the wall: one of he and Father Anthony and Father Joseph at the Italian airport, all three faces full of excitement, one of Christian in Mary's arms shortly after his birth, and one the day he took his vows. He looked back at the newspaper on his desk and shook his head.

Something is definitely wrong.

He drained the rest of his glass and poured some more. That kid had a beef with Christian. He had seen Christian after the blood

incident and had known immediately that he was behind it. And he
had laughed. He had enjoyed it. It was a prank, yes. If that was the
only thing, he might overlook it. But all the other little 'pranks'
added to what he just read made him wonder. Mary, on the other
hand, thought everything was fine. 'Teenage hijinks', she called
them. But they were escalating. *Is this what we get from the savior?*
He drank the last of the bourbon and opened the paper once again.

Local Teen Commits Suicide

Phillip Mayfield, 13, was found Sunday evening hanging
from a rope in the garage of his uptown home. According to
his mother, Suzanne, he left no note and had shown no signs
of depression.
"What can bring a child to kill himself?" she asked. The
answer to that question will remain unanswered for now.
Phillip was an eighth grader at St Michael's School and
active in the church's youth group. Services will be held at
St. Michael's Church on Saturday at 10:00 a.m. The family
has asked that donations be made to the youth group in lieu
of flowers.

Chapter 5

Italy
2013

Carlo cracked a smile as he finished his morning workout. *Finally. After twenty-five years of searching, and God knows how many years of waiting... I've found him.* He wiped his forehead with the towel hanging around his neck. *It's got to be him this time. The age is right, twenty-five. He is unnaturally 'lucky', and people are dropping like flies around him.* Carlo flipped through the Newsweek spread open on the carpet next to him. *Whiz kid's net worth breaks half a billion dollars as he turns twenty-five? Certainly that isn't luck, combined with the fact that much of it was compiled on the deaths of those other CEO's. There seems to be a suicide aberration among American business leaders that he, and he alone has managed to exploit. The article doesn't list his birthplace, but mentions growing up in New Orleans. That fits as well.*

Carlo picked up the magazine and laid it on the desk. He threw the towel on the bed and walked to the small kitchen. He carefully measured 4 teaspoons of psyllium husks into the blender, followed by honey, yogurt, alfalfa, banana, and kiwi. Blended, it made a thick, greenish shake, which he drank without stopping for a breath. Returning to his desk, Carlo scrutinized the article and the myriad of notes he had taken over the last years. *Now, what to do with him? And what to do with those protecting him? How did he compel priests to serve him? I must be prepared to deal with them, also. He must be stopped, that is certain. But, how?* An aged tome on his bookshelf drew his attention. The leather was worn through in places, and showed multiple layers of repairs over the years. He regarded it affectionately. *I wish you had all the answers. You've gotten us this far, but now that he's been identified... I guess the first step is to fly back to America and get more information, before deciding on the correct course of action.*

Carlo opened his closet and dragged out a well-worn trunk. He opened it and began rummaging through the array of weapons within. He ran his hand down the length of a crusader's sword, still sharp after all these years. He carefully put it down on the floor. He held up a felt bag, slowly peeling open the top to reveal an eleven-segment iron whip. He flexed the hinge points to ensure that they were functioning properly. Moving the bag exposed more contemporary weapons, tasers and guns of countless calibers. *I'll have to ship this ahead separately. There's absolutely no way I could get any of this through international airport security.*

~~*~*

New Orleans

"Detective Hooper, over here." The street cop waved Danny past the cordon.

"Jesus, Charles, it's Danny. It's not like we haven't known each other for ten years."

"Yes sir, Detective Danny. And might I say, you don't look a day over forty." Charles grinned.

"That's because I'm thirty-two, ass." Danny's smile faded. "Did he beat me here again?"

"That would be another yes sir, sir." Charles directed Danny past the forensics unit dusting and taking pictures.

"Damn it. There goes my performance review, again." Danny took the steps two at a time but stopped at the door. "What do we have here?"

Charles looked down for a minute. "Stan's been up there for a while. He can give you a better idea."

Danny stepped into the foyer, momentarily stunned by the grandeur. His fifty-dollar dress shoes clicked loudly on the white marble floor. Directly ahead of him, standing on a pedestal that probably cost more than any of the paintings in his apartment was a Chinese looking vase that screamed money. To his right, a carved mahogany railing twisted upwards to the second floor where he could hear his partner yelling at a tech. He grimaced. Upstairs, he worked his way past two more technicians taking pictures as he entered the family room.

"What are we working with, Stan?"

Stan turned away from the cop he had been berating. "Finally decided to get your ass out of bed?"

Danny sighed. "Come on, stop giving me grief. What've we got here?"

Stan pointed to the three bodies lying at odd angles on the sofa. "Looks like another murder/suicide. That makes eighteen this month?"

"Nineteen. Jesus. What the fuck is going on? I think that

makes 169 this year and four months left to go. Who are they, anyway?"

Stan read from his notebook. "Jesse Corkan and family." He pointed to the bodies. "On the left is Maggie, Jessie's wife, then his daughter, Jennifer, and her younger brother, Jordan."

Danny searched the room with his eyes. "Where's Jesse?"

"He's in the bedroom with Maggie's parents." He looked down at the notebook. "Earl and Barbara. They picked the wrong time to visit their daughter."

"It looks like they were just sitting there watching TV. Shouldn't the kids have been off to school?"

"Should've been. Who knows? You see what's in front of them?"

Danny noticed three drinks on the coffee table in front of them. "The drinks? Why?"

"Smell them."

Danny slipped on a glove and lifted the glass closest to him. He inhaled deeply.

"Almonds?"

"Yeah, most likely cyanide. The three in the bedroom have the same."

"It's not staged like your typical suicide pact. Why the two separate groups?"

"Not sure. Maybe the grandparents didn't want to watch their grand kids die?"

"You think they all did this willingly?"

"Danny, do you see any signs of struggle?"

Danny looked around the room. Everything looked neat and organized, maybe too organized for a family with teenagers. It looked freshly cleaned.

Stan tapped his notebook on the back of a wing chair. "I just don't get it. A successful businessman with everything going for him... He's got a wife and kids, an uptown mansion, and two

BMW's in the garage. Why?"

Danny smirked. "Have you seen the stock market, lately. My fucking 401k would barely pay for a trip next door."

"Jesus, Danny. Be serious. Money problems? I doubt it. Here and there, sure, but whole families? In numbers like this?"

Danny's face became serious again. "There's got to be a connection. Are we sure there's no sign of foul play?"

Stan shook his head. "No forced entry and no sign of struggle. They're dusting for prints, but I don't think they'll find anything."

The technicians looked up as Danny slapped his hand on the table, making the glasses bounce.

"There's a reason these folks are dead, god damn it. Find it!"

Chapter 6

Father Michael sat across his desk from Father Anthony and Father Joseph. Both showed signs of aging. They weren't young when the three of them had gathered in Turin, but now they both looked older than their sixty plus years. *This is going to make me look their age before it's all said and done.* Without saying a word, he opened last week's edition of Newsweek and the Wall Street Journal and turned them to face the other two priests. Three headlines jumped off the pages:

Christian McMillan Surpasses $500 Million Net Worth at 25.

FTG Inc. CEO Kevin Delahouse's Suicide Leads to Sell Off.

McMillan Industries Makes Killing Off Company's Misfortune.

Father Mike watched the two skim through the articles. "This should be nothing new to you. I've sent you reports of my concerns. I wanted to have this meeting because I feel you are overlooking the seriousness of this situation. You're like Mary, glossing over what's going on here. Something is wrong. Very wrong."

Father Anthony and Father Joseph looked at each other and then at Father Mike, but said nothing.

"*Come on.* You've got to see that this is not turning out like we'd planned. I've looked for signs. I've looked for miracles. I've seen some impossible things, but I wouldn't call them miracles." Father Mike swept the papers off his desk. "Things are only getting worse."

Father Joseph shifted in his chair. Father Anthony stood up and picked the articles off the floor, neatly placing them on the corner of Father Mike's desk before walking over to the bookcase.

Father Mike pounded the desk to get their attention. "He's not human." He looked Father Joseph in the eye. "Yes, we knew that. But he's not Jesus, either. At least not the Jesus I've read about. Could we have made a mistake?" Father Mike waited for a response. "Say something for God's sake. At least nod your head and pretend you're listening."

Father Anthony turned from the bookcase holding a worn book in one hand. "Michael, calm down."

"Calm down? In the last thirteen years, fourteen people have been killed that I can attribute to him, and you want me to calm down? This blood is on our hands!"

Father Anthony put the book back on the shelf and slowly approached the desk. "First, Michael, these 'killings' were all suicides, am I right?"

"But..."

Father Anthony cut him off. "There is no evidence that Christian caused these deaths."

"Anthony, you haven't been here. You haven't seen the things he does for fun. No. There is no proof, but I am certain. He can be downright inhuman."

Father Joseph reached over and put his hand on top of Father Mike's hand. "Michael, I'm sure you are familiar with many of the letters and writings excluded from the bible."

Father Mike turned back to Father Joseph. "Yes, most of them were invalidated by the church centuries ago. They've been proven to be false."

"Proven? You've proved these actions were caused by Christian?" Father Anthony reached into his pocket and pulled out a pack of cigarettes. "Do you mind?"

Father Mike shook his head.

Father Anthony lit the end of the cigarette and took a long drag on it, holding the smoke in for as long as he could before expelling it.

"The church will never confirm them."

Father Joseph interrupted. "And they never will."

Father Anthony sent him a disapproving glance. "But that doesn't make them untrue." Father Anthony sat down, put both hands on the desk, and leaned toward Father Mike. "A lot of them detail Jesus being mischievous as a child, using his powers in, well, negative fashion when he didn't get his way. Almost like a childish tantrum."

Father Mike sat back in his chair. "Tantrums. Would you call murder a tantrum? Did young Jesus commit murder?"

"Back to murder? Again, all I see is suicides. But as for the other activities you've so meticulously documented, nobody wanted to hear about Jesus throwing a tantrum. Anything like that was deemed unnecessary by early church elders and withheld. They didn't want him to appear less sanctified."

Father Mike looked at him disbelievingly. "Are you sitting here, trying to tell me that you think this..." He gestured to the stack of journals on the shelf behind him. "This is just our Savior throwing a childish fit? And you've based this on what? Unsubstantiated writings that the church has invalidated?"

"They *have been* authenticated by church historians."

Father Mike whirled to face Father Joseph. "What? They have? Then why haven't I heard about this?"

"Seriously, Michael. Do you think any pope would approve releasing something to the public that would have tarnished Christ's image?"

"Oh my God. Now Jesus has an image?" Father Mike shoved his chair back from the desk and stalked to the other side of the room. "The church is just some big marketing group spinning publicity for the 'J.C.' ?"

"We don't need your sarcasm right now." Father Anthony put his hand on Father Mike's shoulder, but Father Mike shook it off. "Think about it, Michael. What would happen if the church gave people a reason to think that Jesus, at any point in his life, was fallible? That he was something less than God? It would be religious anarchy."

"I refuse to believe in Jesus as a brat god."

Father Anthony finished the last of his cigarette and ground it out in the glass ashtray on the desk. "People are already pushing God and Jesus out of their lives more and more everyday. The theory of evolution... technology... People worship their iPhones more than they go to church. Hell, we should have an app. for that."

"I hate to tell you, but science has already won. Cloning is science, incarnate. Science created this *thing*, not religion. We convinced ourselves that we were doing God's bidding. Have you considered the alternative?"

The two priests remained silent. Father Mike grabbed the topmost journal and slammed it onto the desk. The sound echoed throughout the room.

"You've read this, I assume? The *little* things he did to Mary and me... Those things, I could write off, but I'm telling you, he is behind *every* one of those suicides. That is *not* Jesus in those pages."

Father Anthony and Father Joseph exchanged a knowing glance.

"What?" Father Mike looked back and forth between them. "There's more?"

Father Anthony walked back to the bookcase, scanned the titles, and pulled down a small bible. He pressed it to his chest.

"You know the writings of Thomas?" Father Mike nodded, a puzzled look growing on his face. "In some of his writings, he speaks of Lucifer. He wrote about what he can and can't do. Only some of these writings made it into the bible."

"Some?"

"Yes, only some. The rest was omitted. Sometimes I feel that more was left out of the bible than put in. One of the things he wrote..."

With an audible click, they were plunged into darkness. Only the oak shaded sunlight filtering through the small window illuminated their faces.

"Sorry, Fathers, this is a very old building and the wiring needs updating. Hopefully..."

A loud knocking on the door interrupted him. The door opened and Sister Mary Elizabeth entered the room following the lit candle in her hand.

"Father Michael, I think we blew a fuse again. Would you mind checking it? We're the only four here today, and as much as I hate to admit it, I am somewhat afraid of the dark."

"Excuse me, Fathers, we'll have to finish this conversation in a minute. Sister, could you bring some coffee. There's a fresh pot next door. And there are plenty of windows in that room." He smirked and winked at her.

"Of course, Father Mike, and thank you for not making fun of me." She rolled her eyes as she ducked out of the room.

Father Mike hesitated at the door. He turned around slowly, with a scowl.

"This." He indicated the articles on his desk. "This is on us, no matter what you say. It is our moral imperative to make it right, whatever the cost."

No one said a word as he opened the door the rest of the way and walked out.

I know I can't be the only one who sees this as something more than a problem. When he reached the electrical room, Father Mike fumbled with the lid to the fuse box, but it refused to be lifted. He tried yanking on it, but with no luck.

"Come on. Open, damn it!" He slammed his hand against the lid in frustration, raining rust onto the bare concrete floor. Grunting in exertion, he heard a metallic screech as it finally opened. He had to bang the flashlight on the ledge twice to get it to turn on so he could inspect the fuses.

"Damn old building." *We need to get this whole place rewired in a bad way. I wouldn't be surprised to find knob and tube wiring in here.* He unscrewed the blown fuse and looked for a match among the loose ones lying in the bottom of the box.

"Of course not." He pocketed the fuse for reference. *I guess I'm off to the hardware store.*

~~*~*

The candle on the desk flickered with a life of its own. Shadows reached out to the far wall and danced spasmodically. Father Anthony took another sip from his coffee mug and regarded Father Joseph studying the twitching frolickers.

"Could we have made a mistake? We did everything right. It

should have worked."

Father Joseph continued to stare absently into the darkness. "*We* did everything right?"

Father Anthony raised his eyebrows. "You're saying this was *my* fault? We all agreed."

Father Joseph turned from his studies. "You misunderstand me, Anthony. That has been our mistake all along. We misunderstood." He closed his eyes. "We took God's will into our own hands."

"But we meant to bring the greatest good into the world..." Father Anthony shook his head.

"What we meant..." Father Joseph laughed bitterly. "The road to Hell is paved with good intentions. Who knew to take that literally?"

"Joseph, you're getting maudlin. We can fix this, you know."

"We need more light." Father Joseph rose and approached the bookshelf. He opened a box and removed two more candles. "The good thing about a black out in a church is there is always an abundance of candles."

Father Anthony sat back in his chair and regarded Father Joseph with concern. "I said we could fix this. If this was a mistake, then we fix it."

"I believe we already tried the 'means justifying the end' approach. That's what got us here. Now you want to break a commandment?"

"Is it murder if he was made? *You* said we took God's will into our hands. *We* made this, not God. We would simply be cleaning up our own mess."

Father Joseph picked up the empty coffee cups and put the two candle pillars in the saucers. He took a deep breath. "*If* this was a mistake then are you saying that you're prepared to kill? No matter who made what, that's what you're talking about, killing. Ten minutes ago you were trying to convince Father Michael that what he wrote about was merely tantrums, and now you have blood dripping from your tongue?"

"If what we have here is not only not divine, but not human... Then, yes, it's our duty to destroy it."

Father Joseph used the lit taper to light the two pillars, suffusing the room with light. He looked up and immediately dropped the candle he was holding when he saw Christian standing in the doorway. The flame was doused when it hit the floor, splashing molten wax in a Rorschach pattern.

Christian scrutinized the two priests without moving from the door. His Armani suit draped flawlessly across his body. Father Joseph took a step back. Christian turned his gaze on Father Anthony, drowning him in the void that was his eyes. Frost-crystallized darkness exuded from them, giving the room an unseasonable chill.

"I'm not an expert on the matter, but I really don't think it's proper for men of the cloth to be discussing the slaying of a human being, do you?"

"Christian..."

Father Anthony scraped his chair back and backed away from him. "We've been worried about some of the things we've..."

"*Worried?*" Christian's voice exploded. His face contorted for a minute then flattened out again. "Worried *for* me, or worried *about* me?"

Father Anthony's hand fumbled in his pocket. "Worried for you, of course."

Christian burst out laughing. "Of course, of course. The spokesperson for organized religion is worried that I might not be the second coming of Jesus as he planned and wrought." Christian strode into the room, causing both priests to back further away.

"I'm a mistake? *I'm* a mistake? Look in the mirror, you worthless pieces of... No. You're not worth the effort."

Father Anthony removed a small crucifix from his pocket and stroked it desperately.

"Our Father, who art in Heaven, Hallowed be thy name..."

Christian's eyes bored into his. "Does he listen to *you* when you talk to him? I've been calling him for ages." Christian shook his head. "There is a time for words... and then there's a time for actions."

Father Anthony stared at Christian with eyes wide open.

"Thy kingdom come..."

Christian chuckled. "Are you sure you want the coming of a kingdom? Watch what you ask for. I'd think you would have already learned that lesson by now." Christian swept his arms in a wide circular motion. "Do you think all the things you've seen in this world are horrific? Is that why you called me?"

He sat down in the chair Father Anthony had used. Christian's eyes became darker at the same time that all the candles were snuffed.

"Just wait until this kingdom comes."

A bell jingled as the door closed behind Father Mike at the hardware store. *I hate those things. I don't know why, but they drive me up a wall.* He made his way past bins of what looked like fifteen-year old, yellowed-package sundries. At the counter, a mid-twenties tattooed man wearing a name tag that read "Tom" looked up from the book he was reading.

"Whatcha need today, Father Mike?"

"A fuse." He handed over the blown fuse. "I hope you have some of this one on hand."

"Father, I always keep extras on hand just for you. Some days, you're my only customer."

"Trust me, Tom. We appreciate it. Going without lights is

one thing, but when the A/C goes out, that's another thing altogether. It's hard to get people your age in to pray as it is. When it's ninety degrees out with ninety-eight percent humidity, and even hotter inside... Let's just say that when that happens, you've got more customers than I do." Father Mike pulled out his wallet and handed Tom a twenty-dollar bill.

"I'm going to ask the diocese to approve rewiring the whole building. Even if we don't get any new parishioners, hopefully we can keep the ones we've got."

Tom smiled. "Please don't do that. The church is one of our best customers."

Father Mike patted him on the shoulder. "Don't worry, son. The church doesn't spend money that easily. *If* I can get it approved, it'll probably take at least a couple years."

Father Mike reached over to take the bag of fuses out of Tom's hand. He pulled, but Tom refused to let go. Tom's eyes glassed over, as he stared through Father Mike.

"Forgive us our trespasses, as we forgive those who trespass against us..." Tom's voice sounded older and mechanical.

Father Mike grabbed Tom's wrist with his other hand and continued pulling on the bag. "Tom, are you okay?"

"And lead us not into temptation, but deliver us from evil..." Tom began to choke. He let go of the bag and held his hands to his head as hissing noises came out of his mouth.

"Tom!"

Tom looked up at Father Mike as if nothing had happened. He dropped his hands from his head and shut the register drawer.

"What'd you say, Father?" His voice sounded like it always did.

"What were you just saying, Tom? You sounded like you were choking."

Tom shook his head, perplexed. "I said, 'Here's your change.' Choking? Are you sure?" He cleared his throat. "No. Nothing there."

Father Mike swept the change off the counter and pocketed it. He ran out the door, bells tinkling in his wake. He jogged briskly back to the church. Nearing the front steps, he stopped short as he noticed Christian opening the door of his Lexus directly across the street.

"Christian, what are you doing here?" He walked across the street to give him a hug. Christian seemed reluctant about the hug and pushed him away after only a few seconds. He stepped back, admiring Christian's outfit.

"I can't get over seeing you in these fancy tailored suits. You look so... chic."

"Hiya, Mike. You look, well, the same. I was just here checking on some things. Sorry I can't stay and chat. You know how I love catching up." Christian winked at him. "But I've got way too many things to do."

Christian sat down in the driver's seat and pulled the seat belt across his body. "Can't be too careful, Father Mike. Always wear your seat belt." He turned the key and the engine roared to life. Classical music drifted out of the open window.

"Oh." He turned back to Father Mike. "And sorry about the mess." He smiled and smoothly accelerated away.

Father Mike watched him drive off. "What the hell is going on today?" He turned back to the church, heading for the small side door.

Chapter 7

Father Mike screwed the new fuse into the empty spot. The fixture in the hall behind him turned on. He placed the extras in the bottom of the fuse box and swung the door a couple times to loosen it up before he closed it. As he walked back toward his office, he heard dripping sounds coming from the sanctuary.

Oh hell, they've been waiting this long...

He opened the door to the nave and entered. The lights were off in both the sanctuary and the nave, not because of a blown fuse, but to save money. The only lights in the room were the multicolored beams streaming through the stained glass windows. The altar was hidden in the shadows. He studied the rainbow puddles on the floor as he approached the sanctuary.

Definitely something wet sounding. I hope we don't have a roof leak on top of the old wiring.

He stepped in a puddle of brown light that rippled like none of the others had. *What?* He stooped down and touched the surface.

The floor was wet. There wasn't quite enough light to see the extent of the leak, but what he could see of the puddle extended about six feet in diameter. *Damn, there's more money we're going to need. I'd better turn on the lights and see how bad this is.* He walked blindly to the back corner of the sanctuary and flipped the bank of switches. Bright light flooded the room. Father Mike fell backward as the suddenly illuminated altar revealed three human heads.

"Oh shit." He crossed himself before approaching the front of the altar. Father Anthony, Father Joseph, and Sister Mary Elizabeth stared at him with unseeing eyes. Father Mike hunched over and vomited on the floor. He fell sideways into the altar as he crumpled to the floor, causing one of the precariously balanced heads to topple and roll down the aisle. His eyes unwillingly followed it. It came to rest at the edge of the puddle he had been checking out.

"Blood... So much blood..." The pool of blood splashed as something fell from above. Against his better judgment, Father Mike slowly bent his neck to look up. Hanging from the lights, twenty-five feet up, were three headless corpses. They were hung by their feet with the necks facing down, draining to the floor. Father Mike heaved again and stumbled to the front doors.

~~*~*

Danny pulled up in front of the church as Stan was walking down the front steps. He jogged across the sidewalk, catching a glimpse of Father Mike sitting on the edge of the steps with his head in his hands.

"How do you always make it to the scene before I do?"

Stan walked past him without acknowledging the greeting.

He bent over the shrubs at the end of the steps and threw up.

Danny watched him, shocked.

"I've never seen you... What's wrong?" Danny pulled out a handkerchief and held it out for Stan.

"Stan, what is it?"

"This one is definitely not a suicide. What kind of monster does that?"

Danny left Stan at the base of the steps and headed inside to find out what had happened. The scene that greeted him was surreal. The C.S.I. team had set up Klieg lights, filling the church with an unearthly white light. A half-dozen officers meandered about the floor almost directly under where the three bodies hung like giant macabre mistletoe. The two heads on the altar had fallen on their sides, and the third was still lying beside the bloodstain as if contemplating it from the floor's perspective.

"How the hell did he get them up there?"

A few techs looked up, but no one answered him.

"Anyone? They're hanging, what? Thirty feet up? At one hundred plus pounds each? Anyone see a scissor-lift around?"

Silence and shaking heads were his only answer.

"Seriously, how did he get them up there?" Again no response. "I need someone to find out. Look for ladders... something."

He addressed the tech dusting for prints on the altar. "Any idea what he used to remove the heads?"

The tech put down his brush. "No luck yet, sir. We've ruled out bladed instruments. They aren't clean cuts. If anything, they look ripped, as impossible as that sounds."

"Okay, keep looking." He raised his voice so all could hear. "Get me some answers people. This is going to be a media shit-storm. The quicker we get answers, the less shit rains down on us."

Danny headed back out the front doors. Stan had recovered from his nausea and was interrogating Father Mike. As he approached them, he could hear Stan asking Father Mike where he had been earlier this morning. Father Mike started to reply, but appeared unbalanced, reaching out to steady himself on the coping beside the steps.

"Do you mind if I take a short walk? I've got to get away from all this for a few minutes." He looked back over his shoulder at the doors to the vestibule. "I'll be able to answer your questions better once I clear my mind of that..." He shuddered and turned back to Stan.

Stan nodded. "Alright, but be back in fifteen or twenty minutes. We've got to get moving on this thing."

Father Mike walked aimlessly down the street. With all the activity back at the church, the street was deserted. *Sorry about the mess? That's what he said, and with a God damned smile, no less. What'd they do to deserve that? They were instrumental to bringing him into this world.* He loosened the clerical collar at his neck and picked up his pace. *Nowhere to go, but going there fast.* He stopped with a horrified look on his face. *Oh my God. What if he finds my journals? My life will be less than worthless.*

The sky darkened as he continued down the street, and a cold breeze sprang up from nowhere. *What the hell? It's August.* His teeth rattled as the sudden chill whipped through his shirt. *Must be a storm coming. But, damn, it's downright cold.* He hunched over against the growing wind.

Ah, Starbucks. The ubiquitous green and white sign beckoned. *Refuge and caffeine, just what I need.*

He opened the door and breathed a sigh of relief when it closed behind him, blocking off the strangely frigid air. The roasted bean aroma added a little warmth back into his body.

The respite from the weather allowed his earlier concerns to resurface. *What is he going to do next? He obviously has no morals, no compunctions, and seemingly endless resources. He could take over the world in short order if he wanted. What comes after revenge, and am I on that list?*

The barista coughed into his hand. "Can I make you something?"

"Oh sorry, I'm afraid I'm a bit preoccupied." He scanned the menu on the wall, his face clouding in confusion. "Just a coffee, please."

The barista looked at him patiently. "Venti? Decaf? Whole or soy?"

Father Mike's confusion deepened. "When did getting a cup of coffee become so complicated? Just give me something black, full of caffeine, and about this big." He held his hand about five inches off the counter. He tried to hold it still, but it shook significantly.

"No problem, sir. It'll just be a minute. Did you want a pastry with that?"

Father Mike groaned. "No. No food."

The barista gave him a funny look, but continued pouring his coffee.

"Here you go, sir. One medium sized, dark roast coffee, plain." He handed the cup to Father Mike pointing to the side bar. "Lids, straws, and sweeteners are over there."

Father Mike's tremor sloshed half the coffee onto the counter.

"Damn." He reached for some napkins

"Are you okay? Did you burn yourself? That coffee comes out at one hundred and eighty-seven degrees."

Reciting from the manual? "No, no. My fault." Father Mike wiped the coffee with the napkin, but only managed to push it farther across the counter.

"Don't worry, sir... I mean, Father." The barista finally noticed his crooked clerical collar. "I can get that."

"Thanks." Father Mike passed the side bar of lids and sweeteners, deciding he didn't need anything else, and headed straight for the door.

"Hey, Father?"

Father Mike stopped and faced the counter again.

"If you don't pay, it comes out of my tips. It's only a buck ninety-five."

"Sorry. My mind's not all here at the moment." He threw the kid a five-dollar bill. "Keep the change for your troubles."

Father Mike spun around to the door, sloshing more coffee on his hand. He stopped, but the room continued. His eyes couldn't focus as the walls rushed by. His knees felt liquid. His field of vision rapidly shrunk to pinpoints of blurred motion.

Sounding like it came from underwater, a voice addressed him. "Father, what are you..."

He staggered out the door and onto the sidewalk. He leaned against a light post until the world stopped spinning. The sky had not lightened while he was in Starbucks, but it seemed to have lost all color. Drab, monotone-gray clouds lined the sky in all directions, unmoving. Still leaning with his back against the post, he surveyed his surroundings. The neighborhood seemed slightly askew. *What's wrong, here? This isn't the street I was walking on earlier.* Nothing moved. *It's almost like a war zone.* The cars parked on the side of the road were crusted with dust, and some looked burned out. All of them looked like they had been there for years, slowly decaying. A convertible that probably started its existence a bright red, lay on its side fading into a lifeless rust-brown.

A dry blast of air pelted him with sand. He looked down at his feet, half-buried in sand. *Sand? In New Orleans?* Feeling a little less lightheaded, Father Mike pushed himself off the light post and turned around. What he had thought was a light post was actually a cross buried in the ground. Where it met the sidewalk, the concrete was buckled as if from a great impact. Unwittingly, he looked up. A desiccated corpse dressed in a faded business suit hung from the beams. Father Mike stepped back into what should have been the Starbucks, but no longer. The dull metal walls behind him were seamless, showing no signs of doors or windows. *What the hell?*

Farther up the street, he could see more crosses impaled in the sidewalk, all jutting at different angles, all with figures attached to them. He stumbled toward the next closest. As he neared it, he heard a low moan coming from above. Her emaciated face was contorted into a grimace of pain. Most of her dress was hanging in long tatters, revealing angry red welts too numerous to count. *Is she still alive? How can she be? She's all bone, and not even bleeding.* He reached for the oversized nail piercing the body's feet to try to remove it, but it was too high above his head.

He began to feel lightheaded again. It was hard to breathe the air. There was an oppressive weight to it that pushed on his chest, not letting him get a full breath.

Oh, dear God, no. Father Mike could only stare at the next cross. On it, a child hung, clothes ripped and bruised skin showing in numerous places. He ran to the base of the cross, jumping with what little energy he had, trying to reach the child. He fell to the ground, wrenching his shoulder.

"Mikey, Mikey..." A familiar voice echoed condescendingly down the street. "We talked about being careful. Now you've gone and hurt yourself." Father Mike watched anxiously as Christian strolled down the middle of the street toward him. He struggled to rise, gasping as the pain in his shoulder twisted him in agony. He closed his eyes as Christian's dark orbs threatened to suck him out of his body.

Father Mike felt Christian take his hand and pull him up, making him scream in pain.

"Michael, *Father* Michael." Father Mike opened his eyes to see Christian smirking. "Do you know what your name means in Hebrew?" Christian waited for a response. Father Mike wheezed, trying to get more air into his lungs. "It means 'who is like God.' Kind of ironic in this situation, huh? Seems you tried to play God. Look what you got."

Something on the bleak landscape was moving. Dim shadows began to crawl across the concrete, sneaking out of crevices. Dark gray against lighter gray, they were barely visible except for the movement.

"My kingdom comes." Lightning flashed across the sky, leaving a harsh red glow in its wake. Thunder crashed into his body, knocking the breath out of him.

"Look around you, Michael. This is mine now." Father Mike dropped his gaze to his feet.

"*I said LOOK!*" Thunder shook the ground around him, as an unseen force jerked his head up.

Christian pointed to the now endless rows of crosses. "These are *my* souls. This is *my* world." Father Mike could hear moans coming from all directions. "Look at me, Michael."

Father Mike turned his head to face Christian.

"I live and breathe. I can once again affect." His voice softened slightly. "You gave me this. For that, I give you a choice." The thunder was crashing almost continuously. The ground shook so violently that he had to hold onto Christian to keep his balance.

"Behold!" Christian spread his arms wide and a crack appeared in the street before them. The rumbling drowned out everything but Christian's voice as the crack widened. Chunks of concrete disappeared into the void, causing flames to shoot up in their place. Father Mike jumped as a nearby car slid into the rapidly growing canyon. They stood in a five-foot wide island of asphalt in the center of the steaming gap. In a matter of minutes, the chasm stretched up and down the street for miles.

"The time has come." Christian whispered in his ear.

Shadows rose up out of the abyss, joining and metamorphosing into flowing shapes that were painful to watch. His eyes hurt trying to focus on them. Their edges were hard to define, as if they weren't made of solid matter. Their numbers grew every second, larger than any crowd he had ever seen. A vast chittering became audible over the thunder.

Bright shapes flashed into being inter-spaced randomly

among the flowing beasts. They resembled people, except for their height, and what looked like wings adorning their backs. The faces of the closest were incredibly beautiful, but their robes looked worn and torn in spots. The shadow forms encircled the glowing figures in groups, like pets, or squads. They snapped their jaws and appeared to be pulling on unseen tethers, trying to escape.

"Are... are those *angels? How?* "

"Have you never read the apocryphal books? You've been remiss in your education. How quickly your kind dismisses anything that disrupts its happy existence. Not all angels are trumpet-blowing, harp-playing puppy dogs."

Christian beckoned to the creatures amassed before him. His voice boomed over the crowd, silencing them.

"You're either with me..."

Christian pointed to the nearest cross and a bolt of pure white lightning engulfed it, leaving only smoking embers behind.

"Or you're against me." His voice dropped down to normal human level as he regarded Father Mike.

"Your namesake led the *choirs* of angels against me. At God's behest, he turned my brothers against me. I said I would give you a choice, and that I will. What will you do?"

Father Mike looked from Christian to the massed army in front of him. One by one, the shadow beasts resumed their chittering. The volume level threatened to overwhelm him as they all joined in. He clamped his hands to his ears. As one, the angels opened their mouths and every note in the musical scale screamed out. The discord ground at his joints, extracting more pain from his shoulder.

One scream grew louder than the others, overpowering them all. He looked back to Christian, thinking it must be him. Christian smiled, and reached out to lightly stroke his throat. The scream was his.

Chapter 8

The taxi dropped Carlo off at his new apartment as the sun dropped behind the horizon. What was left of the deep reds and blues contrasted with the drab faded paint on the houses surrounding him. Carlo tipped the driver and stepped out onto the sidewalk. *Definitely low rent district, but I knew that. It's a great place to be hidden.* The landlord had warned him over the phone that the rent was low because this was one of the only houses on the block that had been renovated since Hurricane Katrina. Carlo hadn't been sure whether he was trying to talk him out of it or bragging. *Doesn't matter, I'm not here for the amenities.*

He was relieved to see that his trunk had arrived and was safe in the living room. Carlo tossed his satchel on the sofa and checked the lock on the trunk. *Good, no signs of tampering.* He unlocked and opened it. The iron whip was on top where he had last placed it. *That could come in handy. No use wasting time. I might as well do some surveillance.* After placing it in his backpack, he looked for something a little more conventional. *Ah, the H&K P30.* He checked the clip, and then worked the action to put a round in the chamber. He tucked the gun in the small of his back.

Carlo punched the address to Christian's "Global Headquarters" into his GPS. *Not too bad, only a short walk from here.*

It took twenty minutes to walk to the downtown address. *Talk about overcompensation.* The twenty by sixty foot brightly lit sign on the front of the building screamed "McMillan Industries" to the world. *Definitely the right place, but, damn this is big.* He had to step to the opposite side of the street to take it all in. The building stretched a complete city block wide and at least forty stories tall. He could only assume that it took the depth of the block as well. *Well, how's that for nouveau riche ostentatious? It would have cost anyone else a fortune to buy everyone out of that building. In this case, I'm sure there were a handful of untimely deaths.* Carlo frowned as he crossed the street and headed up the twenty marble steps to the entrance doors. All but the central set had some sort of blackout on the glass, rendering them opaque. A large sign covered most of the bottom of the main door, "Entrance by Appointment Only." Underneath was a phone number. *I certainly won't be announcing my presence.* There was no other entrance visible along the front of the building. *There must be a service entrance somewhere.*

Turning the corner, he saw a driveway angling down under the building. *Promising. And no guards posted. Interesting.* He found the elevator in the center of the parking lot. The security camera pointed at the elevator instead of the parking lot. *Strange, but that works for me.* He opened his backpack and pulled out a can of fluorescent red spray paint. Standing on the bumper of the nearest car, he reached around and covered the lens. The elevator was card operated, but a standard key lock safeguarded the stairs. *And this is why God made lock picks!*

Upstairs, Carlo exited into the lobby. It was completely deserted. He noticed three monitors behind the security desk, but no signs that anyone had manned them recently. One screen showed only static. Another showed the front door from outside the building. *Hmm. I didn't see that one.* The last showed a huge,

Asian-carved mahogany door. It seemed totally out of place for the otherwise modern building. Nothing moved on any of the screens.

He surveyed the rest of the lobby. He couldn't find a tenant listing, nor was there art on any of the walls. *Minimalist. I wouldn't have expected that from the exterior.* It took less than two minutes to ascertain that there was nothing in the lobby besides the desk, three elevators, a restroom, and a stairwell. *Curious.*

Carlo climbed the stairs to the second floor. He opened the door to a generic hallway lined with more unmarked doors. Behind each one he opened, Carlo found nothing but empty rooms. Everything had been removed but the walls and carpet. *Even more curious.* The third and fourth floors were the same. *What is going on here?* He pressed the call button for the elevator. Inside, he decided to try the fortieth floor. No muzak assaulted his ears, only silence. A short ride later, he exited into one large space with absolutely nothing in it. Even the walls had been removed. He made a brisk circuit of the floor to ensure that there was nothing else, but could find no signs of the previous layout. It was as if it had always been this way.

Back in the elevator, he pressed the button for the forty-second floor. *The penthouse. If there's anything, it'll be there. But will Christian be there, also? I doubt it. It doesn't seem like anyone's here.* Carlo decided to risk it. He rested his hand on the rail as the elevator rushed upward. *I never realized how annoying an elevator could be with no music.* The bell dinged and the doors opened, revealing a fifteen-foot long hallway leading to the mahogany doors shown in the monitor in the lobby. He found the camera and covered it in paint like the other, before turning his attention on the door. *Strange. I could've sworn that door was Asian.* At closer range, the carvings were definitely African or some other tribal style.

He ran his fingers over the animal figures. *What the?* He jerked his hand back. The wood was warm to the touch, and slightly pliable, like foam, or flesh.

Feeling someone's eyes on him, Carlo spun around. No one was there, but at the end of the hallway, hanging from the ceiling beside the three elevators was a motion detector blinking red. *Damn complacency. I let my guard down. Shit!*

He ran back to the elevators, his mind racing, and pressed the call button. All three elevators opened immediately. *Must be set to standby here.* He pressed the first floor button of the left elevator and stepped back into the hall. He sent the right elevator to stop at the seventh floor before continuing on to the first. Carlo waited thirty seconds before entering the center elevator and pressing the first floor button. He immediately climbed on the handrails and opened the emergency door on the ceiling. He climbed onto the roof of the car and closed the hatch behind him, remaining crouched as the floors flew by. His heart raced as he steadied himself against the air rushing past. Floor after floor, he descended, wondering what he'd find waiting for him when he arrived.

The car slowed to a stop and the doors below him opened with a muffled ding. He could hear voices shouting. *Sounds like two guards. Is that all?* He leaped from the elevator top, reaching for the service ladder attached to the wall. Carlo grabbed a rung with his right hand. His breath was knocked out of him as the rest of his body slammed into it. As he scramble to gain a better purchase, his left foot slipped and jammed between the ladder and the wall. Dangling by one hand, he looked down to see his gun falling from his pants to crash into the metal below. *Crap.* The guards yelling grew louder as he pulled his foot out and placed it gingerly back on the ladder.

"Sam, I've got him here. You take the stairs. I'll watch the elevators in case he comes back down."

Carlo grabbed a rung with his other hand and pulled himself up. Finally getting his feet on the ladder, he was able to climb to the second floor door. He pried the doors open with his fingers and stepped out into the second floor hallway. *Okay, only one coming up the stairs.* He tested his ankle, only slightly sore. He opened his backpack and pulled out the iron whip. *Guess I've got to go old school.* The door crashed open and the guard rushed in, gun raised. Carlo dove to a somersault as the guard snapped off two shots. He rolled out and launched himself upright.

"What the hell we got here? A god damned Indiana Jones? See, boy, that shit only works in the movies. Here, guns win..."

Carlo put all his strength behind a quick whip of the metal chain and barb weapon. The guard tried to sidestep, but was unable to get out of its path. The spike on the end ripped a fifteen-inch long gash in his stomach as it swept by. Carlo followed the arc, spinning around with it until he was once again facing the guard. He snapped his wrist, straightening the chain and impelling the barb deep into the guard's shoulder. Another yank, and he was pulled to his knees.

The guard dropped his gun as he tried to hold his intestines inside his body, and scrambled to pick up what had already fallen on the floor. Carlo slowly edged closer, not wanting to underestimate him. The guard slipped in his own viscera, and struggled to rise.

"Shit, shit, shit..."

Carlo kicked the gun across the floor, out of his reach.

"Who is Indiana Jones?" Carlo swung his foot up, knocking the guard into the wall and watched to make sure he didn't get back up. A voice echoed up the stairwell.

"Sam, did you get him? Sam?"

Carlo quietly opened the door to the stairs and inched his way in. *Now what?* He rested for a second, letting his breathing slow down. He could hear the guard slowly coming up the stairs. Carlo risked a quick glance over the edge of the railing and saw the guard ten feet down pointing his gun at him. He jerked back as a bullet barely missed him. The crack of the gunshot in the confined space was almost unbearable.

"What'd you do to Sam, you piece of shit?"

Carlo gripped the handle of his whip with both hands. The guard's shoes slapped heavily on the concrete steps as he rushed up to meet him. *No time like now.* Carlo swung the length of the iron whip in a wide arc as he leaned over the edge of the stairwell. Before the guard could pull the trigger a second time, the metal segments wrapped around his neck in two loops.

Carlo jerked with all his strength, hearing bones crunch. He continued hauling upward until he pulled the guard over the railing. His arms trembled slightly as he held the guard, swaying for a couple minutes, to make sure he was dead. Carlo released the handle and leaned against the wall, breathing heavily. A satisfying thud followed by a metallic clattering of the whip echoed up the stairwell.

When he reached the landing at the bottom of the stairs, he retrieved his whip and put it back into his backpack. He had no doubt that the H&K was lost in the elevator shaft. He stepped over the motionless guard and continued down to the parking garage.

I'm not sure what I got out of that besides a slightly tweaked ankle. I now know Christian has a strange living environment, and is overconfident. Two guards? Then again, who would take him on? Carlo wiped his forehead with his sleeve and limped up the exit ramp.

Chapter *9*

Father Mike choked out another hoarse scream as he opened his eyes. Beeping electronics drew his attention first. *Hospital? What the hell?* It wasn't until he sat up that he noticed a man in his thirties standing in the corner watching him.

"Are you alright, Father?" He looked vaguely familiar, but He couldn't quite place him. He shook his head, trying to clear it of the vestiges of Christian's Hell.

"Bad dreams? After what I saw at the church, I don't blame you. I'm sure I'll have some doozies over the next couple nights."

That's where I remember him. He was with that other cop at the church. "What?" Father Mike dry swallowed a couple times. His voice was still scratchy. "What happened to me?" He tried to shut out the memories of the crucified boy's charred remains.

"It seems you had a panic attack yesterday at the coffee shop. The barista said you paid him, then started spinning around. Next thing he knew, you were wailing at the top of your lungs and curled up in a fetal position."

"Wow, that's... something."

"Must have been a hell of a nightmare, the way you were thrashing."

"Yeah, that it was." Father Mike shifted in bed and almost cried out from the pain shooting in his shoulder.

"Oh. Apparently you injured your shoulder when you fell. You should be careful with it."

Father Mike's eyes opened wide. *When I fell? Where? In the Starbucks or at the base of the cross?*

"You okay there, padre? You need me to call the nurse?"

"No. I'll be okay, but who exactly are you?"

"Father Michael, I'm Detective Hooper. You can call me Danny." He held out his badge so Father Mike could see it. "My partner, Stan was asking you some questions before all this happened. Do you mind if I ask you some more? The quicker we can get to the bottom of this, the better."

Father Mike nodded. "Sure, whatever you need, detective."

"Really, Danny is fine. Now what can you tell me about what happened at the church, yesterday?"

"Detect... Danny, you saw the same thing I saw. What else can I tell you? It was horrible." *Anyone else would ask 'who could do such a thing?' Just because I know, I should still ask.* "Who could do such a thing?"

"That's what we're trying to figure out. Can you tell me where you were when it was happening?" Danny scooted his chair closer to the bed and flipped open his notebook.

Father Mike's voice croaked when he tried to speak. "Can you get me a glass of water? My throat really hurts."

"Sure." Danny turned on the faucet and pulled a paper cup out of the cup holder. He turned around and handed it to Father Mike, watching as he gulped it down.

"So where were you?"

"I don't know, exactly. The power went out. I had been having a conference with Father Anthony and Father Joseph when a fuse blew."

"How'd you know it was a fuse?" Danny jotted some notes on his pad.

Father Mike laughed nervously. "Cause they're always blowing. The wiring in that building is deplorable."

"So the power went out. Then what?"

"I checked the fuse box, and sure enough, that's what it was."

Danny stopped him. "While you were doing this, where were Father Joseph and Father Anthony?"

"They stayed in my office. Sister Mary Elizabeth was getting them some coffee when I left them." Danny nodded at him to continue. "I didn't have the right fuse to replace it, so I had to go to the store to get it. When I got back..."

Father Mike closed his eyes and gripped the sheets tightly. No matter how hard he clenched his eyes, he could still see the three heads staring at him from the altar. *We brought this on ourselves.*

"Father, I know this is hard, but bear with me. How long were you gone?"

Father Mike thought for a minute. "I don't know. Maybe ten minutes, fifteen at the most. The store is around the corner from the church."

"Ten minutes? Including checking the box?"

"No, I guess not. But only five minutes for that. Why?"

Danny purposefully ignored the question. "Did they have trouble finding the fuse, or did you meet someone on the way back?"

"No, and no. What are you getting at?"

Danny stood up and paced around the room. "Well, did it take a long time to get the blown fuse out and replace it with the new one?"

"Detective, I had already removed the blown fuse. And it was a matter of seconds to screw the new one in. Now, I've told you that it took five minutes to get to the fuse box, and no more than fifteen to get back. That's a total of twenty minutes. There were no other conversations or meetings." Frustration was creeping into his voice. "That's it."

Danny dropped his notebook on the counter and rubbed his eyes.

"Father, I have a problem. You see, the timing makes no sense." Danny ticked his fingers as he spoke. "We have three dead bodies, killed in different areas of the church."

Father Mike sucked in his breath. *That part, I didn't know.*

"They were dragged into the sanctuary and up to the altar. At this point he took their heads off. I say 'took' since they weren't cut, or even hacked."

Father Mike stared at Danny, trying to keep his face expressionless.

"Then he bound their feet and somehow hoisted them twenty-five feet up into the lights, as far as we can tell, without a ladder or any other tool." Danny paused and looked down at his notebook. His hesitation showed on his face. He searched Father Mike's face, trying to judge his emotional stability.

"And somewhere between decapitating and hanging them... Whatever sick fuck did this... excuse the French, Father. Let's just say he mutilated their privates as well." Danny's dropped his head, no longer able to look Father Mike in the eye. "He did things to those people that I can't put into words, and I used to be a beat cop."

Father Mike began to shake, but struggled to hold his composure.

Danny walked over to the sink and rinsed his hands. When he turned back, his face was all business. "Now Father, all of that took a hell of a lot longer than twenty minutes."

"Are you suggesting that I..." Father Mike eyes widened, not having considered that before.

"No, not at all. In fact, I'm almost positive it wasn't you, at least not by yourself." Danny pulled his chair up to the edge of the bed and sat down. He leaned close and lowered his voice.

"*But,* it just doesn't add up. This points to a concerted effort by multiple people. It was most likely planned in advance by someone who knew intimate details about the workings in your church."

Father Mike turned his head away. *What can I tell him? I can't tell the truth. Not only will he not believe me, but I'll probably be thrown in a different kind of hospital. I can picture it now. 'Yes officer, I know who did it. But it was only one person. He has supernatural powers. That explains it, right?'*

"You're afraid, Father. You're afraid of something. Are you afraid they'll come back for you?" Danny leaned in closer.

"I promise you, Father, just give me what I need and I'll protect you. As a former altar boy, you have my word."

Father Mike shook his head. "Protect me?"

"Father, if it's gang related, we can take them off the street." Danny inched back from out of Father Mike's face.

"Gangs?" Father Mike scoffed. "Gangs... if only. You can't protect me."

Danny stood up and paced the room. "Father, we've got a whole division trained to deal with situations like this, but you've got to give us something to work with."

Father Mike ignored him; instead he stared out the window. His voice lowered to a whisper. "You won't be able to protect anybody."

~~*~*

Stan stared at the small kitchenette counter, trying to put together a chronology. The techs had cleaned up the glass from the broken coffee carafe, bringing it downtown to analyze for evidence. The coffee and bloodstained tiles had been left for the church to clean up. Adding insult to injury, the investigators had emptied all the drawers and cabinets onto the counters, and in some places, the floor and left it that way, making it hard to tell what mess had been a result of the crime and what had happened after. Whoever cleaned up this mess, here and throughout the building, would have to clean the crime scene and its aftermath.

Blood splatter painted the walls and even the ceiling. *What kind of rage does that?* Stan stepped over a pile of loose flatware, picking his way back to the door. *If I'm reading this right, this is where he murdered the nun.* He stepped into the hall and around to Father Mike's office. *And here's where he did the two priests. It's a shame the techs took this room apart. It'd be interesting to get a feel for this room the way he left it. Photos aren't nearly as good as a personal walk through.* He picked up an untitled book from a pile of similarly untitled books. He flipped it open and stopped at a random page. Neatly written script covered the page.

"Christian's eyes turned the color of coal and the child fell to the ground, breaking his arm. Christian giggled and went back to his Leggos."

Some kind of weird sci-fi horror. Strange type of book for a priest to be writing. Stan put the book down on the desk and paced the room looking for anything forensics might have missed.

Large bloodstain by the far wall. Probably killed both together. One strong and fast killer or multiple perps? Can't really tell. He followed the trail of blood the bodies had left as they had been dragged out of the room. *Side by side, so, at the same time. Must be more than one person. Don't see how anyone could drag two dead-weight bodies at one time.*

In the hallway, the two trails were joined by a third separate trail. *The nun. No signs of overlap so all three were dragged at the same time. Three perps?* Something on the floor drew his attention, something not quite right. He squatted down to see the marking more clearly. *What? Three blood trails, boot prints in the blood from the techs. Hold on. What is that?* He touched his finger to the heel of one of the boot prints. *Blood. On top of the print. This blood came after... Fuck!* He tried to control the shiver that wanted to take over his body. *Ice. Be ice.* His hand crept steadily to his holster. He had to swallow back the bile that was rising in his throat as he unsnapped the safety strap. He took three deep breaths to steady his nerves. In one motion, he popped up to a standing position and whirled around, gun drawn. He stood still, staring into the shadows and pointing his gun at nothing for a full minute. Finally, Stan let his arm drop. *Holy crap, I'm seriously losing it. This freaking case is giving me the creeps.*

Holding his gun down, but at ready, he followed the trails to the nave. As he entered, he led with his gun, sweeping it left then right, peering down the sight. Nothing moved but the multicolored dust motes floating in the air. He glanced up and his mind filled in the grisly details of the three bodies hanging from the lights as they had yesterday. Three ghost heads returned his gaze from the altar as he crossed the floor. He let out the breath he didn't realize he was holding. *Here's where it gets improbable. Three people or five, it almost doesn't matter. How did they get the bodies up there?* He stared up, contemplating the height. *And why? Why go to that trouble? There's definitely a lot of anger involved here. Someone went to a lot of effort to make a point. But who? Who has a beef with this church? And what is the point, exactly? Whoever they are, they risked being caught at any minute to set this elaborate tableau. They want someone's attention. Well, they definitely have mine.*

Stan holstered his gun and sat down in the first row of pews. He put one arm on top of the backrest of the pew and sat back, trying to learn something by osmosis. He closed his eyes and listened to the building noises. Small creaks whispered from the rafters. A fluorescent light ballast buzzed in the hallway outside the sanctuary. Outside, a car drove by playing a Rebirth Brass Band song. Slowly he tuned these noises out and tried to feel the heartbeat of the church.

Stan jumped up and nearly tripped over the pew cushion as the 1812 Overture blared out of his breast pocket.

"Shit! Motherfucker."

He grabbed his phone out of his pocket. Before answering it, he looked up at the cross.

"Sorry about that."

He put the phone to his ear. "Detective Stanley. You have something?"

"Stan, it's Jim. I'm going to need you to come down here to see this."

"To your office?"

"No, the morgue. I've got to show you something."

"What's this about? I saw the bodies when they came down yesterday. You found something new?"

"Stan, I'm going to have to show you. You're really not going to believe without seeing it."

"Alright. Give me a second to lock down the church. Did you call Danny?"

"He said he was in the middle of something with the other priest. He said you could catch him up."

"Very sharing of him. I'll have to thank him later for that. I'll be there in fifteen minutes."

Chapter *10*

Christian strolled down Magazine Street, casually absorbing the atmosphere. Boutique clothing shops were filled with thirty-something year old women holding up size zero dresses to their bodies and frowning. Ethnic restaurants hosted bored businessmen looking for something different. All around him, voices fluttered.

"Would you believe what my husband told me last night? He's such an insensitive snot sometimes..."

"That'll be three hundred and fifty seven dollars, ma'am. Will that be credit or cash?"

"Can you just bring me the bill, already? I'm in a hurry."

"Did you find out the results?"

Christian perked up as he watched an older couple inside an antique shop in deep conversation. He stepped in the open front door, absentmindedly browsing.

"Yes." the old man's shoulders slumped as he turned his head from his wife.

Christian picked up a silver rimmed crystal ashtray and turned it over, pretending to check the price as he listened. The couple didn't notice his presence.

"He said it's definitely a tumor, and malignant. I've never smoked a day in my life, and this is what I get?" The old man put down the silver pitcher he was polishing. "What am I going to do?"

The woman leaned in and hugged him. Even from twenty feet away, Christian had no trouble eavesdropping on her whispered reply.

"*We* will do everything we can to fight this. Did they tell you what the plan was?"

"Yes." The old man returned her hug for a minute, then pulled himself out of her arms. "Chemo and radiation, but they said I may not be strong enough for it."

She tried to shush him, but he held up a slightly shaking hand.

"*I* don't know if I have the strength for it. They say it's endless misery, constant nausea, pain, and exhaustion."

"Did you set up an appointment with the oncologist?"

"I'm not going to spend my last months on this earth in the hospital, throwing up and losing my hair." He ran his fingers over his head.

"Let's just see what he has to say." She took his hand and they sat down in a pair of matching reproduction Queen Anne chairs. "We don't have to make any decisions today. Today, let's just do something nice together." She smiled at him. Slowly, a small smile formed on his face.

The frown returned as he slapped his hand on the chair's arm.

"Oh, damn!"

"What?" She gave him a worried look.

"I guess it's too late, now."

"Baby, it's never too late. What?"

"I only have twenty-five thousand dollars in insurance

coverage. I'd been meaning to get more, before... Before this."

"Don't worry about that right now. We'll be fine." She grabbed his other hand and turned him so they faced each other. He held her gaze but couldn't manage to return her smile.

"One of my biggest fears is the thought of you struggling through life after I'm gone. I wanted you to be well taken care of."

"Baby, money doesn't mean anything without you. Look..." She shook his hands gently. "We've just started with this thing. Let's not talk about you as if your life's over already."

His face softened as he stood up and leaned over to kiss her.

"Let's get out of here. Play hooky. We can pack a lunch and picnic at Audubon Park. We haven't been there in ages. It's a beautiful day out."

"What about the store?"

His laugh was short and a little tense. "Who owns this store? The bank or us? Wait, don't answer that."

She punched him lightly in the arm.

"We can put a sign up that says *Closed Due to Death in the Family.*"

"Don't you dare. Don't even joke about that."

"Believe it or not, it feels better to be able to joke about it a little."

Christian looked around the store while he was listening in. On one of the walls, he noticed a reproduction of Duccio's *Madonna and Child*. A wry smile broke out on his face. "How loving and worshipful she looks upon you, brother. My mother sees me the same... And soon, so will our father."

The man spun around at the sound of Christian's voice.

"What? Can we help you? I didn't hear you come in."

Christian continued to ponder the painting. Without turning to him, he replied, "James, it's not you who can help me."

The woman's eyes widened. "How do you know his name?"

Christian turned his attention to her. "Angela, I have a very good sense of hearing. You're lucky I stumbled upon your shop today."

"What? How?" Angela edged behind her husband.

"Please, don't be afraid." He held out his hand to shake the old man's. "My name is Christian, and notwithstanding your bad news, today is your lucky day."

"How... How did you know all that?"

"James, Angela, do you believe in angels?" Christian walked to the counter and leaned on it, scrutinizing the pair huddled on the other side.

"If it's money you want, we've only got a few hundred dollars in the register, but take it and leave us alone." James held his arm around his wife protectively. "We've already had enough today."

Christian shook his head. "I told you, it's not about what you can give me. I'm here for you. I've come to show you the way."

"Look, Mr... Christian. Whatever you're trying to sell us, whatever you want us to donate... We don't have it. You came on the wrong day and to the wrong door."

Christian snapped his head away from them as his eyes spit obsidian fire. He took two breaths and pasted a smile on his face before he turned back.

"My dear, I told you, I'm an angel." He pointed to a print of *The Last Supper* hanging on the wall behind the couple. "I see you like religious art. So do I." He gestured and the print floated off the wall and above their heads into his hand. The couple stared at him in astonishment.

"Now what I love about religious art..." Christian continued as if nothing out of the ordinary had happened. "Is that the masters, like da Vinci, put all kinds of symbolism into their works. You never know what you'll find in them."

Christian turned the print around so they could see it. "Take this one, for instance. Numerous scholars have written about countless symbols and hidden codes in this painting. There is significance to the positions of the apostles, what order they're in, even the letters their shapes make. It's fascinating." Amusement showed on his face as he watched the couple staring at the print.

"But..." James interrupted.

"Bear with me for a minute. Let's take a closer look at the central figure." The rest of the print turned fuzzy as Jesus' face began to glow.

"Picture him without the beard and with shorter hair." Christian struck a similar pose as the couple looked at him like he was crazy.

"*Look* at it!"

"Oh." Angela's eyes widened in recognition. "You look a lot like him. Are you... Jesus?"

Christian chuckled as he put the print on the counter. "Close, but no. I am but an angel of mercy. I want to show you something."

The couple looked at each other apprehensively.

"No. No. This is my gift. Sit down."

When neither moved, Christian walked around the counter to help them. "Come on. If I wanted to hurt you, I would have already done it. Now, please sit down."

They reluctantly sat down, not sure what to expect next.

"Now lean back and close your eyes."

Angela pushed herself to the edge of her seat. "What is this all about?"

"Humor me. Please, close your eyes and relax." Christian turned to the front door and waved his hand. It slammed shut and locked with a click.

"Now, now. No peeking. Hollywood would pay a fortune to be able to do what I'm about to do."

The couple grabbed each other's hands and sat back in their chairs. There was a flash of brilliant light, and they found each other hovering over a hospital bed, looking down at their bodies. The James in front of them was curled on his side, his face contorted in pain even as he fitfully slept. His skin was loosely draped over his skeleton and devoid of hair. Angela was clothed in a worn, wrinkled dress and sat in the chair beside the bed looking like a war trauma victim. In the background, they heard a code blue being called and watched, as Angela jerked in her chair not sure for a second if it was for James. She got up and paced the room with a worried look on her face, stopping repeatedly to put a hand gently on his head.

Another blinding flash of light brought them to a small apartment. Angela sat on the couch holding a picture of James. She hugged it tight to her breast, crying softly. On the table in front of her, the couple could see a letter of demand from the bank giving her thirty days to catch up the mortgage or lose the store. She stood up and walked slowly to the sink, full of old, dirty dishes. She stared blindly at them, then abruptly turned and threw the picture across the room.

"Damn you!"

The picture shattered on the far wall, raining pieces of glass into the clutter on the floor. The silence that followed the crash was deafening.

She gasped and ran over, digging through the shards and trash to retrieve the picture. The frame fell in pieces, leaving only the photograph in her hand. Her bleeding fingers smudged the edges of it, but she couldn't see through her tear-laden eyes.

Light flared again, but when their eyes adjusted they were in the same room. It seemed the same, but when they looked around, they noticed some differences. The clutter looked older, more ingrained. The dishes in the sink appeared to have been left for weeks. The letter from the bank was no longer on the table, which was empty except for the photograph of James, folded and age-worn, with dried brown stains on the edges. Angela shuffled out of the bedroom dressed in a tattered and moth-eaten robe and dingy gray slippers.

She opened the small window overlooking the street below. Cold air whipped into the room, making her robe flutter. She seemed not to notice. Multicolored Christmas lights from outside reflected in the tears that rolled slowly down her face. With a faraway look in her eyes, she turned around and walked to the sofa, leaving the window open. She crumpled into the cushions and picked up the photograph. She shook her head.

"Why? Why did you have to leave me?"

Bright light exploded through the scene, leaving the couple back in their shop with Christian. Their hands gripped each other, white from exertion. James took his hand from hers and gently wiped the tears from her eyes, as his produced even more.

"You said you could help us. Can you cure this?"

Christian bowed his head. "Unfortunately, no. I can't change what's happened to you."

"Then what can you do?"

"I can only affect what is to come. I can give you a new life, after this one." Christian picked up a cross from the edge of the counter and held it out to them.

"God did this to you. He listened to your prayers, and allowed this to happen. You are his children, his beloved, and look what he let befall you."

Angela put her hand on James's knee and leaned forward. "What do we have to do?"

"Let him..." Christian looked upward. "Let him know how you feel. Tell him how upset you are. Tell him you don't like being a toy in his toy chest. Then..."

Christian turned back to the couple.

"Take your own lives."

They both gasped and looked at him like he was crazy.

"You can do it quickly and painlessly. Angela, you have enough sleeping pills left in your prescription for the two of you."

James stood up, his legs shaking slightly.

"But what does that get us. Even if it let's God know we're upset, we're dead. Yes, we skip the suffering and torture, but..."

Christian smiled. "But once you've left this life, I can raise you up again, into a new life. Together. Without cancer. No one will know." Christian waved his hand around the store. "Your business will be successful. You can live out eternity here on earth with each other."

"What? What kind of angel are you?"

Christian's smile faded. "I'm the kind of angel that cleans up God's messes."

Angela looked from the painting to Christian. "I know who you are."

Christian tossed the cross onto the counter and walked over to Angela. He squatted down in front of her chair until they were on the same level.

"I'm the one who won't judge you." He held out his hand to help her out of the chair. They both stood up. Christian turned to James.

"Did you follow his ten commandments? Did you put enough money in the collection plates? Did you go to church every Sunday, and on Easter and Christmas? Were you righteous?"

Christian offered a hand to James. "I'm not picky. Did you steal or covet? Hell, did you have naughty thoughts? Everyone does. Why should that exclude you from eternal paradise?"

James turned to his wife, looking dazed. "Is this what I think it is?" He looked back to Christian. "Are you..."

"*I* accept everyone, if they come with me *by choice*. He's big on that free will thing. You will have anything you could want. You've seen what I can do. What I've shown you here is just a small sample of what I can do."

Christian backed away from the couple, and turned to the door. He stopped, and facing the exit, addressed them. "*But*, it must be your choice. You must come to me." He turned his head back to them. "If not... If he sends you to me as punishment... There's nothing I can do. I am bound by his law to bring down every measure of suffering I can upon you, for eternity."

The couple watched as he walked to the door.

"Remember, sleeping pills are painless, unlike cancer. There is no prolonged misery, no sorrow, and no faded photographs. When you wake, it will be to a new world, a world of your choosing. He advocates choice and free will. Look at the possible outcomes. I showed you His path. Is that the direction you want to go? It's up to you."

He opened the door and stopped one more time. "I hope to see you tomorrow." He closed the door as he walked out.

Angela looked at James, then at the photograph of him next to the register.

"I can't. I just can't."

"Shh, honey. It's okay."

"It's *not* okay. I thought I could be strong for you. I thought I could be your peace. But that's not what's going to happen. You saw it. And yours, as painful as it will be, is the easy road. At least it will be over quickly. I... I will become a shell."

"Are we actually considering following the..."

"Don't say it. He didn't have horns and a pitchfork. He seemed compassionate. He cared about us. Even if he didn't offer an eternity of happiness, which by the way, he did, not having to go through what we saw... Isn't that enough? We don't have any children, no living relatives, it can be just about us."

James looked around the shop, at everything they had spent years building up. "Our entire lives are here, in this building, you, me, the store, our home above." He hugged her tightly. "I don't want to lose you, but worse, I don't want you to lose you."

"So..."

James walked to the front door and made sure it was locked. He turned the sign around to read 'Closed.' He turned back and hugged Angela, kissing her head.

"Let's go take a nap."

Her body shook, but she smiled and took his hand as they climbed the stairs.

~~*~*

The afternoon sun shined through the bedroom window, illuminating the couple lying on the bed. They cuddled together with peaceful faces. On the bedside table, an empty prescription bottle lay on its side next to two empty glasses.

The phone rang. Neither body moved. The phone rang five more times before the answering machine picked up and asked the caller to leave a message.

"Mr. Cooper? This is Dr. Pramir. Usually, I don't leave messages, but I thought you'd want to hear this as soon as possible. We reran your tests. It appears the first result was a false positive. We ran it three more times to be sure. Your tumor is benign. You don't have cancer."

"I apologize for the mistake. It only happens once in every thousand tests. I know it must have given you quite a scare, but now you can relax. We would appreciate it if you could give us a call sometime in the next couple days to schedule another appointment. We need to run some follow up tests, but don't worry; it's just a formality. Congratulations, Mr. Cooper."

Chapter *11*

Danny parked his car in the median in front of McMillan Plaza directly across the street from four squad cars with flashing blue lights. He walked to the front door and nodded at the officer manning it.

"So what time did Stan get here? I'm sure he's going to give me hell."

"Stan? He's not here. Something about the morgue, I think."

Danny stopped in his tracks. "Holy shit, I beat him to a scene? That's gotta be one for the record books."

"Don't get too excited. Wait 'til you see this one. It's pretty screwed up."

Danny looked over to the reception desk surrounded by caution tape. "How so? It looks pretty contained."

"Too contained if you ask me. That one..." The officer indicated the young man being questioned in the far corner. "Has an answer for everything."

"He's blowing smoke?" Noting the finely tailored suit, Danny figured it must be Mr. McMillan himself, or maybe his COO.

The officer raised his eyebrow. "I don't know about smoke, everything he says makes sense, but altogether, something stinks. You'll see."

Danny patted him on the shoulder as he passed. It wasn't until he reached the reception desk that he realized it was actually a security station. *That's strange. No reception desk? What company doesn't have a reception desk?*

Both chairs behind the desk were overturned, and two bodies in guard uniforms were lying on the ground. One had a large gash across his stomach and a bloodstain on his shoulder. The other's neck was twisted at an odd angle with dark red marks around it.

"Talk to me. Someone tell me what happened here."

The three officers talking to the young man in the corner looked at him and said something to each other. One of them came over to talk to Danny.

"Sir, what we've got here is a load of shit and shinola."

Danny shook his head. "Isn't that shit from... never mind. How so?"

"What *he* says..." The officer looked over at the young man. "Is that he came in this afternoon and found his two security guards exactly as you see them here."

"How long have they been dead?"

"Approximate time of death is between eight and ten o'clock last night."

"And he's the first person to notice them? No one came in this morning?"

The officer nodded. "That's what he said. He runs a 'lean machine' as he put it."

"Okay, okay. So let's say he discovers them this afternoon. What did he do next?"

"He called us, sir. He says he didn't touch them."

"So, one guard has his neck broken while the other is stabbed to death right next to him?"

"Actually, he was slashed."

"What difference does that make?"

"I don't know, sir, but the stomach laceration is deeper in the middle than at the two ends, indicating a slashing motion. The puncture wound in the shoulder was made by a round, possibly barbed object, like a scuba spear."

"And what are they... Four feet apart? *Slashed* and stabbed while the other is strangled. All behind the desk, here?"

"As far as we can tell, the guard wasn't strangled. His neck was broken."

"Broken? What about the marks?"

"They appear to be made by a chain."

Danny walked behind the desk, stepping over the bodies to judge the space. "How many people can fit back here? Could they have been moved here?"

"That's where it gets a little weird. There's no sign of the bodies being moved."

Danny stopped him. "So what's weird?"

"He..." The officer indicated the guard on the left. "Seems to be missing some intestines."

"The perps took body parts?"

"We don't know, sir. All we know is there are no signs of a secondary crime scene, and there are organs missing."

"So we have missing body parts, a neck broken by a chain, and no signs of a struggle. What are the odds of two impossible cases in two days?"

They were interrupted by raised voices in the corner. The man in the suit was forcibly gesturing to the two officers.

"I've answered these questions twice already. I've given you free reign in my building, what else do you want?" He looked around the room, his eyes settling on Danny. "Who's in charge here? You?"

Danny approached the group. "I'm Detective Hooper. And you?"

"Christian McMillan, and I'm about to be the one calling my lawyer, and not the one to defend me."

"Sir, we're trying to figure out what happened to your employees here. If you could cooperate with us a little longer..."

"Detective Hooper, This is my building, my employees, my... I've answered all their questions more than once. I wouldn't be so irritated if they were asking new ones." Christian glared at the two officers.

"I understand. It's just that there are some... irregularities."

"*Irregularities*? Two of my employees are dead. I'd call that irregular. Your people have been here for two hours, and all they can ask me is how this could have happened. That's your job to find out." Christian's eyes bored into his. "And when you do..."

Did his eyes just... No. I must have imagined it. "Mr. McMillan, please. Leave the crime fighting to the police."

"Then find them, and stop sitting around here asking me the same inane questions."

The two officers gave Danny a look that said, 'See what we're up against?' Danny got the distinct impression that Christian was restraining himself.

"Mr. McMillan, I'd appreciate it if you'd bear with us for a little longer." Danny dismissed the two officers, who shook their heads as they walked away.

"Can you think of anyone who would want to hurt you?"

Christian laughed. "Only the families of a few dozen dead executives."

"What? You killed..."

"No, what am I, an idiot? You must not read the Wall Street Journal. Many of the companies I've acquired had lost their leaders prior to my takeovers. That doesn't engender a lot of love."

"Any threats?"

"None that were serious." Christian dropped his voice to just above a whisper. "Look, I'm only playing in your world because these people made the mistake of playing in mine"

"Are you saying I'm just a peon to *your type* of people?"

Christian laughed. "Think what you will. But do your job. Find whoever did this for me." Christian reached out and straightened Danny's lapel. "I can make it worth your while."

Danny pushed Christian's hand away. "Oh, hell no."

Christian's eyes smoldered.

"First off, I may not mingle in your circles, but this peon is the one who is going to find the people who did this, but not for you and your one percent. I'm going to find them because I like my job. I like feeling good about what I do." He shook his head as Christian tried to interrupt. "No, I'm not done. Your offer of a *reward*, as I'll call it for your sake, is not only insulting, but also borderline illegal. And if I find out you've done anything to impede this investigation or take matters into your own hands, I *will* bring the full force of this department against you."

Christian smiled and clapped his hands slowly. "Bravo." He scrutinized Danny, looking him up and down. His eyes narrowed. "You have made a decision today, a decision I'm quite sure you will regret. Be that as it may, I am a busy man, so either arrest me or call my lawyer when you need me again. I am leaving."

Christian turned without waiting for an answer and stepped into the elevator.

Danny stood unmoving as he watched him leave. *Fucking rich people think they own everybody. Well that didn't get me any points.*

He took a second to compose himself, and then waved the two officers back.

"Did we canvas the building?"

"Yes, sir. Nothing out of the ordinary. Offices with people running around and making phone calls."

"No signs of a struggle anywhere else?"

"No, sir."

"So, how do we call this?"

"I believe that's your job, sir. I'd call it fubar, but no one but you is asking."

"Damn, Captain is going to fry my ass. I guess we'll have to play this one like it seems for now."

Danny's phone rang. He pulled it out of his pocket and answered.

"Detective Hooper."

"Detective Hooper? This is Dr. Graham at Memorial Hospital. You asked me to let you know when we were releasing Father Michael. He should be ready to leave in thirty minutes."

"Thank you, Doctor. I appreciate the heads up."

He shoved his phone back into his pants and grabbed his keys. As he passed the officer at the front door, he smiled.

"Make sure they don't fuck this thing up any more than it already is."

"I warned you, Danny."

"You should have warned me not to get out of bed this morning." He gave a mock salute as he headed for his car.

Stan hated the morgue. He hated the perpetual cold and the stark white and stainless steel. *I don't know how you could take more feeling out of a room.* Seeing a dead body, matter of factly spread out on the table with precision cuts and no blood was somehow worse than any gruesome crime scene itself. At least crime scenes felt real. This was so... antiseptic, emotionally removed, and almost inhuman.

"Stan, glad you made it."

"Hey, no problems, Gerry. You know I love a trip to Antarctica every so often."

Gerry unsnapped his glasses and let them hang from the strap around his neck, and beckoned for Stan to follow him. "Let me show you what I found. It's unbelievable."

"As in amazing?" Stan followed Gerry into the next examination room where the three bodies were laid out side by side on stainless steel tables. The head of each body rested a few inches past the severed neck.

"No. As in utterly unbelievable, as in Ripley's Believe It or Not, as in Area freaking 51."

Stan studied Gerry to see if he was being serious. "Really? What's got you so worked up?"

"Okay, so look closely at the neck." Gerry pulled the magnifier over so Stan could get a close up. "See how ragged the skin is?"

"Yeah. So?"

"So we know that no bladed weapon was used to do this."

"And how is that unbelievable?" Stan backed away from the lens.

"Do you know the amount of strength it would take to remove a head from the body without some sort of instrument? All three victims had broken necks with the bones completely shattered."

Stan shook his head. "I guess that would be a lot."

"That would be impossible enough."

"Enough? There's more?"

"Look again. Look at the wound area."

Stan leaned over the magnifier and studied the skin. "All I see is ripped skin and bone fragments. What else am I missing?"

"Look at the direction of the tears."

"What do you mean?"

"What direction is the skin torn? Look closely."

Stan angled the lens to get a better view. "To the left?"

"What side are you looking at?"

"Come on, Gerry, stop beating around the bush." Stan straightened up. "What are you getting at?"

"Stan, look at the right side."

"Oh, shit."

"Yes, it's torn to the right. In fact, all the skin and bone fragments seem to have moved from the inside out. Not twisted. Not pulled. There are no compression marks on the skin on either the head or the body that would have been left if they had been pulled apart."

"Wait. What are you saying?"

"In each of these cases, it seems that the neck exploded from the inside and was blown off the body."

"With a bomb?"

"Oh, no. There's no gunpowder residue. There's no residue at all. Like I said, Area 51, call Mulder and Scully, 'cause I've got nothing else."

"Danny's going to love this. Keep me posted if you come up with anything else." Stan shivered, not sure if it was the temperature or the surroundings. "Where else is this one going to go?" *And how the hell do I write this up? Two priests and a nun were strung up by their feet, twenty-five feet of the ground after their heads were blown off their bodies without explosives. The media is going to be all over us. Just what we need.*

Chapter *12*

Father Mike studied the release papers as he was wheeled to the hospital exit. *Anti-anxiety medication. Doctors figure pills will fix about anything. I wonder if pills can fix Christian.* He laughed. *Pills to fix the anti-Christ... Not that he'd ever take them.* The young man wheeling him looked at him strangely, wondering what he found funny.

"Thank you," he told the attendant as he stood up. "I'm not sure why I need to be rolled in a wheelchair to the front door if I'm okay enough to walk out on my own, but thanks, anyway."

"It's hospital policy, Father. We wouldn't want you to get hurt while you're still here."

Father Mike smiled and shook his hand. "No worries, son. I'm just giving you grief 'cause I hate being cooped up." He patted him on the shoulder and turned to walk out the door.

As Father Mike exited the hospital, he noticed Detective Hooper leaning against a bright red Mustang. His shirt was wrinkled, but the car was in pristine shape.

"Mid-life purchase? They must pay detectives well."

"It's my baby. Having no wife or kids leaves me with a little spare change."

"I take it you're waiting for me?"

"I thought you might need a ride, Father."

Father Mike smiled. "Please, call me Mike."

Danny held out his hand. "And call me Danny. Let's call this an off the record ride for both of us. It'll just be two new friends riding in a car."

Father Mike shook his head. "I guess you're cheaper than a cab."

Danny mimicked a formal bow. "In that case, Father... Mike, I'm at your service." He opened the passenger door for Father Mike. "Back to your apartment?"

"Oh, no. I can't go anywhere near there right now."

"Yeah, I guess not. Where to, then?" He turned the key and smiled as the car roared to life.

Father Mike held up his discharge papers. "You think these things say I can't have a drink?"

"Now you're talking my language, Father. Mike, sorry. I'm having trouble calling you Mike with that collar on. It's that Catholic upbringing. They drill it into you like at boot camp."

Father Mike unbuttoned his clerical collar and folded it into his shirt pocket. "There, now maybe if you put that badge away also, we can be those two friends."

Danny held up both hands in mock surrender. "What badge, Mike?"

"Exactly." Father Mike ran his hand appreciatively over the dash. "Hell of a machine. One of the things I miss being a priest is having my own car." As his fingers trailed over the buttons, the stereo turned on. Bon Jovi's *Wanted: Dead or Alive* blasted out of the speakers on full volume.

"Sorry. My one vice, eighties hair bands." Danny turned the volume down. "Okay, maybe not my only vice, but certainly one of the more enjoyable, and legal." He looked over at Father Mike and laughed. Father Mike wasn't smiling.

"Danny? Are you much of a churchgoer? I don't recall seeing you at the church."

"I thought you put that collar away, Mike." Danny turned his eyes back to the road.

"No judgments. I'm just curious."

Danny tapped his fingers on the steering wheel. "To be honest, I don't see much reason to... In my line of work, I don't see a lot of proof of God's existence, or the power of prayers."

Father Mike mumbled under the growl of the engine, "That might be about to change."

"What?"

"Nothing, just mumbling to myself."

Danny parked in front of O'Reilly's Bar and placed his badge on the dash.

"One of the perks of the job. I also don't have to pay for most of my drinks. Contrary to popular belief, we don't all hang out at the doughnut shops."

"Sad to say, Danny, but it's one of the perks of my job, too. Although, I get some strange looks with the collar on and a scotch in one hand."

"I can imagine. Here..." He opened the door to the bar. "You'll get strange looks ordering a scotch no matter who you are here. Try a Bushmills sixteen-year old. I think you'll like it." An older man at the bar waved at Danny as they passed.

They sat in a booth in the back of the bar. Danny ordered two Guinness Stouts.

"It might be better if we start off slow. Let's keep the whiskey for a little later in the night."

"Danny, have you ever read the Bible?"

"Don't you remember I told you about that strict Catholic upbringing? Yes, I read it, although not recently." Danny sighed as he took a big gulp of his beer. "And I can't say I read it from front to back."

"Do you remember the Book of Revelations?" Father Mike emptied his beer and ordered another.

"Yeah, the weird part. Something about the end of the world and the anti-Christ, right?"

"Very good. I'm impressed. You're probably not going to believe what I'm about to tell you, but I've got to tell someone, especially after..." Father Mike paused as the waitress brought another round.

"What if I told you that neither God nor the devil created the anti-Christ?"

Danny put his beer down and gave Father Mike a serious look. "I'd say you might have had a few beers too many. And I'm not sure I like the use of past tense."

"Man created him. I created him." Father Mike put his face in his hands. "And now he lives among us."

"I'm sorry, Mike. I didn't here that last. What did you say?"

Father Mike looked up. "I said he lives among us."

Danny laughed. "Good one, Mike. I didn't realize you had that kind of sense of humor. What do you have some kind of chemistry lab back at the church? I bet there's no sugar or spice in that recipe."

Father Mike looked seriously at Danny.

"I'm sorry, Mike. Please go on."

"Before I do, let's get a couple of those Bushmills you were talking about. You're going to need it."

Danny flagged the waitress down. "Two Bushmills sixteen-year over ice, please." She nodded and walked off.

"Danny, let me tell you a story of hubris. I'm sure you've heard of the Shroud of Turin."

"Yeah, supposedly it's the cloth that covered Jesus after he was crucified. But didn't they prove it wasn't old enough? With carbon dating or something."

"It is true that the carbon dating placed the year of origin to be many centuries after Christ, but it didn't take into account all the candles that had been burnt around it for so many centuries, or the fire that almost destroyed it. All the smoke and the heat from the fire affected the carbon content and skewed the results."

"So you're saying it's real?"

"Yes, besides, no one in the Middle Ages knew what a photo negative was to try to replicate it."

"What do you mean, photo negative?"

"I guess most people forget. The most common pictures circulated of the shroud show the positive image that is much easier to see the features, but the actual image on the shroud is in negative, just like a photo-negative. How could someone who didn't know what one was create it, and why?"

"Okay, but what's this got to do with the anti-Christ?"

Father Mike sniffed at the Irish whiskey, rolled his eyes, and took a sip. "Not bad." He put his glass down and looked at Danny gravely.

"The Shroud has blood on it. Father Anthony, Father Joseph, and I..."

"Wait. You're not trying to tell me that twenty-five years ago, three priests..."

"And a nun, Sister Mary Elizabeth."

"Three priests and a nun played Russian roulette with blood from the Shroud?"

"If you want to put it that way. We thought we were bringing some good back into this world." *We played God.*

"I didn't know cloning was understood back then."

"The Germans discovered it years ago, but lost the process. We found the scientist, or, rather he found us."

"So, you cloned the blood of Jesus, but got the devil instead?"

"It's my belief that we cloned the body, but not the soul. He's the first human born soulless."

"So, you're saying the devil used this... soul vacuum to enter the body? Sort of a back door into humanity?"

"Danny, I have no idea. I'm just guessing at some of this. For years, we hoped that the things we saw developing in him were anomalies, but..."

"Wait! You know who it is? You're hiding him? Now I know you're pulling my leg."

"I'm not hiding him, so much as trying to hide from him. Yes, I know him. You've probably heard of him."

"If you say George Bush, I'm going to hit you."

"Seriously, it's Christian McMillan, the Newsweek wonder child."

Danny spat out the sip of whiskey he had just taken. "Shit. Christian McMillan? From McMillan Industries? You do know that he'd have an army of lawyers after you for libel if he heard even a little bit of this conversation... Oh, crap."

"What?"

"I've already crossed paths with him. Earlier today, in fact, and I'm pretty sure I didn't make the best first impression."

"Be careful, you don't know what he's capable..." Danny's phone ringing cut him off.

"One second, Mike." Danny put the phone to his ear and turned away from Father Mike.

"Hey, Stan. What do you have?"

"I'm sorry, say that again?" He looked back at Father Mike with an incredulous look on his face.

"Is he sure?" The fingers of his left hand drummed the table nervously.

"Okay, look, I'm with Father Mike right now. I'll call you back in a bit." He put his phone away and turned his attention back to Father Mike.

Danny waved the waitress over, and ordered another round of whiskey.

"Danny, don't you think we've had enough?"

"Mike, I'm not sure they can make enough. You tell me you've created the anti-Christ... I'm not sure where to go with that, but what does it have to do with the murders at the church?"

"I know you see where I'm going, you just don't want to believe it, to follow it to conclusion." *I wish I didn't.* "Danny, I know that society likes to have a solid, scientific proof for everything, a CSI society with its forensic tools to prove without a shadow of a doubt who the killer is. Everything needs to have its own neat place in a box on the wall where Wikipedia can reference it."

Father Mike grabbed Danny's hand as he reached for his drink. "The power of faith is underrated. Faith, by definition, is the act of believing in something that can't be proven. You've *heard* what I said, but you don't truly believe it."

"Okay. But you're talking about superstitions."

"Superstitions? Did you just call part of the bible a superstition?"

"You know what I mean. All that apocalyptic stuff, that's just metaphor, cautionary tales."

"Metaphor, tales, theory... A theory is nothing more than faith. It hasn't been proven yet. A tale is just a future that hasn't happened yet."

"Yeah, but Father..."

"Hold on. When you go to sleep at night, you fully expect to wake up in the morning. The sun will rise each day to greet you, right? There's no proof that it will happen, just a history. Yet, you expect it each day. That's faith."

"In my line of work, faith is worthless. I can't bring faith to a prosecutor. If I don't have concrete, verifiable evidence, then there's no case. Nothing. Nada. Bad guy walks."

"I beg to differ. Policemen exhibit faith all the time."

"How?"

"How many times have you been stuck on a case, no line of

evidence to follow? Don't you sometimes have a hunch? A gut instinct? Police intuition? You're basically trusting in something that has no proof whatsoever, but without that faith in your instinct, you wouldn't be able to find the proof. Armed with that faith, you seek out the truth and find it."

"Alright, so cops have faith. How do I get from following hunches to believing in an anti-Christ out to destroy the world?"

"I could tell you all the things I've witnessed him do over the years, but without seeing, without your proof, I doubt you would have enough for belief."

"What about the three murders I'm trying to solve?"

"You wanted to know what I was scared of. I've told you."

"But you weren't there when it went down. How do you know?"

"Faith, Danny. Faith and confession."

"He confessed?"

"All but. I told you that I didn't stop to talk to anyone on the way back from the hardware store. That was a lie. That's a venial sin, unlike my other." *How will I be judged?* Father Mike looked down at his hands. "Christian was in front of the church when I got back. He was getting into his car. Before he left, he apologized for the mess he'd left inside." He took a long gulp from his drink.

"What would your gut instinct be?"

"To be honest, Mike, I don't know. It's a lot to swallow."

"You told me that this case had inexplicable aspects. I'm giving you the explanation, just not the one you want."

"So, you're telling me that my number one suspect in a triple homicide is the anti-Christ, who, by the way, you created? I can see where this interrogation would go. He's such an ass when answering questions."

"You've already questioned him? How did he come up in your investigation?"

"Not in this one. Another case. Two of his security guards were killed last night in his building."

Father Mike choked. "What? Who would... Who could do that?"

"He's still flesh and blood, right? They killed Christ. Why not the anti-Christ?"

"Jesus died for us. He allowed himself to be killed. Christian won't."

"Pardon my French, Father, but you don't really believe this shit do you? I mean, I'm not trying to question your faith, and I've heard everything you've said tonight, but an omniscient, omnipotent criminal? I'm giving you more benefit of the doubt than I've ever extended to anyone, but I don't buy it."

"I don't think he's omniscient, and I'm sure there are limits to what he can do, but I think you're missing the point. Anti-Christ or not, who is after Christian? I'm assuming it didn't look random or gang related."

Danny shook his head. "Can't the church help you with this. What do they say?"

"Believe me, I don't think the church would acknowledge this if it knew."

"Are you telling me that you were trying to clone Christ, and no one in the church knew about it? How did you get the Shroud?"

"We only took part of it, and no one knew, another sin. We thought the ends would justify the means. There were only ten of us involved. Unfortunately, three of us are now dead. But none of us have tried to take him on. And if not us, then who?"

"Father, if what you are saying is true, and I'm *really* not on board, yet, he'll go after the rest of you. I'm less worried about a loose cannon gunning for Christian, than... Wait, you could be next."

"He could have killed me yesterday. He didn't. I don't know why." *He wants me to make a choice.* "I think I'm safe for now. Call it a hunch."

"Faith."

"Yes, faith."

"You know, I'm going to have to question him."

"I wouldn't..."

"Father, you have your job, which you've done as you've seen fit. No judgment, but I've got mine, and I've got to do it how I see it. So, I'm going to call a cab and try to sleep off some of these drinks before I go talk to him again tomorrow."

"Yes, well, if we're going to talk to him, I think we need to prepare."

"We?"

"Don't you think it would be smart to take a priest with you?"

"Mike, I don't know what to think anymore, but I won't turn down any help."

Danny helped Father Mike get out of the booth. "You know, if it turns out you're nuts and this Christian is just a psycho and something happens to you, I'll lose my pension."

"Danny, losing your pension should be the least of your worries."

"I wonder how all this will sound tomorrow after the whiskey wears off."

Colored shadows crossed the floor of the nave at St. Michael's Church. The light from the street lights filtered randomly through the stained glass windows, and was the only light illuminating the area. Dark shadowed angel statues appeared more like monsters in the half-light. Christian sat silently in the back pew. He nodded at one and sneered at another.

"Fat lot these humans know."

He stood and stretched. "You know, it's hard to get used to muscles and eating. These *people* have a lot to distract them. I can see why you made all these strict rituals for them to follow. It's a shame they perverted them." Christian regarded the cross on the wall, as he walked up the aisle.

"This is too easy. It's not even fun. Okay, I lied. It's a little fun."

He paused in front of the crime scene tape surrounding the bloodstain on the floor. He waved his hand and watched the tape flutter to the side. Standing in the center of the stain, and looking up where the bodies had hung, Christian spread his arms and slowly spun in a circle. A black-light glow effused from his body, highlighting the bloodstain and making it glow on its own.

He stopped, facing the cross again. "You know your mistake, right? The worst thing you could have done was instill in them fear, self-preservation, and free will. That combination will always result in stupidity in this kind. It has from the beginning. Did you change anything? Of course not. Has anything changed for them? They pull the same shit on you they pulled from day one. And you *love* them."

Christian reached into his pocket and pulled out a cut crystal glass. He walked back to the holy water font, and brushed his fingers across the surface, watching it turn green. He dipped the glass, filling it halfway.

"La fée verte. Your humans have found so many amusing ways to occupy themselves over the years. Absinthe is one I've always wanted to try."

He approached the altar and started to genuflect. "Oops, just kidding." Christian placed the glass carefully on the altar and removed the sterling slotted spoon from his pocket. He dipped a sugar cube in the alcohol before balancing the spoon across the top.

"I know traditionally, water would have been poured over the sugar, but I favor the flame method." He lit the cube with a lighter and watched blue flames lick across the mouth of the glass.

"Look into flames for long enough and it's like being hypnotized." He tipped the spoon and let the burning cube splash into the liquid, quickly covering the glass with his hand to douse the flame. Picking up the glass, he swallowed the contents in one gulp.

"Ah, warms the gullet. Although, I'm not getting any of the hallucinations I've read about." Christian clenched the glass tightly before flinging it at the cross. Glass flew in all directions.

"Why don't you stop this? Save your *children.* You know I'm not going to stop. I can't. I can't stop even if I wanted to. I am what you made me."

Christian turned from the altar and walked over to the Stations of the Cross. "Eternity is such a long time. You made my brother wait three days. *Three days!* Sure, he was a goody two-shoes. So was I, how long ago? You loved me once, as I loved you. Before the imperfect *humans.* Why can't you again?"

"You love these *people* unconditionally. Prove it. You know what it'll take to end this. It's not even that much."

Christian paced the aisle. "Nothing?" He walked back to the holy water font, now filled with alcohol. Flicking the wheel of his lighter, he held the flame inches above the surface.

"I could burn your house down. I could burn them *all* down. Would that get a rise out of you?" He dropped the lighter, smiling as the flame whooshed above the font. The dancing blue flames cast his shadow, jumping across the altar.

"Did you get the *holy men* I sent you? I can still feel their energy. It's like bathing in the sun." Christian pushed the font over, spilling the flames across the floor.

"Stop this. Only *you* can stop it."

The flames slowly sputtered out.

"That's not what I meant. Say it, and this will all end."

Christian sat down in the pew.

"I can wait a long time. But I get bored easily. And when I get bored, I find things to amuse me."

"Anything?"

"I didn't think so."

Chapter *13*

Italy
1046 AD

Abbot Thomas led Brother Stefano down the hallway toward the storeroom. Their heavy robes flapped noisily as they rushed away from the living area.

"Pull your cowl up, Stefano. I fear Bishop Ruiz has eyes and ears everywhere."

"Yes, Abbot."

The abbot peered furtively down the hall, looking for anyone who might be following them. When he was satisfied they were alone, he closed the door behind them. Dust motes floated in the air as Brother Stefano waited for Abbot Thomas to speak.

"I know I must seem incredibly paranoid, but you haven't seen the missives the bishop has been sending to me."

"It's not my place, Abbot."

"Please, we are alone. Call me Thomas. With everything that has been going on, I think we may end up on common terms soon enough."

"What do you mean?"

Abbot Thomas pulled a large sack of grain off the stack and gestured to Brother Stefano to sit down. The abbot scowled, trying to think of a good way to say what he needed. *How do you tell a monk that his bishop is scheming to bring down his monastery for earthly gains?*

"Stefano, we've known each other a long time. You are like a younger brother to me, in deed as in title. I've been trying to keep this from you, from all of you, in case my fears were unfounded."

"Fears? Of what?"

Abbot Thomas kicked at a rat that scurried undaunted from between the bags of grain and twitched its nose with distaste in their direction.

"I have so many things to worry about. The daily workings of this abbey are enough to take eighteen hours out of every day, leaving little time for prayer." The abbot worked his hands with worry before turning back to Stefano.

"Everything we've built here... Years of service to the Lord... It's going to be taken down stone by stone by that appointed *fool.*"

"Abbot?"

"I'm sorry. I've got so much on my mind." Abbot Thomas sat down next to Stefano, patting him on the back. "Did you bring the journal like I asked?"

Brother Stefano pulled a leather-bound portfolio from under his robe. The worked leather glowed as it passed through the light streaming in from the high-set window. "Right here, Thomas. Why?"

It might be the most important thing in the world. We must unravel the riddle of the prophecy or mankind could be lost. The abbot took the book from Brother Stefano and turned it over as if inspecting it. He held it up and inhaled deeply, sniffing the journal.

"It seems so insignificant, like any other journal. But this is what started it all. Brother David died giving us these words..." Abbot Thomas stared past Stefano, lost in thought. "But ever since I reported Brother David's death and the actions recorded in this journal, it seems like Bishop Ruiz has been out to rid himself of our community... of me."

"Surely not? It must be your imagination."

"He's always wanted more... more money, more power. This inexplicable event has given him the excuse he needed." *He paid for his position. He knows the power of money.*

Abbot Thomas opened the journal and flipped through the undecorated pages filled with Brother David's words and the actions of that night. Memories of what he witnessed flashed unwittingly through his mind.

Brother Stefano cleared his throat. "Excuse? To do what?"

"Don't you see, Stefano? The bishop wants our land. Meager as it is, he must see some value in it. Now he is out to destroy me... destroy us, to get his hands on it."

He slammed the book down on the sack, raising another cloud of dust.

"Damn them all! Thieves, the lot of them. Why can't they leave God's house untouched?"

A muffled crashing filtered through the closed door.

"Brother Franco must have dropped the kettle again." The abbot sighed. "There goes more food, wasted."

"Thomas, what are we to do, then?"

"There isn't anything *to* do, my friend. I sent a letter to the pope months ago, but got no response. It was the pope who appointed that greedy dolt. I fear the end is inevitable."

"But what's going to happen to us if he takes our abbey? What about you?"

A scream echoed down the hallway, followed by a loud clanging. Brother Stefano and Abbot Thomas looked at each other questioningly. A muffled voice yelled indistinguishable words, obviously commands by the tone of them.

"What is going on out there?"

The abbot opened the door and entered the hallway, followed by Brother Stefano. Thirty feet down the hall, two men with swords stood facing a monk in robes, holding his hands in supplication. Before Thomas or Stefano could utter a word, one of the armed men jabbed his sword into the monk's chest. Abbot Thomas heard a quiet grating sound as it slid past bone and exited his back. The armed man was pulled forward as the monk sunk to the floor, his eyes wide in pain.

"No!" The abbot felt Stefano pitch against him from behind, his hands grabbing Thomas's shoulders to retain his balance.

The two soldiers turned at the sound of his voice and smiled at the sight. "Oh, good. Two more lambs to the slaughter. "

The abbot lightly shoved Stefano to the side as he sprinted toward the armed men. The man on the left laughed as he watched him run at them. He stepped back, letting the other shift to the middle of the hall. "You take this one. I've got the other."

The soldier raised his sword and cocked it slightly back, readying for Abbot Thomas's approach. Two steps before they met, the abbot shifted slightly, altering his trajectory by a few inches. He lowered his shoulder and slammed into the soldier's chest. At the same instant, he felt a tearing burn in his side. As the soldier lurched backward, Abbot Thomas reached down to his side. He grabbed the handle of the sword that had cut him and steadied it. Still surging forward, he spun the armed man sideways until his sword faced the second man, caught unawares. Before the second soldier could raise his own sword, the first soldier's sword plunged into his abdomen with a sucking sound.

The abbot shoved forward with his shoulder as he twisted the handle of the sword. The first soldier slammed into the wall as the second slumped forward with glazed eyes. Abbot Thomas pulled the sword from the man and turned to the still breathing soldier.

"Who are you? Why are you here?" He let the sword hang loosely from his hand, blood dripping from it and from his hand. He sucked air in raggedly, trying not to think of the searing pain in his side.

The man stared at him with a calculating look. He glanced at the bloodstain spreading on the abbot's robe. A smile slowly broke out on his face.

"Prayer cannot save you now, and you will not be so lucky a second time." He levered himself off the floor with his elbows. "You will pay for what you did to Antonio. I'm going to make it last for you. We'll have a good time. Well, *I* will, at least."

Abbot Thomas turned back to Brother Stefano to see that he hadn't budged from where he had shoved him, his eyes wide in disbelief. As he returned his attention to the soldier, the man launched himself upward from the floor.

The abbot expertly flipped the sword to a fighting grip pointed at the soldier's chest. The man continued to surge to his feet directly into the point of the sword. He looked shocked as he was pinned back to the ground by his own sword.

Brother Stefano found his voice. "Abbot? How did you?"

Abbot Thomas slid the sword out of the soldier's body.

"Misspent youth, Stefano. I've been trying to make up for it for the last twenty-two years. Some of the old skills do come in handy every so often." He knelt down before the soldier and rifled through his clothes.

"What are you looking for?"

"Anything to explain what's going on."

They both jumped as they heard a pair of bloodcurdling screams. The abbot grabbed the dead man's hand, turning it over. He slumped back.

"What?"

"His ring... He's from the Bishop's guard." He turned to face

Stefano. "It has started."

Stefano grabbed his arm to help him back to his feet. Abbot Thomas screamed in pain.

"Are you hurt?"

Brother Stefano stepped back, noticing the blood on the abbot's robe concentrated around a long tear.

"He caught me on that first charge. Not enough to put me down, but I'm definitely feeling it now. Grab his shirt."

Brother Stefano ripped the shirt off the dead soldier's body. Abbot Thomas opened his robe, exposing a six-inch long gash in his side. He wrapped the shirt around his torso and tied it tight, trying to staunch the flow of blood.

"That's going to have to do for now. Do you still have the book?"

Brother Stefano held up the leather journal and smiled weakly. "While you were saving our lives, I saved a book."

"That book may be more important than our lives. For all I know, the bishop destroyed the copy I sent him. That may be all that is left of Brother David's words."

The clanging of metal sounded like it was getting closer.

"I fear there isn't much we can do here. One wounded sword wielding monk won't make a difference in this attack."

"But Thomas, they'll kill them all."

"Some may escape, at least, I hope so, but there isn't anything to be done." *I'm sealing their death warrant, but if the book doesn't survive, how many more might die?* He studied the bodies of the dead soldiers. "We must protect this journal, and that means we need to get out of here alive."

"Can't we just hide until night?"

A loud crash interrupted their conversation. Laughter echoed down the hallway.

"Stefano, take off your robe." The abbot gingerly began peeling his robe off his shoulder, trying not to pull at the shirt tied around his wound.

"What?"

"We're going to put on their clothes." He pointed at the dead bodies. "Help me pull them into the storeroom. If we're lucky, they won't be found until we're long gone."

Abbot Thomas grabbed the man with his one good arm as Brother Stefano pulled with both, sliding him across the floor. After both were lying in the room, they began to undress them. The abbot shuddered in disgust as he removed the ring and held it to the light.

"*Men of God*, killing other men of God. What has the church come to? Damn you Ruiz. Damn you for besmirching the office of bishop. Damn you for these men you slaughter simply for being in your way."

"Abbot, we must hurry."

"Yes, Stefano. Wear the ring as well. Hopefully we'll pass a quick inspection."

"But? Where are we to go? This was our home. Who'll take us in?"

"We are no longer monks of this church. We might be homeless for now, but not homeless monks. The church doesn't want us. I guess I'm okay with that. We'll have to find our way without it. But first we have to get out of here. Grab the other sword, it'll help you look the part."

The abbot and Brother Stefano ran down the hallway. Slowing as they reached the opening, they edged into the courtyard. Stefano stopped when he saw other soldiers milling about. Abbot Thomas urged him on.

"Boldness will see us through," he whispered.

Halfway across the yard, a soldier hurried over to them. He scrutinized them, not recognizing their faces. His eyes lingered on the bloodstains on their clothes, not noticing the rips where the sword had entered, and shrugged.

"I see you've had your bit of fun. This part is mostly wrapped up. I need you two to head out to the countryside. We haven't found the abbot yet. I don't see how he could escape, but the bishop wants to make sure he doesn't. Make a circuit around the abbey and report back before sundown."

Stefano and the abbot stared dumbfounded at the soldier.

"What are you waiting for? Go!"

Abbot Thomas tried not to wince as they ran for the front gate. *God works in mysterious ways. First he allows this to happen, and then he gives us our escape.*

Thomas looked back at the abbey he had directed for the last ten years. And sighed. The sun was riding low in the sky as they left the gate behind them. The cross jutting from the top of the main building was back-lit, sending spears of sunlight to their feet. *We must find our own way in this world, but always, we will be lead by God.*

"Come, Stefano."

"But, abbot..."

"No. We are Thomas and Stefano now, nothing else, two pilgrims seeking enlightenment."

Chapter *14*

New Orleans
2013

Just one more snooze. Searing light burned Danny's eyelids as he rolled over. *Crap, who opened the drapes? Maybe that last whiskey wasn't the best idea in the world...* He cracked his eyes, wincing as the morning sun assaulted his senses. Grabbing the bottle of Advil off the bedside table, he dry swallowed four. *I guess there could be worse things than a hangover... Like the anti-Christ. That's some serious craziness. Father Mike either had one over on me, or maybe the stress got to him. An all-powerful anti-Christ?* He sat up, rubbing his eyes. *One of these days, I've got to clean up this house.*

Danny picked his bathrobe off the floor and wrapped it around his body. Stepping over the previous nights clothes, he made his way to the door and headed downstairs. *I wonder what's in the news today, Anti-Christ Plunges World Into Chaos? Or just another murder. I'm not sure what's worse, a murder every day or the infamous anti-Christ. Since this particular anti-Christ isn't too happy with me at the moment, I guess I'll take the murder.* He opened the front door and walked out onto his front porch, searching for the Times Picayune.

As he bent over to retrieve the newspaper, his head began pounding. He felt a huge pressure building from inside, looking for release. *Holy shit... That Advil should be hitting by now.* His vision closed in, narrowing to a small circle, almost drowned out by a hazy blackness. Danny dropped the paper as his hand slammed into the porch, barely keeping him from rolling to the ground. The world spun past his tunnel vision in a kaleidoscope of scenery, all out of focus.

What appeared to be a field of old, dead grass with one leafless oak tree raced by. *What the hell? Where's the sidewalk and street?* The tree sped by, and then again, the only landmark in a field of grass. *I think I'm going to be sick. Will the world stop spinning for one god damned second?*

The rotating field of view slowed marginally. *No noises? Where are the big city noises? And where's my fucking house? Where am I? All I can hear is my own ragged breathing... and my stomach grumbling.*

The tree circled slower with each cycle. He could discern little else but the mass of branches. His house had disappeared along with the street and the rest of the city. As the spinning finally dragged to a halt, all he could see was the burnt out tree, alone in a vast field of grasses. Danny leaned over and heaved out the contents of his stomach, mostly liquid. *I'm going to have to lay off the Irish whiskey for a while.*

The monochromatic grass dominated his vision, reaching halfway up his calves almost to the edge of his robe. Slowly, the tunnel vision opened, giving him a wider view of the sepia-toned grass. His nausea diminished, Danny straightened up to get a better look at the rest of his surroundings. *What the hell? Am I stuck in an antique photograph?* He could see no clouds or sun, only a dull ocher glow pervading the sky. He reached down to grab a handful of the grass. *Feels real enough.*

The field of monotone grasses continued as far as he could see. As he turned around, he heard the beginnings of a noise, the first since he stepped out of his front door. He listened, as it became a rushing, like a wind, but backwards. It built in volume as he turned, looking for the source, until it roared to a stop, leaving... everyday sounds: grasses swaying against each other, a normal wind, and several voices moaning in the distance. *Well, that last is not so normal.*

Across the field of lifeless grasses, a half dozen people wandered aimlessly. They were far enough away that he couldn't discern their specific attire, except that they seemed ragged and dirty. Five wavered in a loosely collected group, not walking the exact same path, but more like a flock of birds going the same direction, each following their individual trajectories. The last lagged about thirty feet behind the others. All of them shuffled at such a slow pace, he found it hard to figure out their intended destination. *Not that there's anything out there for them to be traveling to.*

As he watched, mesmerized, the sixth fell to the ground and was hidden momentarily by the tall grass. He rose slowly, as if in pain, limping after the group.

Danny turned his head as he noticed a rustling in the grass a hundred yards back from the motley group. It appeared to be more than one object, all racing across the plain. Their destination was more obvious; they were on a collision course with the moaning crew. The six people seemed oblivious, continuing their zombie-like walking across the plain. *They're being hunted. They're sitting ducks.*

"Hey!" Danny jumped up and down, waving his arms. "Behind you. Come on. Look up!"

As the rustling approached the group, Danny could pick out seven or eight individual disturbances making up the whole, and he began to hear growling. A pack of *dogs?* Two of the animals split off to either side, cutting off all avenues of escape. *Damn smart, whatever they are.*

"Come on. Look out!" He shouted again, trying to get their attention, but they continued their oblivious shuffling. *What's wrong with these people?*

The pack converged on the lagging figure in a seething fury. Danny could see splotches of fur as the animals climbed over each other to get at the man. A dog's head popped out of the grass, stopping for a second to look in his direction before diving back into the fray. *Shit, I don't have my gun, or even shoes.* "Jesus Christ, people, look behind you. You've got to help him!"

The dogs snapped at each other as they fought over the man, shaking their heads violently, trying to rip off pieces for themselves. He dropped to his knees as more dogs reached him and he was unable to carry their weight. Throughout the ordeal, he uttered no other sounds but the low moaning he had been making before. As the two dogs that had split to the sides reached him, he fell beneath the surface of the grass, which was rapidly turning red.

Holy shit. And the rest are still walking along as if nothing happened. The upheaval in the grass began to dissipate, as one by one, the animals separated from the group, taking with them whatever prize they had won. Danny's stomach tried to heave again, but there was nothing left to come up.

What the fuck is going on here? If this is a dream, it is the most vivid one I've ever had. He slapped himself in the face. *Yep, that stings.*

Cold and bony talons gripped his shoulders, spinning him around. He watched, stunned, as two branches retracted back to the tree, shortening to their former length. Danny turned his head side to side, looking for a witness to corroborate what he saw. *This is seriously messed up. I'm pretty sure all I had was beer and whiskey last night.* His attention was jerked back by a splintering noise as the massive tree trunk split open vertically. Danny watched, mesmerized as the crevasse widened. Out of the corner of his eye, he noticed that the remaining people had turned and were headed his way, shambling slowly but purposefully in his direction.

The two sides of the split trunk separated with a grinding sound, leaving tooth-shaped shards on either side. They continued to spread, impossibly wide, revealing a hollow core. Laughter erupted from its depths.

"This can't be good." Danny nervously stepped back, edging away from the tree. "Really? Where the hell am I?"

In the distance, he could see rustling in the grass where the dogs had been, turning toward him and surging forward. *Shit. Zombieland and Cujo all in one movie. I'm seriously disliking the starring role in this one.*

"Where the hell are you, indeed? Well said, Detective."

Fuck me. Christian stood in front of the gaping maw in the tree trunk, no longer wearing Armani, but dressed simply in a flowing cotton robe.

"Yes, and that is exactly where you are." His unnaturally loud laugh echoed across the plain. The five souls shuffling his way stopped, covering their ears in pain. "Pleased to meet you. Hope you guessed my name."

"Christian. Mr. McMillan. What are you... What's going on, here?" Movement to his left caught his attention. Two of the dogs were close enough to be visible, racing through the grass twenty feet away. Their oversized jaws dripped blood as they snapped open and shut.

"See ya, Danny."

The nearest dog opened its mouth as it launched itself at him, roaring out an ear-piercing clanging. Its jaw clamped down on his arm and it clanged again. *What the... Why doesn't it hurt?*

A brilliant beam of sunlight burst through the ocher sky, blinding him. "Christian? What are you doing?"

The clanging resolved itself into the ringing of his phone. He opened his eyes, rolling over to see a red digital 7:00 a.m. blinking at him. His brain couldn't quite figure where he was at first. *Phone. Damn, for once, I don't mind being woken up by it. Seven a.m.? Shit, what happened to my alarm?* Slowly lifting his head from the sweat-damp pillow, he checked the caller I.D. *Stan.*

Oh shit! I'm late to some crime. Danny jerked the phone off its cradle, almost dropping it in his haste.

"Hey. Yeah, I'm up." His breath rasped into the phone. "No. No. I'm okay. I had a bad dream, that's all. What's up?" He sat up quickly and his head almost exploded in pain. *Damn. I still have a hangover. I guess dream Advil doesn't work in the real world. That sucks.*

"Danny, get up, take a shower. I don't know, get a strong cup of coffee, whatever you need, but get down here as soon as you can. There's something you really need to see."

"Down where, Stan? What's going on?" Danny rolled out of bed. Holding the phone to his ear, he barely missed tripping on his robe lying on the floor.

"The station." Danny heard a slight tremor in Stan's voice.

"What's wrong?"

"Just get over here. It's a mind fuck."

"*It's* a mind fuck. Try living *my* life." Danny looked at his face in the mirror over his dresser and frowned. *That looks a little worse for the wear.*

"Just get here, and on a normal person's schedule, not yours."

"Yeah, don't worry. I'll be there in a few."

Danny tossed the phone on the bed, on his way to the bathroom and grabbed the bottle of Advil. *Second time's the charm, right?* Cupping his hands, he chased the pain reliever down with lukewarm water, and then splashed some on his face. *That's what I get for mixing priests, murder, and alcohol in one night. That was one intense dream.* He rubbed the arm the dog had latched onto just before he woke up. *Is that a mark?* He held it closer to his face. *Guess it's just my imagination. You'd think I was a schoolboy the way this thing's affecting me. Shake it off.*

Danny was brushing his teeth when he heard a rustling in his bedroom. *What the hell? That can't be anything good.* He dropped his toothbrush, looking for anything he could use as a weapon. *I don't think an electric razor's going to scare anyone. Trimming shears... I guess that'll have to do.* He tiptoed to the door and peeked through. *Nothing?* Holding the sheers in front of him, he burst through the door. He turned each way, looking for in intruder. *Rats?*

Out of the corner of his eye, he caught sight of a figure, crouched to attack. He spun to meet him, and burst out laughing. The figure reflected in the mirror of himself, in boxer shorts and a t-shirt, holding a pair of trimming shears at ready with eyes bugged wild certainly made for a formidable opponent. *I need a drink. But I know where that leads. I need some breakfast, at least a sausage biscuit or something.*

He put the scissors down on his nightstand and turned to his closet. Reaching for a shirt, he heard the rustling again, this time followed by scrabbling. Danny turned around, eying the scissors he left on the table just out of reach. *What the hell is making that noise?*

He inched toward the table, eying the rest of the room, wary of any motion. Grabbing the sheers again, he made a slow circle, looking for anything out of place. *How the hell am I supposed to see anything out of place in this mess? Maybe I should clean up once in a while.*

The only place left is under the bed. Boogeyman land. His chuckle died half formed. *Damn, I am kind of spooked.* He put his hand on the edge of the bed as he leaned down to check underneath. *Nothing. That's not entirely true. There are my hand weights that I haven't been using.*

A low growl sounded from on top of the bed. *Oh shit.* Danny shoved himself back and held the sheers with white knuckles in front of him. On the bed, one of the dogs from his dream crouched, ready to lunge, dripping blood from his bared teeth on his duvet. *Seriously? What the fuck?*

The dog growled, never taking its eyes off him. Danny looked from the shears to the dog. *They never talk about bringing scissors to a dogfight, but that's got to be as bad as running with them.*

Quicker than seemed possible, the dog leaped and grabbed his outstretched arm, causing him to drop his only weapon. Danny screamed as the dog's teeth ripped into his arm. The dog almost pulled him down on top of it as it jerked its head from side to side. He pounded its head with his good hand to no effect. Gritting his teeth against the pain, Danny grabbed the dog's neck with his free hand, and using both that grip and the wrist held tightly in the dog's jaw, he swung it in a wide arc that ended in a satisfying crunch as it hit the doorframe. The dog let go of his arm and fell motionless to the floor. He gripped his wrist where the dog's teeth had torn his skin and turned around searching for something to tie around it to stop the blood flow.

"Fuck me." Another dog stood at the foot of the bed, ready to attack. Its eyes moved from him to the fallen dog and back. Danny searched frantically for the scissors. *Not that they did a lot of good on the last dog.* He saw them, out of reach under the bed. Next to them, he saw his shoulder holster and gun. *Thank god, finally, something I can use. If I can get to it before the dog gets to me.*

Danny dove toward his gun, rolling into a somersault as he grabbed it. He flipped off the safety while pulling it out of the holster. As he came out of the roll, he expected to use it like a club to fend off the beast, but it stood in the same position as when he had leaped. *Thank god. Finally a break.* He aimed at the dog's head. As he pulled back on the trigger, the dog opened its mouth to growl, but what issued forth sounded like no sound an animal would make. A phone rang loudly in its place. The dog glared at him as if nothing was out of the ordinary.

What the... The dog opened its mouth again and the phone rang a second time.

Danny rolled over in bed, staring incredulously at the red 7:00 a.m. on the clock. *God damn it. Again? What is this? Groundhog Day?* He grabbed the phone, wincing at a pain in his wrist.

"Hello?" He examined his wrist. A red crescent faded as he watched. "Fuck."

"What?" Stan's voice issued from the phone. "No. Never mind. Danny, get up. Take a shower. I don't know..."

"Get some coffee, Stan? Get down there as soon as I can? What's going on? Is it a mind fuck?"

Stan remained silent after Danny's tirade. "Danny?" Danny heard papers rustling in the background. "Those were the exact words I was going to use. What is this? Did you call the Psychic Friends Network or something? Next *you're* going to tell *me* what's going on over here."

"No. I was hoping you could do that for me." Danny looked around the room for signs of violence. *Freakin' dreams. They're going to be the death of me.*

"Sorry, wise guy. Get your ass down here as quick as you can."

The line clicked and went dead. Danny stood next to the bed staring at the bed skirt. Nothing moved. He put his hand on the bed as he bent down. He paused as he started to lift the bed skirt.

"Fuck that."

He dropped it back in place without looking and picked up his robe on the way to the bathroom.

Chapter *15*

Father Mike stared at the front of his church. From the outside it looked the same as it had for the last twenty years. *But it will never be the same.* He walked up the steps, hesitating at the front doors. He took a deep breath and sighed. Opening the doors, he stepped in. *Two days later and it's still not cleaned up. Who knew you had to get a licensed crew to clean up crime scenes? There goes the electrical work, of course, that's the least of our worries.*

He looked down the aisle and three heads nodded to him from the altar. He stopped in his tracks. Their forlorn eyes beseeched him. *What do you want?* Father Mike closed his eyes and shook his head. When he opened them again, the altar was empty. *Ghosts.*

He looked down and saw the brown stain saturating the runner down the middle of the aisle. His eyes were irresistibly drawn upward, but the only thing he noticed was the light fixture hanging slightly askew. He shuddered. *Definitely, ghosts.* He turned around, looking at the church he called home.

Hold on. What happened here? On the floor past the toppled holy water font, he noticed what looked like a scorch mark. *How'd I miss this on the way in?* He looked up at the altar. *Oh, yeah. Preoccupied. There wasn't anything in the report about a fire.* He knelt down to get a better view, feeling the carpet around the mark. *Sticky. That's odd. I'm pretty sure none of this was here, yesterday.* He sniffed his fingers. *Smoke and... anise?*

He stood and hesitantly approached the altar. *What lofty goals we had. What hubris.* Father Mike ran his hand along the surface of the altar where he had seen his friend's heads. *You paid dearly for yours. I'm afraid my reckoning will be much worse.* He continued to the giant cross on the back wall, pleading with his eyes. *Lord, what can I do? We thought we could do this ourselves, but I can't... we can't stop him alone. Please help us.*

Something crunched under his heel. He reached down and picked up a piece of broken glass. *That's strange.* He sniffed it. *Anise as well. What's this all about?* Glancing around the sanctuary, he saw that the floor was littered with more broken glass. *I guess the cleaning crew can get this also.* He dropped the glass shard on the floor with the rest, and jumped as he heard breathing from the pews. He spun around and peered into the nave, looking for anything out of the ordinary. *Nothing. These ghosts won't be exorcized until after this whole Christian thing is done, one way or the other.* Father Mike stepped down out of the sanctuary and eyed the door to the hallway. *I've put off going to my office long enough.*

Walking down the hall, he tried not to step in any of the trails left in the carpet. He reached his office and stopped outside, staring at the partly opened door. *Cops left more of a mess than Christian.* He opened the door the rest of the way and walked halfway across the room before he realized that someone was sitting at his desk.

"Damn!" Father Mike stumbled back, not recognizing the muscular man in front of him.

"Who are you, and what the hell are you doing in my office?"

Carlo leaned back in Father Mike's chair and pursed his fingers together in front of him. "Interesting choice of words, Father Michael. My name is Carlo." He reached into his jacket and laid a handgun on the desktop.

"I'd rather not use this, but I will not hesitate if I feel it is necessary. But, in the spirit of honesty, which I hope you'll embrace, I thought I'd reveal it to you."

Father Mike looked at the gun, bigger than most he'd seen up close, then at Carlo. *Why does he look vaguely familiar?* "So, you have my attention. What do you want?"

Carlo spun the chair absentmindedly from side to side, rubbing the leather arms. "I really love this chair. I wish I had one like it back in Italy. You Americans know how to make utilitarian things into luxury items. But your office is... How do you say? Dirty?"

"It is a mess. We had an incident."

"Incident? I'd call it more than that. What happened? Your *pet* get loose?"

Father Mike couldn't take his eyes off the gun. "Pet? What do you mean?"

"Oh for heaven's sake. Here, I'll put it away if it'll make you more talkative." Carlo slipped the gun back inside his jacket and turned his attention back to Father Mike. "Your grand experiment, Christian."

"Who the hell are you?"

"That doesn't matter. All I want to know is who are you? What are you and the church trying to do with Christian?" Carlo patted his jacket where he had put the gun away.

Father Mike sat down and gave Carlo a defeated look. "First of all, it's not the church. Most of the church knows nothing of this. It's just ten of us... seven, now."

"Your pet turned on you?"

"What's your point? Are you trying to make me feel bad for what we've brought about? You can't make me feel worse than I already do. We were just trying to bring some good into this world. Belief, in this age of technological wonders has fallen to an all time low. Turn water into wine? We can do it. How polarizing would the second coming of Jesus be? The world would have been a better place. We needed something to combat the apathy."

Carlo slammed his hand on the desk. "The audacity... Did you not trust God to do his own will? What were you thinking? Some of the most evil and vile things done throughout history were done with the best of intentions." Carlo turned his chair to face the window. "The devil would not exist in this world if we did not continually open the door and invite him in."

Father Mike looked down at the floor, flinching when he saw the bloodstains. "And how did you even find out about him... about us?"

"Father, I've been waiting for this for a long time. The signs aren't hard to follow for one who is looking. What I need to know from you..."

"No." Father Mike stood up, taking a step toward the desk. "We made a mistake. A huge mistake." He gestured to the spot on the floor. "And we're paying for it."

"Along with the rest of us."

"But what gives *you* the right to come in here and rub my face in it?"

"Because, Father, I'm here to fix it."

"Fix it?"

"Yes..."

Mary ran into the office and launched herself across the desk at Carlo. "No, you can't hurt my baby." Father Mike grabbed her around the waist, pulling her back as she flailed her arms ineffectually.

"This is what I came here to find out. Who will stand against me? I know my enemy, but what I need to know are who his allies."

"There's nothing wrong with my boy. He's special." Mary's voice rose, bordering on hysterical. "Why would he be your enemy?"

Carlo turned to Father Mike. "Is she really asking that question?"

"Give me a second, Carlo." Father Mike pulled Mary into the hall.

"Mary, it's okay. He's not going to hurt Christian. You misheard part of a conversation."

"But he said..."

"Mary, go back to the sisters. They'll take care of you and I'll take care of him. Christian will be fine."

Mary sighed. "Okay, Father Mike. If you say so."

"I'll see you for Sunday supper. We can play bingo with the nuns."

"That would be fun. I'm sure Christian will be there this week."

Father Mike frowned. "Hopefully, Mary. Now you head back. I've got some things to discuss with this man."

Father Mike entered his office and walked over to his emptied bookshelves, kicking his toe through the books strewn across the floor. Carlo waited patiently.

"She hasn't been the same since Christian was born. I think it may have something to do with carrying him in her body for nine months." He turned to Carlo. "Have you ever seen *Rosemary's Baby*?"

Carlo shook his head.

"She doesn't see wrong in anything he does. To him he's an angel, the second coming. She's been, I don't know, a bit simple since then."

"As long as she doesn't get in my way. And you? Where do you stand?"

I've been given a choice. If he actually lets me choose... I can't say that. "Tell me Carlo, how do you plan on killing him? Is it even possible?"

"Now why would I tell that to someone who might try to stop me?"

Father Mike laughed, his face looking wild in the light from the window. "So you don't have an idea. You know, I was rooting for you. It would be nice to let someone else do the dirty work for me. But I guess that is going to be my burden alone. My father always told me that it's your job to fix what you broke."

He put his hands on the desk, looking Carlo in the eye. "You do what you have to, and good luck to you. I certainly won't stand in your way, but I don't put much stock in your chances of success. Do you know what he's truly capable of? Have you seen him? No matter how much *research* you've done..."

"Until you've walked in his world," He winced at the memory. "You have no idea."

"Father, I've dedicated my whole life to finding and stopping this abomination. I've been studying... I have a good idea what may stop him. I think you will find that you don't know me either."

Father Mike shook his head. "I'll pray for you."

Carlo stepped from behind the desk, patting his jacket as he walked past Father Mike. "Just don't do anything to make me come after you. I will not hesitate to take you out if the fate of humanity relies on it."

"Goodbye, Carlo," he whispered as Carlo stalked out the door.

~~*

From the front page of the Times Picayune:

Shroud Of Turin Missing

Church officials discovered Monday that the Shroud of Turin was no longer in its container in the Guarini Chapel, part of the Cathedral of St. John the Baptist complex. Scheduled to be brought out for display at the end of the month, the shroud was being removed for last minute preparations. Italian police have no leads on the missing relic except for some old unauthorized electronic monitoring equipment found hidden under a loose stone in the altar. The equipment had been disconnected and no further evidence was found.

The Shroud of Turin is believed by many to be the shroud that covered Jesus when he was buried. The controversial carbon dating that showed the Shroud was not in existence at the time of Jesus has since been called into question. No explanation of how the image was imprinted into the cloth has ever been found.

During its last exhibit in 2008, the Shroud was rolled out in its aeronautical alloy and bulletproof glass display, built to protect it in public. It was the first chance to see the Shroud since the controversial 2002 restoration. Until it was transferred to its display case, it had been stored in a light-free container surrounded by an argon and oxygen mix designed to protect the cloth. The one thousand kilogram storage case was left behind, seemingly untouched, along with the support and runners. "It's as if the Shroud was teleported from inside the case. It is quite puzzling," Detective D'Amato reported.

Church officials are not sure when the theft occurred over the five year period since its last removal, making the investigation that much harder. The Pope is scheduled to issue a statement later this week.

Chapter *16*

Carlo leaned forward in the rental car, watching Christian sitting on a bench at the park, while sipping casually from a wine glass. He was close enough to see that Christian's eyes were coal black. *Interesting. I wonder if he doesn't have any more bodyguards or if he thinks he doesn't need them?*

Parents stood nearby, watching their children swinging and climbing on a jungle gym. Cyclists sped by on the bike trail, paying no attention to the pastoral scene as they passed. Carlo swallowed the last of the burger he had been eating and tossed the wrapper in the back seat. *Americans have certainly perfected the art of fast food. It doesn't taste like it should, but it tastes good, although I think I can hear my arteries clogging.* Carlo twisted his head, looking for hidden guards.

At the corner, three men perched atop scaffolding, painting the side of an office building. *None of them are paying any attention to the park. Besides, he's not that subtle.* He turned back to Christian, still enjoying his wine. *The anti-Christ is having a relaxing day at the park? It must be exhausting work, continually trying to subvert the will of God. This would be a great time to catch him off guard, but this isn't the place to confront him. There are far too many people around.*

The midday sun shined through the leaves of a one hundred year-old oak tree and played across the ground in front of Christian. The wine bottle at his feet sparkled verdantly in the light play. Nobody noticed him, one of a handful of people picnicking, only Carlo. *Isn't this just too quaint?* Carlo wrote a few lines in his notebook. *Soon. Soon, you won't be able to hurt anyone.*

Christian tossed a handful of torn bread pieces on the grass, looking content as four pigeons fought over them. He smiled as he watched a young mother push a stroller along the sidewalk in front of him.

Carlo could hear the baby crying from his car. The mother stopped and squatted down to calm the child, making cooing noises. She reached into her diaper bag and gave a pacifier to the baby. Christian looked amused as he followed her progress. Walking around to the back of the stroller, she didn't see her baby drop the pacifier onto the ground.

Christian put his wine glass down under the bench, accidentally knocking it into the empty wine bottle he left there earlier. As the bottle rolled slowly across the sidewalk, Christian leaned over and picked up the pacifier. Turning it over in his hand, he studied it for a minute, and then reached into his pocket. Carlo leaned forward. *What's he doing? Did his eyes just turn blue? Why the color change?* Carlo jotted down his observations in his notebook. Christian pulled out a handkerchief and wiped down the pacifier. He pocketed his handkerchief and jogged after the woman and child. As he caught up to them, he tapped the woman on the shoulder.

"Excuse me."

The woman jumped, loosing her grip on the stroller. It began rolling away before she could grab it, angling off the sidewalk toward the busy street. She looked at Christian for a brief moment before sprinting after her child.

Christian's wine bottle rolled under her feet, tripping her. She sprawled forward into the concrete as the stroller continued to roll toward the street. Her scream cut short as her head hit the ground. Christian appeared hesitant, leaning toward the fallen woman.

Tires screeched as motorists realized what was happening. Carlo reached for the door handle, knowing he was too far away, but feeling the need to do something. *Now what's he doing?* Carlo sat back, stunned, as Christian leaped over the fallen mother and raced toward the runaway buggy. *Is he trying to save him?* He reached the stroller a foot before the curb, stopping it before it could roll into the street.

Several picnickers and cyclists who had stopped to watch the unfolding drama applauded as he rolled the child back to his mother, who was slowly getting up off the ground. She sat up, rubbing her jaw where it had hit the sidewalk, and almost fell back down with relief when she saw Christian returning with the stroller and her child.

"Oh my god! Thank you."

Carlo could see Christian's face cloud over briefly before breaking out in a grin. Christian released the grip as the woman reached in to grab her baby.

The anti-Christ is a hero? What next?

While the woman hugged her child, Christian leaned over, searching the ground between the stroller and the curb. Carlo watched him with a questioning look in his eye. *Now what? Your wine glass is back by the bench.*

"Yes!" He shouted, holding the pacifier in his hand as he stood up. "This is what I was trying to give you when I startled you. He threw it out in front of me."

"I can't thank you enough." She took the pacifier and gave it to her baby, quieting him down. "You were like his guardian angel." She hugged her baby tightly, spinning around in giddiness, before holding out her hand.

"Alyssa. What's your name?"

"Christian." He took her hand as if to shake it, then leaned down in a short bow and kissed it. "At your service, milady." He pulled out his handkerchief, reaching over to dab at the blood running from the corner of her mouth.

Alyssa blushed. "I think you've done enough, already. I couldn't ask for anything more."

"Oh. I'm sorry. I guess your husband wouldn't approve. Don't worry, I'm all bark and no bite."

Is he flirting with her? What is going on here? It's almost as if the anti-Christ is on vacation, or time out. Carlo looked over at the street as a car honked its horn. A water delivery truck was double-parked, blocking traffic as its driver carried a five-gallon water bottle under the scaffolding to the door. The driver of the car was shouting obscenities at the delivery man. *People can be so impatient.*

"No." She frowned. "He died in Afghanistan last year, while I was still pregnant."

"I'm so sorry, Alyssa. Please know that I truly appreciate what he was doing over there."

I bet you do. Carlo swallowed back the surging bile as he listened to Christian's conversation.

Christian reached into his pocket, pulling out a small white object. "Here's my card. Call me if you ever need to talk. I'm a great listener."

Alyssa examined the card before putting it in her purse. "McMillan? Like the building?"

"Yes, just like the building."

"Well, Mr. McMillan, it was nice meeting you, although next time, maybe without all the acrobatics?"

"Definitely." Christian sat down on the bench and retrieved his wine glass, watching Alyssa walk away.

Definitely flirting. Bizarre.

The driver honked his horn again, laying it on for a full ten seconds. Christian turned to see what was going on. Carlo watched him stare at the car, then up at the scaffolding. He turned his head to observe the traffic passing steadily in both directions, then across the park at the picnickers. *This cannot be good.*

Christian emptied the bag of shredded bread pieces onto the ground. Pigeons began landing in front of him, first one or two, then almost a dozen.

Tires squealed as the driver punched his accelerator and darted into the oncoming traffic. Everyone turned to the noise except Christian and Carlo. Christian scanned the onlookers, holding up his hand with splayed fingers as if measuring distances. Satisfied, he looked down at the birds grouped at his feet, before turning to the street.

Christian smiled broadly as he kicked his foot through the birds, scattering them into the air. Flapping in all directions, one flew in front of the accelerating car and smashed on its windshield. The driver took his foot off the pedal and reached out his window, trying to dislodge the bird off his windshield. *Oh man! Watch out for the truck!* Carlo reached for his door handle again as he realized that the driver was no longer paying attention to an oncoming truck in his lane.

A louder horn blasted as the oncoming truck tried to warn the car driver. He took his eyes off the bird and turned his wheel to the right as hard as he could, swerving off the road. As his car jumped the curb, he jerked the wheel back, overcompensating. His fishtailing rear end slammed into the deliveryman, throwing him and the water bottle into the street, before taking out the support beam for the scaffolding.

Seeing the deliveryman flying into the street, the oncoming truck driver swerved to his right to avoid him, sideswiping Carlo's vehicle before jumping the curb into the park. Carlo's head smacked into his door as it crumpled. *Holy Mary...* Carlo slumped down in his seat as he lost consciousness.

As the scaffolding collapsed, two of the painters jumped to the grass, but the third rolled down the platform and into the street. A rapidly decelerating car swerved to avoid him, slamming head on into the water truck. The next driver, distracted by the exploding water bottles ran over the fallen painter.

Christian took another sip of wine while surveying the chaos.

A cyclist ran into Alyssa's baby stroller, trying to veer out of the way of the out of control truck. The stroller rolled away from Alyssa for a second time as the truck crashed into a tree, erupting in steam.

Christian held up his hand, ticking off his fingers to a countdown. Five... Four... Three... Two... One... The tree cracked and fell in slow motion, engulfing a handful of bystanders running to help.

For a moment everything became quiet. Carlo sat up, rubbing his head and gasped as he saw the extent of turmoil. He jerked on the door, but it wouldn't budge. He climbed over the seat and let himself out the passenger door. *Oh my God. This is insane. One bird... and one anti-Christ. So much for time outs.* Screams and cries cut through the air. People were running in all directions. Some were running away to escape any further carnage, while others were rushing to the aid of the fallen. Christian nonchalantly drained the last of his wine.

Carlo sprinted toward Christian, not sure what he was going to do when he got there. Christian turned to face him and raised an eyebrow. Carlo realized there was nothing he could do with what he had present and altered his trajectory to the people laying in the street.

Christian followed his progress then shrugged and walked toward the fallen tree. At the edge of the tree, the stroller stood unscathed.

Christian faced the sky. "Nice touch..." As he walked around the stroller, he noticed Alyssa pinned beneath a huge branch, unmoving. Blood pooled around her head. The smell of gasoline from the wrecked truck permeated the air.

His eyes flashed obsidian as he clenched his fists.

"Oh... well played." He shoved the stroller, barely hearing the baby cry. "Well played, indeed."

Christian bent over, fingering through the contents of her purse, strewn haphazardly through the grass. He froze when he touched his card. Picking it up, Christian stood and threw an angry look at the sky. He spun the card unknowingly between his fingers as he surveyed the chaos he created.

"But I think I won this battle." He shrugged and flipped the card away as he walked down the street. It flew straight for eight feet before it began to tumble end over end, fluttering through the air. It landed on the front of the truck face up. Flames erupted from the hood. Christian didn't flinch as the thunder of the trucks explosion ripped through the air.

Carlo looked up from the cyclist he was helping at the sound. *What was that?* He put more pressure on the wound, trying to slow the bleeding.

"It's going to be okay. I can hear the ambulances coming."

Chapter *17*

Italy
1357

Terrence and Antonio sat across the table from Constantine in silence, watching the door. Antonio pulled a piece of bread off the loaf sitting on the rough wooden platter. The other two men looked at him sharply.

"What? I'm hungry."

Constantine fingered the hilt of his sword, shaking his head. "We're in the catacombs. It's dark and damp, and we're surrounded by crypts."

"So, a man can't be hungry in strange surroundings? I haven't eaten all day, and we've been waiting at least an hour past

when Brother Edward said to meet here, at least by my reckoning."
Antonio punctuated his statement by ripping a huge bite out of the
hard bread.

Constantine cringed. "Please, no 'brother', even here. I know
these meetings are secret, but we don't want bad habits to form. The
church is still ignorant of our existence and it's best that it remain
so. Remember the Templars."

The three men made the sign of the cross. Antonio put the
remaining piece of bread on the table, and picked up his wine. He
gulped from the chalice, spilling as much down his shirt as he
swallowed. He pulled at the shirt, flapping the edges where it was
buttoned.

"I'm not sure I still see the point of this. This group has been
meeting in its various incarnations for over two hundred years and
accomplished nothing except the continuation of our brotherhood."

"Antonio, you have doubts?"

"Doubts? I don't have doubts, all I have are fireflies."

"What?"

Antonio met their questioning looks. "We have a two-
century old journal filled with half-mad ravings and the only thing
we've been able to come up with is that firefly rain *may* refer to
Chinese fireworks. The rest is as much a mystery as it was when
Abbot Thomas first wrote it down."

Constantine looked shocked. "But the fate of mankind is in
our hands, no one else's. The church spurned this message. Not only
that, they let that sniveling little..." Constantine sighed. "Look, we
are the only four alive who even know about the threat. Don't tell
me that you're no longer convinced of the evil that is coming."

"No. Between the words of Brother David and the notes
from Abbot Thomas and Brother Stefano, I'm convinced something
will happen. Whether we'll find out what or when remains in doubt.
It's been two hundred years. What do we have? Hearts of glass?
Hordes of locusts acting as one?" Antonio brushed the crumbs from
his beard, and pushed them around on the table without looking at
them.

"We are the fifth generation of our brotherhood to study this journal and the best we have is *maybe* the firefly rain? I think we're just not smart enough."

Constantine covered Antonio's hand, stopping the nervous motion. "But it is a valiant effort, and one we've dedicated our lives to pursuing. We weren't the first, and we may not be the last, but the answers must and will be found."

"I agree with you. It's just that... It feels like such a daunting task with no end in sight. And..." Antonio frowned, and then pasted a smile on his face as he freed his hand to reach for the bread. "Daunting tasks make me hungry. What say you, Terrence? You've been awfully quiet."

"Not me."

"Not you? You're not frustrated?"

"No. I lose my appetite when working on enigmas. I'm not hungry." He grinned, watching Antonio tear another piece from the bread.

"Still, Antonio has a point. It is hard to go on year after year with nothing to show for our efforts. We've devoted our lives to this undertaking because we believe in it, but it would be nice to see some results. By the enthusiasm he showed in his last missive, I hope that Edward has found something in France."

"Shhh. Did you hear that?" Constantine cut them off with a wave of his hand.

Metal rang through the air as all three jumped up, drawing their swords. Antonio and Constantine flanked the door on either side, signaling each other to be ready.

As the door opened and the man entered, Antonio grabbed him from behind, putting him in a choke hold. Terrence and Constantine looked at him down leveled swords.

Constantine sighed in relief. "It's okay, Antonio. It's Edward."

"Let me go before I drop this." Edward clutched a carved box to his chest.

"Can't be too careful, you know." Antonio slapped Edward on the back, before sitting down and picking up the piece of bread he had left on the table. "You never know who might be coming for our bread."

"Coming for your what? Oh, never mind. We are well met, my friends. I'm glad you could make it." Edward set the box lightly onto the table. "Sorry I'm late. I was making sure no one followed me."

"Why the long faces, fellows?" Edward opened the padlock on the box and put the key back in his pocket.

"We were sitting here lamenting the fact that our life-calling has been so fruitless." Antonio reached for the bread but stopped short with a look from Constantine.

"Ah, that again. Maybe what I have in here will spark your interest, then." Edward pulled out the familiar leather journal and laid it on the table.

"I think we've seen that enough. I can almost recite it by heart. Is there anything else in there?" Antonio reached for the box. "Some lamb would be nice."

Edward swatted his hand away. "Sadly, there is no lamb, but I do have something else that might perk you up. First, however, I think we need to talk about the prophecy. Why don't you sit down, please?"

Antonio groaned. "The prophecy," he muttered. "As if we haven't talked about that enough."

Constantine and Terrance shot him an angry glance and sat down waiting expectantly for Edward to continue.

"I think we may have been going about this whole thing wrong."

"In what way?" Constantine sat forward, interest playing across his face.

"We've been dwelling on what is supposed to happen, an evil greater than the horde that acts as a single beast, the beggar and a thief, and a hollow thing. We've turned these phrases inside-out to no avail."

"That's exactly what I was saying," muttered Antonio.

"Shh. Hear him out."

"We've tried to figure out when it was going to happen, sometime after golems walk through firefly rain and mankind lives in glass hearts." Edward held the journal up to the candlelight. "For two hundred years, no one has been able to shed any light on that, either."

"Edward, we know all this. We have tomes filled with the scribblings of our forefathers speculations about just those things, but we are no closer to an answer."

Edward slammed the book on the table, causing the other three to jump in surprise. "And we may *never* find it." He turned his back to the table before continuing. "Prophets see more than the words they relay to us. They try to paint a picture with those words from an image they see in its fullness. They must try to translate the fullness of that vision into scribblings with quill and ink. The prophecy we read can never match up to what was lived."

He turned back to face them. "How can we hope to measure the distance between two objects painted on canvas and expect to get an accurate reading?"

Antonio frowned. "We can't. We'd have to travel to the place that was painted to get anything close to the truth."

"*Exactly.* We'd either have to be prophets ourselves, or be present at the place and time of the event prophesied. Unfortunately, none of us is a prophet, and fortunately, we do not appear to be in the time foretold."

Constantine cleared his throat. "So, if we've been wrong all this time, what do we need to do?"

"We have been trying to solve the unsolvable."

"That's comforting."

"Antonio, if your sword was as sharp as you think your wit is, you would wear far fewer scars."

"Ah, but the others look far worse." Antonio chuckled.

"The point is that while I don't doubt your martial or mental prowess, so far they have not been up to the task. So, instead of pounding our heads against an impregnable fortress, we should sneak in the back way."

"Is this what you learned in France? Metaphor?"

"Actually, in France, I believe I discovered where the back door is."

The three men sat in stunned silence.

"I spent some time visiting with Jeanne de Verey, widow of Geoffroi de Charnay. You may have heard of him."

"One of the greatest knights in recent history. Yes, I've heard of him, and his widow. Isn't she parading about with what Goeffroi claimed to be the shroud that covered our Lord?"

"Yes, and quite an impressive piece that is. It's huge, and not what you might think. You have to stand back from it some distance to make out the features."

Constantine stepped in when Edward paused. "But didn't the Bishop of Troyes all but deny its veracity? I've heard rumors that it was merely a cleverly painted fraud."

Edward nodded. "Almost. He prohibited veneration of the shroud. But we all know how selfless some bishops can be. The descendents of Bishop Ruiz still hold the land that housed our old abbey. Besides, the shroud is not like a standard painting. It's... off."

He reached in the box and passed out some sketches. "The shading is the opposite of what you might expect. It gives it a rather ghostly effect, don't you think?"

Anthony held the paper to the light. "What does this so called shroud of Jesus, interesting as it may be, have to do with our puzzle?"

"We've been searching for the when and the what unsuccessfully, when all we really needed to know was the how." Edward smiled smugly.

"The how? How does that help us?"

"If we know the how, we can guard it until the moment has come, and fight to stop it."

"So, you're saying that the Shroud of Jesus is that 'how'?"

"Yes."

"But how can a piece of linen that may or may not have covered Jesus cause the world's greatest calamity?"

"I have no idea."

The other three men mumbled under their breath.

"However, I still see this as a turning point for our brotherhood. We need to change directions."

"Stop studying the journal?"

"No, Antonio, we can continue that as well, but I think we need to watch and guard the shroud."

"Why the shroud? What makes it special? I mean to us."

"'It will come from the upside down and the inverted,'" Brother David said. "Look at those sketches. What do you think?"

Antonio turned his sketch around, looking at it upside down. Constantine slapped his head.

"Not literally, you idiot. Edward, I see what you mean, but it could refer to any number of things. Are we really going to focus on this one object with only generalizations pointing to it?"

"True, it may be coincidence, but the fact that it's a religious relic makes it less so. However, that isn't all. The painted looking glass..."

Constantine jumped up, holding the sketch closer to the candle. "Yes. I see it. I don't know why I didn't think of that earlier."

Antonio looked from Constantine to Edward with confusion in his eyes. "Care to enlighten us idiots?"

Constantine laughed. "Sorry, brother. You know I mean you no ill." He put his sketch down

"It's a reflection, right?"

Edward nodded. "That's my thought. It's like a painted reflection of Jesus, the painted looking glass."

"Okay, I guess I see that. But now what? What do we do? Burn the thing?"

"I thought about that, but I don't think that's the way these things work." Edward picked up the sketches, putting them back in the box before locking it.

"The evil is coming whether we close the door or not."

"What does that mean?"

"Better to have a known weakness than one unknown. If we destroy it, we destroy the only link we have with the prophecy, and with it, our only chance to stop it."

Terrence sat forward. "I think you're right. Better to guard this shroud. Remember the prophecy? The evil will come from it, but so will the weapon to stop it."

"How can a piece of linen be a weapon?"

"We don't know, just as we don't know how it can be a vehicle for the great evil, but if that truly is the image of the Lord, who knows what it is capable of?"

Edward grabbed the leftover piece of bread, tearing it in half. "So, we're agreed? We have a new mission?"

As one, the other three responded, "Yes."

"But..." Anthony looked doubtful. "How do we guard that which is not ours without revealing ourselves?"

"We need resources," Constantine whispered.

"What's that?"

"You heard me, Edward. We need money. You, of the four of us are the only one that has a substantial amount of money. How else have you funded all your travels in seeking this answer?"

Edward hesitated, and then sighed. "You're right, but we'll all need to add to it as we can, and invest. This could go on for a couple hundred years for all we know. We need to make this sustainable."

"We also need to continue to train ourselves physically. We don't know what we'll be called upon to do." Antonio patted the hilt of his sword.

Edward nodded at Antonio. "Who knows what will be required of us. We must be prepared, but foremost, we need to ensure the continuation of our brotherhood. We fail if we disappear before the time comes. We need to remain small to avoid exposure, but we must constantly search for new recruits."

"What do you think we need to do first?"

"I think one of us needs to take residence close to the shroud, and stay near at all times. Constantine, you speak French. Will you take first duty? I've already been seen frequenting the area and asking questions, and may draw suspicions should I return this soon. We must remain invisible."

"Of course I will go, but what should I do if the prophecy comes to pass?"

"Once we've determined that the evil has arrived beyond a shadow of doubt, we must take steps to retrieve the shroud. It is the only thing that can stop it, and therefore must be our first priority at that point. We must become guardians of the shroud. Meanwhile, we all continue to study the journal for clues as to how the shroud can be used to thwart whatever is coming."

Antonio picked up the last of the bread and dunked it in his wine. The other three watched him with amusement.

"Did, uhm, anyone want any more?"

They all shook their heads as one.

Chapter *18*

Father Mike sat at his desk and looked around his office. *It took over five hours to straighten this up, but thank God I don't have to stare at those bloodstains anymore. I think this room looks better in hardwood floors, anyway. Fortunately they were in pretty good shape under the carpet.* The stack of journals on his desk drew his attention

What happened? We did everything right. We should have gotten the second coming. The body is identical. Cloning seemed like such a straightforward affair, like making a photocopy. He has powers, but did that come from the DNA? Did we get a soulless body? Maybe Satan is merely man's attempts at describing a person with no soul. Or did something fill the void? Either way, he must be stopped. Carlo, whoever he really is, doesn't have a clue. Guns and knives can't stop Christian, but what will? Anthony and Joseph seemed to have an idea. Maybe I can follow up on that. I should give Father Vincent a call.

Father Mike picked up the phone and dialed.

"Yes, I need to place an international call. The Vatican. Yes,

I can wait."

Father Michael listened through interminable static, numerous clicks, and dead space. He had almost decided he must have been cut off, when he heard a voice coming through.

"Ciao. Questo è Vincent." The voice, laden with accent, sounded hollow through the long distance connection.

"Father Vincent, it's Father Michael. How are things in Italy?"

"Michael! It's been awhile since I've heard your voice. The Vatican is as the Vatican always is, a rock. And you? Have you, Anthony, and Joseph found an answer to the anomalies?"

"They are more than anomalies." Father Mike lowered his voice. "He killed Anthony, Joseph, and Sister Mary Elizabeth. We found them..."

Father Vincent interrupted him. "I don't need to know the details." He paused. "I'm not ready to give up on him, yet. He represents mankind's greatest chance for salvation. He has the power to unite us all, to eliminate petty bickering and war. We could enter a new golden age."

"Vincent, have you been watching the news? Things are getting worse, and faster. He's escalating. It's only a matter of time before he begins acting on a worldwide scale."

"That doesn't mean Christian is Lucifer, Michael. Maybe he needs better guidance."

Michael held his tongue, not wanting to reply to the barb. "Have you been reading my reports over the last twenty-five years? We've given him the benefit of the doubt on far too many occasions, while showering him with love and caring at every turn. We gave him the best upbringing in school and in the church. At some point, we have to face it. Christian is not Jesus, quite the contrary. And we created him. We brought him into our world. We're responsible for everything he has done, for everything he will do. Christian will be held accountable for what he does, but so will we."

The phone remained silent.

"Vincent, are you still there?"

"Yes."

"This was a mistake from the beginning. We should not have taken it upon our hands to be God. Unfortunately that is the past and we cannot undo it. But, to turn our backs on it now, to do nothing... That would be an even greater sin. It would not only be dangerous for our souls, but our bodies. What he's capable of doing in this physical world is unfathomable."

"Michael, I see your point, but if we try to stop him and succeed, and he *is* the second coming, then we would be no different than Pontius Pilate. You're asking me to be another Judas Iscariot without the silver coins."

"Are you saying you need compensation?"

"No, no. Of course not. All I'm saying is that I don't want to be the one who kills the Son of God."

"Fine, you don't have to have anything to do with that. I just need some information. What I need you to do is get into the Vatican vault."

"Into the vault? Without anyone knowing? You don't ask for much. What do you need there?"

"There are scriptures which never made it into the bible, scriptures that hardly anyone alive today has read."

"How do you know about them?"

"From a conversation I was having with Anthony and Joseph, right before he decapitated them and hung them upside down from the lights."

"Okay, I get it."

"There must be something in one of those forgotten scriptures that will tell us how to defeat Lucifer."

Father Mike could only hear clicks and static on his end.

"Are you still there?"

"Yes, Michael, but..."

"Listen, if he's not Satan, then anything that is supposed to get rid of the devil will not affect him. You won't be Judas. It will merely affirm that he is not Satan, and we have to take a different tack."

"But if he is Satan, doesn't he know we're doing this? Won't he stop you?"

"He has many powers, but thankfully omniscience appears to not be one of them. He has gotten in my head at least once, but while he really screwed with it, he did not know what I was thinking... At least as far as I could tell."

"So, all you want from me is information?"

"Yes, I will carry the burden of action. If I'm wrong, you will not be Judas."

"From your lips to God's ears. I'll see what I can find."

"And Vincent?"

"Yes, Michael."

"Be careful, but please... Be swift."

Father Mike hung up the phone and looked up to see Father Simon in the doorway with a look of confusion on his face.

"Father Simon. How long have you been standing there?"

"Long enough, I think. What is this all about?"

"Come in and have a seat. I have a story to tell you, a story of pride and good intentions gone awry." He gestured to the leather sofa across from his desk.

"It's time to let our demons out, so to speak."

"Michael, is this some sort of confession?"

Father Mike looked up, surprised. "Yes, as a matter of fact, it is."

~~*~*

Danny walked through the doors of the precinct station. The lobby appeared calm, but he could hear frenzied sounds coming from the rooms beyond. Detective Williams waved at him from across the room, headed in the opposite direction.

"Danny, did you hear about the cluster fuck at the park yesterday?"

"I heard the sound bite on the way in. Are you on that one?"

"Yeah, talk about seriously messed up. We had six dead and over fifteen injured all because some idiot couldn't wait for a delivery truck."

"Sounds crazy."

"You don't know the half of it. If you study the scene, it looks like a freakin' Mouse Trap game board. The stars had to align just right, or wrong in this case, for it to have happened exactly like it did."

Stars aligned all right. Crap. Christian is certainly being a busy boy.

He walked past the main desk and through the door toward his partner's desk. Stan sat behind his desk, engrossed in his computer terminal and didn't notice Danny walk up until he put his hand on his shoulder.

"So, partner, what's so important that you needed to interrupt my beauty sleep to get me to come down in person?"

"Hang on a sec." Stan continued to type on his keyboard, before looking up. "Beauty sleep?"

"Don't say I'd hate to see you without it."

"Actually, I was going to say that you shouldn't have still been asleep at seven o'clock. There's way too much weirdness going on with these cases to sleep late."

"About that weirdness..."

"Before you tell me what you found out from Father Michael, I've got something here I want to show you. Follow me."

Danny followed Stan to another terminal where a uniformed officer was diligently working. Stan tapped him on the arm.

"Gene, can you show us the fingerprint found at the church?"

"Which one, sir"

"The strange one."

Gene double clicked an icon and a picture of a fingerprint covered half his screen.

"That fingerprint was taken from the church. Actually, it was lifted from the blood left in the kitchen. It was repeated in the sanctuary and a number of other areas that were part of the crime scene."

"Okay. So we know it was from the afternoon of the murder."

"Yes, and when we run it through AFIS to find a match, this is what we get."

Gene punched some keys, and a mug shot of a Hispanic man in his late thirties pops up on the screen.

I thought Christian did this. Father Mike could have been having one over on me, but what about this morning?

""Well, it appears you've found our guy, then. Let's go pick him up."

"Wait, Danny. Here's where it gets strange. David Garza, age thirty-eight, died four years ago. Gene, exclude him from our search and start over."

Gene tapped his keyboard again, and another photo popped up, a Caucasian male from Los Angeles.

"Jimmy Zins, age 42, incarcerated in Los Angeles County Jail since June of 2012.

"What the hell? How's that possible?"

"Wait, Danny, that's not all. Gene, do it again."

"Whatever you say, sir."

After typing again, a picture of an African American female popped up.

"Again."

Next came a picture of a seventy-two year old white male.

"Again."

"Hold on, Stan, I get the point. What is it? Some kind of computer glitch?"

Stan shook his head. "Nope. We tried running prints from other scenes and they come out fine. We've tried running other prints from this scene and no problems there, either. It's just this print."

Danny paced away and back. "What is it about this print? Could there be something wrong with it?"

Gene looked up from his computer. "We thought of that, sir. We ran the others we lifted from in the sanctuary. Same print, different location... Same results. Or rather same random results."

"How is that possible?"

"I said it was a mind fuck, remember? There's no way it's possible. When we initially ran the print, it came up Leon Washington, a thirty-seven year old African American man from Indiana. He's been in Angola State Prison for the last five years. We've gotten a teacher from Minnesota, a construction worker from Florida, even a web designer from Alabama."

"Did anyone else corroborate these results?"

"Yeah, we sent them to Baton Rouge. They got the same thing. I'm starting to get a bad feeling about this one."

"Starting? Stan, you think *this* is a mind fuck?"

"Well isn't it?"

"Yes, but wait 'til you hear what my last day was like, it started with my conversation with Father Michael, off the record by the way. Crazy as that was, it didn't compare to my morning before work today."

"I thought you slept late this morning."

"If you want to call it that. I'm about ready to wash my hands of this whole thing, if I could. I feel like I'm on the edge of a black hole, getting sucked in; there's no escape."

"Danny, are we still talking about a couple murders and

some messed up evidence?"

Danny gestured to Stan to follow him as he walked away from the desk. Stan looked at him questioningly. Danny pointed to Gene and shook his head.

"I'm going to have enough trouble trying to convince you that I'm not crazy, I don't want rumors spreading through the force." Danny opened the door to 'the tank' and flipped the lights on.

"Have a seat. You're going to need it."

Father Simon stared at Father Mike in silence.

"Simon, please, say something."

"Mike, what do you want me to say? Do you realize how crazy you sound?"

Father Mike tossed Simon the top journal from beside him.

"Here, read some. It's all there. Twenty-five years of insanity." He pointed to the stack of journals. "You saw what happened to Anthony and Joseph. He is capable of anything. He has no morals, and I think, an underlying hatred for the rest of us humans."

"But Mary speaks so highly of him. Is she just covering? She seems so genuine."

"She does. I think she's under his thrall... Something about carrying him in her body changed her. I can't give you solid proof for any of this. You have to take it as a matter of faith. In the end, it comes down to whether you believe me or not."

"Mike, in the ten years I've known you, you've done some crazy things, more than I knew about apparently, but I haven't seen any signs that you are not in control of your faculties. What you've just told me is extremely hard to swallow." Father Simon stood up and walked over to the window, looking out before turning back to face Father Mike.

"I'm a priest. I believe in a loving God. I guess I believe in a devil, but I always thought he was a part of us. I never thought of the devil as a separate entity, more like that part of us that didn't listen to God when he talked to us, that part that was outside of God. Now you're saying that not only is that wrong, but the devil is made man and walking among us?"

"I know it sounds insane. I was like you until he brought me to his Hell. Trust me, it's not someplace you want to visit twice, much less end up for eternity. I really don't know what I could do to convince you."

"That's the problem. I do believe you. Do you have any..."

"Way ahead of you, Simon." Father Michael opened the drawer of his desk and pulled out a bottle of scotch and two double old fashions. "Sorry I don't have any ice. They had to throw out the refrigerator, it was pretty banged up from..." Father Mike was lost in thought for a moment. "Sometimes I wish I had taken up smoking. Here, have a little liquid courage."

"Thanks, 'cause if what you say is true, then we're in the end times." He took a swig of the scotch. "And end times call for a lot of courage."

~~*~*

Stan stared at Danny over the stainless steel table with no expression on his face.

"Say something, Stan. Let me have it."

Stan sat motionless, looking through Danny.

"Come on. Tell me I need a psyche eval. Say I'm crazy. Hell, tell me I need a vacation, but say something."

Stan shook his head. "Okay, you're nuttier than a fruitcake. Is that what you want to hear? Fuck the vacation. I should tell them to put you on leave, but then I'd never be able to get any time off for myself."

"It's not funny. You should have heard him. I could see it in his eyes; he's scared. If Christian isn't the devil, then he's the next best thing. When I saw him coming out of the teeth of that tree..."

"Whoa. Slow down there little doggie. When you saw him *where?*"

"Oh yeah, I was about to get to that. Remember when I said my morning was even crazier than Father Michael's story? I did some kind of groundhog day in Hell kind of thing."

"Like fire and brimstone?"

"No. Weirder. It was all monotones, like an old movie. I kept getting attacked by these Hell hounds, and every time I woke up, they were still there."

"Sounds like one hell of a dream."

"That's what I thought the first time I woke up, and then there was the bite mark that stayed on my arm even after I woke up the final time."

"And Christian was there?"

"Oh, yeah. Gloating, like he was orchestrating the whole thing."

Stan stood up and walked over to the two-way mirror, picking a piece of food out of his teeth.

"Well, I guess I'm going to have to brush up on my bible."

Danny let out his breath in a rush, not realizing he had been holding it.

"So you believe me?"

Stan shook his head, smiling. "I still think you're fucking

looney, but that doesn't matter. You may never be on time, but you're always there when I need you." He turned back to face Danny. "Besides, you don't have enough imagination to make up a vision of Hell so far off the mainstream. And, yes, I have faith in you."

"Faith. Seems like we're going to be needing that in record amounts soon."

Stan's phone rang and interrupted them.

"Stan, here. What have you got?"

Stan nodded in response to the conversation.

"Okay, we'll be there as soon as we can." He hung up and putting his phone away, he looked up at Danny.

"Another suicide, this one at an antique shop on Magazine Street."

"Are they sure it's suicide? No signs of foul play?"

Stan shook his head. "It's an older couple, in bed with sleeping pills."

"Do you think it could be connected to... This?"

"He said there's a note."

"What are we waiting for? Let's go."

An ambulance was parked outside the shop when they arrived.

"Where are they?"

The uniformed officer opened the door for them. "They're upstairs. There's an apartment above the store."

"Is there anything missing or out of place down here?"

The officer raised his eyebrow. "In an antique shop? Really?" He glanced around the shop. "I can't tell if anything's missing. What I can tell you is there was no sign of a struggle. They've apparently been up there for two days."

"Alright, thanks. Danny, let's head upstairs."

Danny set the print of The Last Supper down on the counter where he had picked it up and followed his partner up the steps.

In the bedroom, two officers and a paramedic were gathered at the bedside. The man and his wife were fully clothed, lying side by side on top of the blanket, holding hands. An empty pill bottle lay on its side next to a letter on the side table. Stan slipped on a pair of latex gloves and picked it up.

"With all the pain and suffering in the world, we got along as best as we could. The day I met my wife was the happiest day of my life. The day she said yes was my luckiest. That luck has run out."

Hmm, long winded for a suicide note.

"I don't want to suffer. I can't do the pain and indignity of cancer. My wife doesn't want it for me either. Nor does she want to go on without me."

Stan let the paper fall as he studied the two bodies. Both looked at perfect peace.

"Today, we were visited by an angel. He showed us a better way."

Danny leaned over Stan's shoulder, trying to get a better view of the note. "An angel?" He whispered so only Stan could hear. "Anti-Christs and angels. Not good."

"Since we have nothing to leave behind and no one to leave it to, we leave only knowledge. I know it sounds crazy, but the angel is real. He promised us a better life than God gave us. Know that we die in God, to be reborn to a new life. It's the beginning of a new life."

"That's it?"

"Yep, and then they both signed it."

Stan handed the note to the officer, who slid it into a plastic bag.

"Sir, that's not the kicker."

"There's a kicker?" Danny and Stan asked in unison.

"Yes, sir. The message light on the machine was blinking when we got here. It was his doctor letting him know he didn't have cancer. I guess that angel was more of a devil, huh?"

Danny led Stan to the other side of the room.

"Definitely sounds like Christian, but what was he doing here? I mean what's the point? An old couple?"

"Who knows, but the bodies are starting to pile up. We're following his trail now, but at some point we're going to have to think about how we're going to stop him."

"I know. That's what scares me."

Chapter *19*

Father Vincent fidgeted at the entrance to the lower levels of the Vatican Archives. He patted his hidden pocket to ensure his iPhone remained in place.

"State your business."

Vincent pointed to the paper in the curator's hand. "You have the letter of permission from Cardinal Ventura. I seek information."

"Yes, but entrance into the sub-levels is highly irregular. There is no reason stated in this letter. Maybe I should call the archivist. Cardinal Richoud might have some questions for you."

"From what I understand, Father *Rinaldi*, a reason is not required."

The curator flipped the paper over, looking for more information on the back.

"No, it is not required. However, in my tenure here, I have never seen a letter of permission with no purpose stated."

Father Vincent bowed his head in deference. "Even so, as it is not a requirement, it must have slipped his Eminence's mind when he drafted the letter."

"Will you not enlighten me yourself, then? What is your purpose?"

"I apologize, but it is a matter of both urgency and secrecy. You understand, I'm sure."

Father Rinaldi raised his eyebrow. "No, I do not. But as you say, you have the required documents. I assume you know the rules."

Vincent nodded, the over dry air making his voice crack. "No photography or electronic recording devices of any kind."

"And yet you have no pencil or paper, either. How will you record your findings?"

"It is a small but important piece of information I seek. My brain will be sufficient for the task."

"Are you sure you don't want to let me know what you are searching for? I've looked through many of the papers down there. Maybe I can save you some time."

"Again, I must apologize. I am under strict instructions from the cardinal."

Father Rinaldi sighed "Very well. Ring the bell when you are ready to leave and I'll come unlock the door." He punched his access code into the panel and opened the door for Father Vincent.

"Don't forget, the archives shut down at six o'clock. That only gives you four hours."

"If I can't find it today, then I will just have to return tomorrow."

Father Rinaldi shrugged and walked back toward his office, looking over his shoulder as he turned at the end of the hallway.

Vincent breathed a sigh of relief as he disappeared out of sight. He climbed down the narrow spiral staircase, scraping his elbows on the rough stone walls on two occasions. Unlike the often-ostentatious architectural details found in the upper levels, this little used floor had low ceilings and sparse lighting. The aisles wound in serpentine fashion in all directions, often ending in unexpected cul de sacs. There were unsubstantiated stories of researchers getting lost for hours in the maze-like rows. Worse yet, in many cases the papers were so old that they weren't bound in book form, instead, they were bundled and placed in acid free storage boxes with sometimes-cryptic labels.

Vincent sat down at one of the two small desks at the base of the stairs, letting his eyes wander around the seemingly random stacks of bins. *Where to start?*

Crrrrrrrrk.

Vincent flinched. *What was that?* He looked as far down the aisles as he could see, but could see nothing suspicious. *Something's giving me the creeps. Old buildings make noises.* He pulled out his iPhone. *I never broke the rules before this venture. I hope Father Rinaldi doesn't call Cardinal Ventura. He might be surprised to find he wrote that letter for me.*

Father Vincent started down the aisle to his left, reading labels and looking for anything that might seem relevant. *Where do I find scriptures kept out of the bible? So far this looks like church land deeds from the ninth and tenth centuries.* He wandered down the aisle until he reached a crossroads. Deciding that right was as good as any direction, he turned and continued to study the bin labels, hoping for anything that might be of interest.

This might be good. "The Infancy Gospels of Thomas." He took the box back to the desk and began to pull out papers. *It's written in Syriac? Oh, thank God, some translations to Latin.*

"When Jesus was five years old, and playing at the side of a stream, He dug a pool with his bare hands and let it fill with water. With just his words, he made it pure. He then took mud from the bottom of the pool and fashioned twelve clay birds from it."

"Being unlawful to fashion from clay on the Sabbath, the other children rebuked him and ran to tell the Pharisee. When confronted, Jesus commanded the clay birds to take flight, and they did, making much noise as they flew away."

I've definitely never heard this story before.

"The son of a scribe took a stick and destroyed the pool and drained the water Jesus had blessed. Jesus, seeing what the boy had wrought, said to him, 'Your roots shall wither and your branches fall to the earth.' And instantly that child died."

"While he was traveling away from the stream, another child ran into him and knocked him down. Jesus said unto him, 'You shall no longer go with us.' And that child died as well."

Holy cow. No wonder these writings didn't make it into the Bible. That's pretty intense for five years old. Father Vincent took a picture of the page with his iPhone. *I'm not sure that passage will help Father Michael, but it might shed some light on Christian's childhood.* He put the scriptures back into the bin, being careful not to damage any.

Searching through the aisles, he had trouble finding where he had gotten the box. After backtracking a few times, he located the spot and replaced the box and continued down the aisle, looking for anything else of interest.

A loud crash startled him, sounding like it came from the next row over. He rushed to the end of the aisle and turned the corner. A bin was overturned on the floor, spilling documents in all directions.

"Hello? Is anyone here?"

"Shhhhhh."

"What? Hello? Who's there?" *I'm supposed to be alone down here. Who would be following me? Father Rinaldi? He seemed like the overly curious type. But is he trying to scare me? If so, it's working.*

Sweat stung his eye as it dripped down from his forehead. He backed down the aisle, keeping his eye on the far end. Something poked him in the back and he froze. *What? Who?* Nobody moved. Father Vincent counted to ten, then spun around as quickly as he could, hands raised and ready for a fight.

"Oh, my God. Books." *A dead end, and I spooked myself on books.* He straightened the jostled titles, letting out his breath in relief. *But what was that whispering?*

"Shhhhhh."

He retraced his steps to the staircase, finding nothing out of the ordinary. Now, he could distinctly hear a faint rattling in conjunction with the whispering, both too faint to recognize exactly what they were.

Both sounds abruptly ceased with a mechanical clunk. *Damn dehumidifier. I am seriously wound up. These things should not be getting to me like this. I've got a limited amount of time to find this information.*

Vincent decided to try going the opposite direction as he had before. He sifted through boxes of missives written to popes, proclamations by popes, and papal journals for over an hour.

"Sssssss."

Vincent jumped. *No. I am not going to overreact again. Concentrate.*

He pulled down a box labeled "Thomas". *Hmm. Apparently this must be different from the other Thomas writings. It's on a whole other row.*

He walked back toward the desk with the box under one arm. After turning right and following the aisle to a dead end, he began to suspect that the stories of people getting lost while searching for books might have more than a kernel of truth to them. *Which way was it?*

"Ssssssss."

"Oh, shut up. Air conditioning, dehumidifier, whatever. I've got work to do." *Michael, you owe me. You have no idea how much you owe me.*

He wandered the aisles for another five minutes before he found the way back to the desk. He sat down and poured over the writings. *This is more like it. Aramaic, but with translation again, thankfully.*

"The life of the fallen angel is real. His sole purpose is to collect as many souls as possible. He who believes in the Lord must therefore also believe in the opposite. The fallen angel has power slightly lesser than those of our Savior and Lord. For only with His blood and His blood alone shall the light replace the darkness.

When Lucifer walks among us, we will be at our darkest. Our Lord, Jesus Christ has shed his blood that we may be free of eternal night."

That's it. That's what we need. If I'm reading this right, the blood of Jesus will defeat the anti-Christ. Father Vincent sighed. *But where do you get the Lord's blood now that the shroud has gone missing? Let me get this to Michael, at least. Maybe he can figure something out.*

Father Vincent took more pictures and attached them to an email to Father Michael. He hit the send button and watched the progress bar move slowly toward one hundred percent. *The wonders of technology never fail to amaze me. Deep in the bowels of the church's archives, I can send a message to my friend in America. How long would that have taken just a couple centuries ago?*

"Sssssss."

Really? I'm so over this place.

At ninety percent, the bar stopped. *Oh, come on. Send, you stupid phone.*

"Ssssssennnnd."

What? Tell me I'm hearing things.

"Ssssssennnnt."

It's just the stupid air again. And yes, it needs to finish and say sent. The bar edged to ninety-two percent and stopped again.

"Vinnncennnt."

Oh shit. That was not the air.

"Who's there? What do you want? Father Rinaldi?" Vincent searched frantically for the source of the voice, but nothing appeared out of the ordinary.

Father Vincent boxed the papers and walked down the nearest row of books. Shadows loomed ahead, seeming to track him. He looked down at the phone. *Stuck on ninety-four percent now. Hurry up, damn it!*

"Vincent."

He spun around, hearing the whispered voice as if it was just over his shoulder. *Nothing?* Behind him, a whole shelf of books fell to the floor with a crash.

Vincent ran back the way he came. As he exited the row and neared the desk, the papers on it blew off and flitted to the floor.

What the? There's no wind in here.

"Vincent!" The voice was more insistent, becoming louder.

He veered sharply down another aisle, slamming into a shelf before straightening out. He took the next right and knocked down two bins as he careened into them. Ten feet ahead of him, four boxes fell from the shelf, blocking his way. He turned, looking for another direction to run.

"Vincent. *Vincent. VINCENT.*"

He picked his way through the scattered books and papers, and ran to the next corner.

The sound of a gale force wind tore through the archives, but not as much as a breeze hit his face. Vincent took the next turn he came upon, thoroughly lost. He ran at full abandon, fleeing on instinct only.

"*VINCENT! VINCENT!*"

Damn it, dead end. Behind him, bookshelves on both sides of the aisle tottered and fell into each other, raining books and boxes all over the floor.

"*SHHHHHHHHHH.*"

The sound of the wind increased in volume, becoming unbearable. Vincent dropped his phone and clamped both hands on his ears and slumped to the floor.

"*SHHHHHHHHHH.*"

"*VINCENT!*"

When he thought he could bear the sound no more, it stopped suddenly. In the unexpected silence, his ragged breathing sounded like a small army marching across the frozen tundra. A bitter copper taste flooded his mouth.

Before he could stand back up, the lights turned off. In the complete darkness, Father Vincent began scrabbling across the floor, searching for his phone. *Is that breathing? Oh, that's me. Where's the stupid phone?* His hand closed on the rubber case. *Thank God.* He pressed the home button, and light from the screen illuminated his immediate surroundings. *Damn, still ninety-eight percent?*

Father Vincent held up the phone and began climbing the hill of books spilled when the two cases fell against each other. *It's back to silence, what happened? Is it gone?* Books slid from under his feet as he tried to reach the top. *Oh, come on. This is the only way out.* He reached the midpoint and could see to the end of the shelves where the path was clear.

The books below him shifted. Vincent dropped the phone as he scrambled to steady himself. He began sinking slowly but inexorably into the massive pile. *No, no, no.* Reaching over to the nearest shelf, he tried to grip it, but couldn't gain purchase on the edge. His phone fell down the far side of the pile and flipped screen down, plunging the area into darkness. *Perfect.* Suddenly, it seemed like the pile was moving of its own volition, dragging him further down. Hip deep in the pile, he could barely move his feet. *Is that groaning coming from the books?* As the books started to crowd his chest, claustrophobia set in. He flailed his arms desperately, flinging books in all directions.

I'm an idiot. Father Vincent straightened out his legs, touching the floor under the books. He shoved books to the side, pushing his way to the other side. He picked up the phone and held it above his head to get a better idea of which way to go. *Hmm. That way looks somewhat familiar.* Ten minutes later, he was still wandering through the rows. *Still ninety-eight percent, but now I only have twenty percent power left. All this stone must be blocking most of the signal. I need to find the exit quickly.*

Vincent turned right and saw empty space at the end of the row. *Thank God.* He passed the desk and took the stairs two at a time up to the door. He pressed the button to ring the bell for Father Rinaldi. Nothing happened. He pressed it again. Again, nothing. He peered through the glass and to the side, sighing when he saw that the keypad's light was out. *Damn power. Everything's high tech and then it doesn't work.*

He banged on the glass with his right hand.

"Father Rinaldi! Help! Let me out!"

Father Vincent stopped banging on the door and listened to see if Father Rinaldi was coming. All he could hear was rustling behind him at the base of the stairs. *Oh, crap.* He banged on the door with both hands, dropping his phone and shattering the screen on the stone step. Behind him, the sound of wind was added to the rustling.

"Vinnnncennnnnt."

Oh, please. "Father Rinaldi!" Over the furor of the wind, Vincent could hear flapping. *Bats? Don't turn around. Just don't turn.* He yanked on the door handle repeatedly, hoping it would give.

"Father! Please!" He jammed his thumb on the button for the bell until the plastic cracked.

The flapping and rustling had arrived at the top of the stairs. He could hear it directly behind him. He shut his eyes tight. *Don't turn around. It'll go away. Just ignore it.*

Father Rinaldi looked at the clock on the wall. *Six o'clock, and no word. Damn these priests, they're worse than secular researchers, always making me stay late.* He walked down to the door to the sub-levels and punched his code in. The light turned green. He turned the knob and pushed on the door. It opened an inch then stopped as if blocked. Father Rinaldi pushed again, but only managed to move it another two inches. *What is this?*

He leaned his shoulder against the door and shoved, putting his whole body into it. The door slowly swept open, moving something behind it as it went. *Why are the lights out?* When Father Rinaldi flipped the switch beside the door, the lights showed papers piled almost a foot deep all over the floor of the landing.

"Father Vincent. What have you done? These are historical documents." He bent down, seeing something black peeking between some of the pages. *A cell phone?* "Father Vincent. Where are you? You will be answering to Cardinal Richoud for this." He looked at the screen. Through the cracked glass, he saw the screen change from ninety-eight percent complete to 'email sent.'

"Father Vincent!" Father Rinaldi let the door shut behind him as he prepared to go down the steps. As it shut, he saw Father Vincent lying in the papers face down. *What?*

Father Rinaldi rolled him over and gasped. *Oh, my God!* Father Vincent's face was gray, staring at him with glazed over eyes open wide in fright. His jaw was unhinged and his mouth stuffed with paper. Father Rinaldi pulled out eight crumpled pages and could see more down his throat. *Why would you try to eat paper? I've got to call Cardinal Richoud. He obviously totally lost his mind.*

Chapter *20*

Carlo finished his morning workout and buried his face in his towel. *Father Michael has so little faith in me. No matter. If he had more faith of his own twenty-five years ago, then we wouldn't be in this mess now.* He tossed the towel on the bed and reached up for the almost one thousand year old journal. Cradling it in his hands, he scanned the writings from his memory. *The painted looking glass... There is a weapon strong enough; I only hope I have the vision to use it properly.* Laying the book on his desk and closing his eyes, he placed his hands on the cover. He wished he could use osmosis to absorb the strength of all who had come before him. He tried to visualize Christian's destruction. In his mind, he jabbed a spear wrapped in the shroud into Christian's side. He opened his eyes. *First, however, time to knock him a little off balance.*

Carlo dialed an international number, waiting only one ring before it was picked up.

"Signore Demonte? Carlo?"

"Yes, Joseph, it's me."

"How is America? Is everything going as you wish?"

"It's on track so far, but Joseph, I need you to do something for me." He picked up the journal and carefully replaced it on the shelf.

"Yes, sir?"

"I need you to liquidate the holdings and buy shares of McMillan Industries."

"How much, sir?"

"All of it."

Carlo listened to static, waiting for Joseph's response. "Sir..." Carlo could hear Joseph swallow loudly. "That might take a while."

"Not if I don't care to make a profit off of them. I need you to sell off everything you need in order to buy every outstanding share of McMillan stock."

"Do you think that is wise? If you give me a few weeks..."

"Joseph, if I'm not successful in this endeavor, none of the money in the world will be worth the paper it's printed on." Still standing in front of the bookshelf, he fingered a copy of Dante's *The Divine Comedy* while he waited for Joseph. After a few seconds, he heard him sigh.

"How public do you want this to be?"

"The purchases themselves should be highly visible. I want some murmuring, however, I want our names to be hidden, a mystery wrapped in a shell corporation. We've got a handful of those, don't we?"

"Indeed, sir. It will be as you wish. Will there be anything else?"

"Wish me luck, Joseph. If you and I are alive this time next week, we can lament the fact that all of our holdings in McMillan Industries are worthless, but at least our lives will not be."

Carlo hung up and opened his footlocker. He lifted out a large metal case, taking extra care not to drop it. *So this is what all the hoopla is about? A bit of temptation mixed with miracle.* Carlo rolled his eyes. *Just because we are capable of doing something, doesn't mean we should. Ha. I can hear Father Michael now, "But what if?" 'What ifs' have led to many a downfall.* He fingered the edges of the box. *But at least we have a chance at redemption. God gave us the tool and the knowledge, and now it's time to wield it.*

~~*~*

Danny held out his hand and stopped Stan as they approached the door to the St. Michael's rectory.

"Are you a religious man, Stan?"

"Not so much. I guess when the bullets are flying, I thank God that I made it to the next day. Other than that, I haven't been to church in... I can't remember how long."

"Me either." Danny stared at the cross, mounted above the door, noting the peeling paint. *Father Mike needs to do some work on this place.* He shrugged his shoulders and turned to Stan. "How did we get dragged into this?"

"Fucking anti-Christ."

"Did you ever think you'd be trying to collar the devil?"

Stan shrugged and managed a weak smile. "Just another perp."

Danny choked on a laugh. "With superhuman powers and magic fingerprints?"

"Like I said, just another perp. Just another day for the N.O.P.D."

Danny reached for the bell, pausing inches away from pressing it. He turned back to Stan. "Who thought it would be a good idea to name the anti-Christ, "Christian"? That blasts right past irony and heads straight to WTF!"

"Come on, Danny, let's get this over with." Stan pushed Danny's hand into the button, listening to the distant buzzing halfheartedly.

Father Mike opened the door, looking like he hadn't slept in days. His shirt was wrinkled, hanging loosely on him, and his breath smelled of sour whiskey.

"Detectives?"

"Father Mike, this is detective Muzzo. You met him the day after..."

"Stan, please." Stan held out his hand.

"I filled him in on our chat about Christian, and everything going on."

Father Mike shook Stan's hand. "And where on the belief scale are you?"

Stan laughed. "Maybe you're not so crazy, after all." Stan shoved his hand in his pocket. "I'm here because none of this makes any sense unless you and my partner, here, haven't lost your minds completely, and even then, I'm not sure it makes a lot of sense. If you're wrong, then I'm just humoring you. If you're right... Fuck if I know what to do, but at least we'll all be clueless together. But either way, hell if I'm going to bow down to that shit."

"Fair enough." Father Mike stepped back into the hall. "Come on in. Let's go sit down. I've got an interesting development to tell you about." Danny and Stan followed Father Mike inside.

What is an interesting development when you're chasing Lucifer? Is there any chance it could be good?

Father Mike gestured to the chairs. "Have a seat. Danny, I called one of our group at the Vatican."

"Wait. I thought the rest of the church was ignorant of your activities."

"The church, yes, but we needed contacts in many areas. One of those happened to be the Vatican. He has been able to get us valuable information from time to time. Yesterday, I asked him to do some more research for us."

Danny rolled his eyes. "Research? Did he find a way to stop this thing?"

"Very possibly. In some of the scriptures withheld from the bible, he found an answer."

Stan reached into his pocket and pulled out a crumpled pack of cigarettes. "I only thought I had given these up." He shook his head. "Father Michael, how can writings that weren't even good enough to make the cut help us? Look, you're on a short leash with me. You've hooked my partner to some degree, but I'm just looking for a way to stop the madness, so please get to the point."

"Father Vincent emailed me a passage of scripture from the unpublished gospel of Thomas. It was kept from the bible, not because it wasn't *good enough,* but because of what it says. Its main subject is Lucifer. One section, in particular, talks about his destruction. It says that Satan can only be defeated by the blood of Christ."

"The blood of Christ?"

Father Mike smiled. "Yes, so he can be defeated."

Stan looked at Father Mike like he'd just lost his mind. "Father, I hate to burst your Prozac bubble, but Bill and Ted, we aren't."

"What my sarcastic partner here is trying to ask is how do we go back in time to get His blood?"

Father Mike gave Danny an encouraging smile. "Come on, Danny. You know the whole story. Where can we get His blood? You know the answer."

Stan stood up and slapped his hands on the desk between them. "Let's cut the shit, Father. I haven't had nearly the alcohol you've had this morning and don't have patience for these games. If we can stop him, then how?"

"Wait, Stan. It's the shroud isn't it? That's where you got the DNA to begin with."

"Danny, what are you talking about?"

"They had to get DNA to clone Jesus. He bled on the shroud. They started this whole thing by getting blood from the Shroud of Turin. If we get the shroud, then we can use it to destroy Christian." Danny had a look of smug satisfaction on his face. It quickly melted away. "But how are we going to get the shroud? Isn't it locked up?"

"It's already arranged. I talked to Father Vincent last night after he sent me the email. He's on his way to Turin right now with some very official looking documents. The shroud is scheduled to be displayed soon, so it's being removed from its regular secure place, which we did infiltrate twenty-five years ago, to a display case, which makes it easier. Father Vincent assured me that he could get it and will be on a plane to meet us tomorrow."

"So, on a day's notice, your priest friend is off to steal a religious relic? Just like that? What the hell is wrong with you people?" Stan sat down, looking incredulously at Father Mike.

"Stealing is a sin, Detective. We're just going to borrow it."

"There goes the pension."

"We're on the verge of Armageddon, I think we will be forgiven for small transgressions. The point is that we will have everything we need to defeat him by sometime tomorrow."

"Isn't that the kind of thinking that got you here?"

"Can we begin the incrimination after we stop him?"

Stan glanced over at his partner. "Danny, are you drinking the Kool-Aid?"

"Stan, I've been drinking the Kool-Aid since my morning activities."

"That was just a bad dream. Look, I'm here because we need to stop this killer. I'm somewhat on board with the craziness. But we've now got a priest stealing the Shroud of Turin from the Catholic Church so we can use the blood of Jesus to defeat the anti-Christ, who, by the way, is Newsweek's poster boy of the year, all at the urgings of an alcoholic priest. Do I have it right?" Stan watched Danny for a reaction.

"Detective, the end times will not be infused with logic. The world does not go on as normal. And yes, I have been drinking, thanks for noticing. I realize the enormity of what is happening here, and it is greater than any one person can handle. I am glad that you two have decided to help, but if you don't want to sign on for this, I understand. It all sounds insane, I know, believe me, I wish this were all the ramblings of a priest out of his mind. I have had a drink or two already this morning, but that doesn't change the fact that the anti-Christ is out there and the killing will only escalate."

"I hear you, Father, and Danny, it's not that I don't believe you, but I'm a cop. I live and breathe evidence. As much as I tell myself that this is really happening, I think I need to talk to Christian at least once, hear what he has to say for himself."

"Stan, you've *got* to be kidding? He's seriously crazy."

"Actually, Danny, I think it would be a good idea for Detective Muzzo to meet Christian. Maybe coming face to face with actual evil will convince him. You could ask more questions about the murders that happened at his building. That was your case, wasn't it, Danny?"

"Yes, but aren't you coming with us? You said I'd feel better with a priest with me, and I definitely agree."

"At this point, I think you might be safer without me. As long as you don't pose a threat to him, you'll probably be fine."

"Probably? I'm not sure I like the sound of that."

"Right now, you're not associated with me in his mind except for questioning with the church murders. If he sees you with me in another context, you might become a threat, and anyone who seems a threat to Christian has a very short life expectancy."

"Threat? His body count is already in double digits. If he did it, then he's going down, even if we need to use the shroud or Harry Potter's wand to do it."

"Be careful. Remember, he can get into your mind without you knowing it."

Stan looked at Danny. "He's not going to find much there."

"Seriously, dude. He already messed with mine. Don't joke about this guy."

"Detective, faith is your only weapon. Right now, both of you need to have faith. Faith that what I've told you is true, and faith in each other."

Father Mike stood up, placed his hands on their heads, and blessed them. Danny bowed his head involuntarily, smiling as he looked up. "Thank you, Father. Any extra bit of protection is welcomed." Both detectives stood up and shook his hand.

"Call us if you find out anything on the shroud front before we get back to you."

"Sure."

Danny and Stan walked back to their car, neither speaking until they were seated and the doors were closed.

"You know he's crazy, right? Nine in the morning and his breath was giving me a buzz."

"After the little I've been through, I'm thinking of joining him, so don't hold the drinking against him. And when you call him crazy, you're calling me crazy. I went somewhere, to Hell, wherever. How do you explain the inexplicable?"

"With good police work, my friend. I may be a skeptic, but I'm still here. If this is my best chance of solving these murders and bringing the perp, businessman or anti-Christ, to justice, then I'll follow you two down the rabbit hole. Just know that if you go too far off the deep end, or if this all pans out to be nothing, I'll be the first to check you in."

"I'm good with that. At this point, I'd welcome a restful stay in an institute as long as there was no crazy demon out here trying to destroy the world."

"Let's go get some answers from the horse's mouth."

~~*~*

Christian poured two fingers of Laphroaig into a cut-crystal double old fashioned glass. He dropped in one ice cube to open it up. *Humans have come up with a few things that are almost worthwhile.* He closed his eyes, inhaling the peaty smoke smell and sighed. *I almost hope I fail, so I can experience this plane more.* He laughed. *Nah, not really. Humans stink. Freaking cattle.* Christian tilted the glass back and swirled the liquor in his mouth, savoring the slight burn combined with the explosion of flavor. *Ten o'clock, never too early for debauchery of any sort.*

Christian waved at the over-sized fire pit set in the center of his suite, watching as the flames swelled, reaching for the ceiling. Shadows danced on the walls around him, caressing the half dozen marble statues encircling the room. The pained expressions of the angels and demons caught in otherwise normal poses, appeared to move as the shadows passed over them. He walked to the oak triptych painted by Hieronymus Bosch, *The Garden of Earthly Delights.* Trailing his finger over the raised oil paint, he looked upward.

"Soon. Soon. My voice grows louder every day. He must answer soon or lose all."

A persistent beeping announced someone outside the door. Christian nodded and a monitor over the door flashed on, showing Peter Anderson, his C.O.O. standing awkwardly, trying not to stare at the fluid sculpture in front of him.

"Come in." The door opened silently, leaving Peter on the threshold, staring wide-eyed into Christian's suite.

"Oh, please. How many times have you been in here? You act like you've never seen it before."

"It's always... a little unsettling."

"Be that as it may, I assume you came here for a reason, not just to be unsettled."

"Yes, sir. There is some disturbing news from Wall Street."

"I really don't care what they think about what I'm doing. They can all go to Hell for all I care." Christian chuckled. "No, never mind, not Hell."

"No, sir. No one is saying anything about your activities. It's just that..."

"Oh, spit it out."

"Apparently there is a hostile takeover." Peter stood rigid, looking straight ahead.

"Who cares? I've participated in many myself. Who's the company? Maybe we can get in on the action."

"That's the problem, sir. The company is you. Over forty percent of the outstanding shares of McMillan industries have been acquired by..."

"*What?*" The fire roared up, flames licking the ceiling. In spite of the extra flames, Christian's face remained hidden in the shadows.

Peter backed up from Christian's wrath, looking behind him at the closed door with regret.

"Who would dare such a move?" Christian spoke it as a whisper, but Peter shivered at its force. Shadows that had been randomly flitting about the room began to concentrate behind Christian, seething in a roiling mass.

"I asked you a question." Christian's voice lacked emotion, but his eyes became twin obsidian sinkholes.

"It's a shell corporation, T & S subsidiaries."

"And who owns that?"

"Another shell corporation. And before you ask, we've been able to drill down through five layers of companies, but haven't gotten to any names yet."

"That is unacceptable." Blackness crept forward, slithering over the floor. Larger shadows engulfed smaller ones, growing as they did.

Peter's body shook as Christian approached him.

"Sir, you've paid me well for my services, but I feel like you expect too much from me. I'm not sure that I'm the best person for this job."

Christian's eyes flashed. "Are you trying to quit? The only way to leave is..." Several of the shades wound their way around Christian's ankles. He spun and walked to the fire, seeming to step into it. Turning around, he smiled broadly, and sauntered back to him, looking thoughtful.

"You know what? You're right." Christian touched Peter's cheek, slowly dragging his fingertips down to his chin. "I'm sure you've done everything you could, both to prevent this from happening and to find the person behind it." He walked over to the bar and took a sip of his unfinished drink, letting it sit for a moment on his tongue.

"I think maybe you should take some time off and regroup. Don't be too impulsive. We can talk about your employment after you've rested some. Does that sound reasonable?"

"I think..."

"Before you finish that sentence with something both of us might regret." Christian chuckled. "Actually, I regret very little, but you might. Please, take a week and relax. I'll handle this situation myself. When you come back, then you can make your decision."

"Alright, Mr. McMillan." Peter edged back toward the door, not taking his eyes of Christian. "I'm not sure what difference a week will make, but I'll try it."

"At a boy, Pete. That's the spirit." Peter flinched as Christian clapped him on the back. Christian steered him to the door, opening it for him and leading him to the elevator.

Christian stopped Peter and held out his hand. "No hard feelings, okay, Pete. We'll get through this."

Peter had trouble meeting his eyes as the moving figures on the door distracted him. "Yes, sir. Thank you." The elevator dinged behind him.

"Well, off you go. I'll see you in a week."

Peter turned and stepped through the open doors into the empty shaft. "What?" His scream cut off short with a whoosh as flames rushed up the elevator shaft and into the hall, surrounding Christian.

"Take your time, Petey. You'll have all you need. I'm sure you'll come up with the right decision."

He stepped back into his suite. "Hostile takeover. They don't know the meaning of the phrase."

Stan craned his head back, absorbing the mass of Christian's building.

"It's something, isn't it?"

"Yeah, I wonder what he's trying to compensate for."

"So, are you ready for this?"

"Ready for what? To meet Satan? I've gotta tell you, I'm a little bit edgy. You and Father Mike have set him up to be... well, how can you be worse than the devil? I've seen the crime scenes. If this is that guy, devil or not, he is crazy, and with the resources Christian has, he could do some major damage and maybe even get away with it. What about you?"

They jogged across the street, dodging a car that paid no attention to them. "I'm not too sure I really want to do this. He's an ass in person, but in my head, he's a horror show. But if you feel it's necessary, then, let's do it and get it over with."

As Danny grabbed the door handle, lightning bolts of ice shot up his spine, paralyzing him. The sky dimmed and his vision narrowed. *Oh, hell no. Not again.*

"Are you going to open that today?"

Danny opened his eyes and took his hand off the handle.

"Did you feel that?"

"Feel what, buddy? Are you okay?"

"Never mind." Danny yanked the door open. "Let's get this over with."

They entered the lobby and headed for the security desk. Seated behind the desk, a girl in her twenties, decorated in numerous tattoos and piercings chewed gum noisily.

"Can I help you guys?" She barely looked up from the book she was reading. Danny could barely make out colorful illustrations, like a comic book.

"I'm Detective Danny Hooper and this is Detective Stanley Muzzo." They held their badges for her to inspect. After a cursory glance, she popped a bubble and turned a page of her book, holding it up between them like a shield. Danny read the title, *Maus,* with a neo-Nazi type symbol. *Typical.*

Stan pulled the book out of her face. She looked at him, emotionless and blew another bubble.

"We're here to see Christian McMillan."

"Yes?"

"Can you page him, let us up, something?"

Before she could answer, they heard a falling scream echoing out of the elevator. It stopped with a rushing sound.

"What the hell?" Both detectives waited for a crash that never came.

The receptionist picked her book back up. "I find it works best if you don't ask."

Stan straightened his shirt. "Seriously, we need to speak to Mr. McMillan."

"Go on up. I paged him when you first walked in. He's waiting for you. His suite is on forty-two." She rolled her eyes. "Anything else I can do for you?"

"Up that elevator?" Stan pointed to the elevator that the scream had come from.

"Yep. If that's a problem, I'm sure he can make an appointment to come see you next week sometime."

"No. Come on, Danny, let's go."

Chapter 21

Mary sat virtually motionless, staring out of her second story window at the manicured hedges in the courtyard below. She watched a squirrel run along the power line, its tail swaying side to side as it scampered toward the outreaching branches of a magnolia tree. She barely noticed as it disappeared out of view.

"Mary, sweetie, come on, let's get you some fresh air."

Mary turned to the older lady dressed in her black habit. "Is he here, sister?"

"No." She sighed. "You've been staring out that window for hours. At least come down to the public room and mingle with some of people for a while."

Mary turned back to the window wistfully. "It makes no difference where I am, Sister Anne"

The nun reached out to her and helped her out of the chair. "Come on, leave that." Mary had tried to pick up her sweater. "It's not cold. The air conditioner has been broken for two weeks. You know that." The nun wiped sweat off her forehead. "The humidity is the worst part."

"I'm always so cold, sister. I need a sweater or blanket or something."

"Mary, it's ninety-three degrees with at least ninety percent humidity, and no air conditioning. You can't be cold."

"I'm sorry." Mary bowed her head. "I don't mean to be a burden. It's just that..." She looked up, her eyes showing more life than they had in many months. "Whenever he's not here, I can't stay warm."

The nun shook her head. "Fine, bring your sweater, as long as we can get you out of this room for a while."

Mary lowered her eyes as she walked past the cross hanging on her wall, mumbling a short prayer. She crossed herself, and then followed the nun down the hallway.

"Everybody, look who made it down." The nun led her into the room enthusiastically. Two women were seated across from each other at a worn folding table, playing cards. Another woman, closer to Mary's age, sat on a love seat watching a small television.

"Mary, so nice to see you out." The two women interrupted their card game to greet her. "Would you like to join us?"

Mary shook her head silently. Sister Anne led her to the love seat. "Here, Mary, why don't you sit by Lenora? I'm sure she'd love the company."

Lenora nodded without actually looking over, engrossed in the news playing on the television. As Mary sat down, Sister Anne walked away, shaking her head.

A perfectly manicured voice from the TV finished reporting on Saints football training camps, his voice droning on about the newest free agents. Mary turned away from the set and stared at the painting of Mother Mary on the wall.

A new voice, sounding frantic, blasted from the speakers, interrupting her thoughts.

"No one can say for sure what triggered the horrific chain of events that resulted in six dead and dozens injured."

Mary jumped up as the camera panned across pandemonium

at the park. The two women at the table looked at her, concern showing on their faces.

"However, it came to a tragic halt when this tree fell after a truck crashed into it." The camera pulled back, giving a wider shot of the chaos. Mary rushed to the television, placing her hand on the screen.

"Hey, I'm trying to watch that." Lenora shifted to her left to get a better view of the screen.

Mary watched Christian walking away from the burning truck. He turned back to the camera as if he knew it was there. While she watched, his lips began moving. She couldn't hear his voice, but she could read his lips. *This is for you, mom. I love you.*

Sister Anne came running back into the room as Mary screamed and crumpled to the ground. "What happened?" She implored Lenora.

"Don't ask me. She jumped up and blocked the TV, then just started screaming bloody murder."

"He's my baby. He's my baby." Mary curled in a fetal position on the floor, repeating the phrase like a mantra. Sister Anne stooped down and hugged her.

"It's okay Mary. What's wrong?"

Between sobs, Mary sat up and stared at the TV, now showing commercials. "Sister, is there any kind of sin that can't be forgiven?"

Sister Anne kept her arms wrapped around Mary, consoling her. "My child, forgiveness is to be had by all. One needs only to ask."

"But what if what we've done has brought about true evil?" Her voice dropped to a whisper. "What if we aren't worthy?"

"All children of God are worthy, even if they don't know it. You have to want it in your heart, be contrite, and you must atone."

Mary whispered back, "Atone..." Her face contorted.

~~*~*

Danny and Stan stepped out of the elevator to see a door open in front of them. Danny could hear a fire roaring in the condo. *Fire? It's ninety degrees out.*

"Come on in. I've been waiting for you." Christian's voice echoed out of the doorway.

Danny entered the room, noting the large open fire pit below a huge hood vent hanging from the ceiling. Flames leaped up from the floor, almost meeting the vent ten feet above. He shook his head in confusion as he swept the rest of the room. Marble statues of angels and demons eyed him from all around. Renaissance paintings, most looking like originals, depicted Heaven and Hell on all walls. The only place to sit was on a bar stool tucked in front of the marble bar at the far end of the room. Christian was nowhere to be seen.

"Interesting taste."

"Stan, what did you expect?"

"Well he is..."

"Shhh. Not here."

Danny felt his nerves jumping every time he saw movement out of the corner of his eye. The flickering flames softened the hard edges in the room and projected motion on the walls. Even the painted figures seemed to be gyrating on their canvases.

Christian walked into the room with a glass filled with amber liquid held in one hand. "Welcome, Detectives. I'm just finishing up lunch." He downed the glass in one gulp and placed it on the edge of the bar. "Please, come in. Make yourself comfortable. Please excuse the cold, my HVAC system is on the fritz, hence the fire." Christian gestured at them to move in out of the doorway.

Cold? I'm sweating in here. As Danny approached the bar, a massive beast with hunched shoulders and bristling fur pounced into the room. Danny jumped back as the twin of the Hell hound from his dream bared its teeth and a low rumbling issued from its throat.

"*Cerberus. Sit.*" The dog sat, obediently, its eyes trained on Danny and seeming to be filled with intelligence. "It appears he still doesn't like you, Detective." He flashed his teeth at Danny. Danny rubbed his arm where the dog had bit him.

Stan stepped in front of Danny. "Still?"

"Oh, please. Can we stop tip-toeing around this?"

"Mr. McMillan, we have a few questions for you about the occurrence at St. Michael's Church."

"Okay, if we're going to play it that way. I was raised at St. Michael's."

"Really?" Stan turned to mouth to Danny, "Did you know that?" Danny nodded.

"Yes. My mother had very little when I was born. My father left us, you see. He cast us off like we were nothing." Christian sighed. "The priests at St. Michael's took us in. Father Mike and Sister Mary Elizabeth are like family to me. I saw them just a couple days ago."

Stan took out his notebook. "What was the nature of your visit?"

Christian grinned. "You're assuming I saw them at the church."

Stan sighed. "Danny, is he always like this?"

"You're the one who wanted to play this game."

"Let me be more specific, then. Where did you see them?"

"At St. Michael's, of course. I was in the area and thought I'd drop by. I hadn't seen them in a while."

Stan waited for more. Christian reached for his glass, frowning when he realized it was empty.

"And what happened while you were there?" Stan tapped his

pen on the paper, frustrated.

"Let's see. I saw Sister Mary Elizabeth, and those two older priests that were visiting. I think I met them when I was younger. Father Mike wasn't there at the time, but I did say hi to him as I was driving off."

Christian clicked the glass on the counter. "I appear to be empty." He waved the glass in the detectives' general direction. "You guys want any?"

They shook their heads, watching Christian fill the glass. He bent over and opened the door of the ice maker, pulling out one cube and dropping it in his drink. He turned back to face them, swirling the liquid slowly.

"The secret is the one ice cube. It cools it and allows the scotch to open up to get the full flavor."

Stan closed his notebook. "Okay, look, let's get straight to the point."

Christian stopped swirling his glass "I was trying to at the beginning of this *friendly* conversation."

"Did you kill those priests and the nun?"

Christian looked at both detectives while he savored a long sip of scotch. He closed his eyes, putting the glass down. Sitting down on a stool, he drummed his fingers on the counter.

"Why would I do that?"

"I don't know. That's what we were hoping you would tell us."

"Now why would I do that?" One side of Christian's lip curled up slightly.

Stan looked at Danny, who shrugged. "Are you saying you didn't do it?"

"I'm saying that I don't know why I would have done something that horrible."

Stan took a step toward Christian. "Cut the crap, Christian. Stop this semantics dance."

"Oh, he's got vocabulary. Apparently there are some brains

behind the brawn." Christian took another sip of his drink. "I tell you what, I'll allow you two to continue if you tell me who killed my guards."

Stan looked at Danny. He shook his head. "We don't have any leads, yet."

Christian laughed. "Of course you don't. Two of my employees are brutally murdered, and all you can do is ask me about how people I consider my family died."

"Just tell us what you were doing while you were at the church."

Christian stirred his drink with his finger. Sticking his finger in his mouth, he sucked the excess liquor off. "You know, I'm just not motivated to do that."

"What?"

"Hey, are you too cool? I think I feel a draft." Christian tossed a log on the fire, causing glowing cinders to rush to the ceiling. The flame's glow painted emotions on the statues surrounding them. Danny edged back, feeling like they had moved closer than when they first came in.

"Mr. McMillan, you can either answer our questions here, or down at the station."

Christian cast a glance at the fire pit and the flames immediately reduced to normal height. He leveled his gaze at Stan.

"It doesn't matter if I answer your questions or not. It doesn't matter whether we talk here or downtown. It doesn't matter whether I did it or not. Frankly, detectives, it doesn't matter who lives or dies." Christian pushed the stool back and squatted down to pet the dog that had curled up at his feet.

He looked up at Stan. "Do you mind if we drop the charade? It's quite tiring, amusing at first, but in the end, boring." The dog's eyes narrowed and it began to growl lowly.

"All humans die. Some have accidents, some are murdered, some die violently, and some peacefully. The point is that the human condition is temporary. As such, the race as a whole is temporary. I used to wait for the day when you imploded, somewhat helplessly. Oh, I had some influence, sure, but I had to rely on your particular faults to push you over the precipice. No longer." Christian patted his body. "I can now affect. You were motoring along well enough on your own, but sometimes people need a gentle push. You see, after your little flash in the pan of excitement and novelty is past, there are beings that will still be here, will always be here. Five hundred years may seem like an eternity to you. I've blinked for longer than that."

Christian patted the dog's head, lovingly and they both stood up. Firelight reflected in the dog's eyes, giving them a red glow. Danny's eyes were drawn to a painting of demons frolicking in a garden. He couldn't tell for sure, but it seemed like they were actually dancing in real time.

"You see, I really could care less about your questions, but there is one you should be asking yourself. Do you want to be a part of this?" Christian spread his arms indicating himself and the rest of his condo. "Or not?"

"Who the hell do you think you are?"

Christian laughed. "Exactly. I am who I am."

"What does that mean?"

Danny nudged Stan in the back. "Stan, remember, we talked about this." Stan shrugged him off.

Christian smiled. "Are you really sure you want to know? Seems to me, you've been told, you just don't want to embrace it."

Stan frowned. "Consider me stubborn."

Christian pushed down on the dog's rear end, making him sit. "Stay, Cerberus." He walked up to Bonifacio's *St. Michael Vanquishing the Devil*. As he approached it, his shadow passed across the canvas. He stepped to one side, tapping the ornate gilded frame. "What do you see?"

Stan regarded the painting and realized that the two figures had flipped. The emaciated and bat-like devil now had the upper hand, plunging a sword down toward St. Michael.

"All you have to do, Detective, is look around you. The answers have been there all the time. In fact, the answer has been there throughout time." The flames roared up at a glance from Christian, casting orange light and shadows to all corners of the room. Angel and demon statues alike loomed toward each other, as if to attack.

Christian rose up, looking to be over eight-feet tall. "I am who you blame for *your own* faults. I am the beast. I am legion, and we are many." Christian's shadow burst into thousands of dark shards, flitting across the wall behind him. They coalesced into two huge wing shapes emerging from his back. He pointed at Danny.

"I am the one who comes in your dreams, and makes them nightmares." Danny backed toward the door.

"I am the one you were taught to fear your whole life." He pointed to the devil in the painting, now chewing on the arm of St. Michael. "Why do you paint me as such a hideous creature? Look at me. Do I resemble that contemptible beast?"

"Are you thoroughly insane?"

"I am the favored one, the most beautiful. Before *you* I was his closest..."

"Before me?"

"You, and by you I include all of your kind, are incredibly slow. I am the fallen angel."

Stan shook his head. "I get what you're saying. You can stop rephrasing it. I still find you loony tunes."

Christian's face clouded over, before he laughed. "That's funny, Stan. After you leave here, you might question your own sanity, but don't. I want you to know that everything is real." He stalked toward them, his shadow looming ominously behind him, growing as he neared them. Cerberus followed closely behind him, saliva dripping from his teeth.

Stan bumped into Danny as he backed away from Christian's approach. Danny turned to the door and noticed it was still open. They both kept their eyes on Christian as they backed out into the hallway.

Stan swallowed nervously. "Yeah, okay. That's all we've got for now." He put his notebook in his pocket, watching Danny press the elevator button. "But don't go anywhere. We may have some more questions later."

Christian chuckled. "Of course, Detectives. Oh, and by the way, watch out for that elevator. I've had some problems with it lately." He burst into laughter. He stopped suddenly, commanding their attention with his eyes.

"I know I provoke fear, but that isn't what I really want. I'd much rather have loyalty, or even submission." He held his hand out, stopping the dog from lunging into the hall. "Sometimes..." He looked wistful. "Sometimes, I just want some attention."

Stan jumped as the elevator dinged and the door opened behind him. Christian walked past, pressing the button for the lobby.

"Have a nice day, gentlemen."

The elevator bell signaled each floor they passed. After thirty, Stan turned to Danny and broke the silence.

"Holy shit. That was seriously messed up."

Danny leaned over and vomited in the corner. "Sorry, He has that effect on me. So, what are you thinking now?"

"I don't know. Nobody will believe us."

"I told you."

"I don't believe me, but one thing is true."

Danny wiped his mouth on his sleeve. "Oh yeah?"

Stan hardened his eyes. "That mother fucker is going down."

"It's not like we can go in there with guns blasting. What would that accomplish?"

Stan grinned. "It might work, besides I'd love to see his smug little face."

"But what if it doesn't. I saw enough to cement my opinion. What do you think? Is he human and crazy, or the devil?"

Stan tapped his foot as the elevator signaled the passing of the tenth floor. "I take option number three."

"Three?"

"He's the evil *and* he's crazy. Can you picture bottling up his issues and neuroses for eternity? Sure, he's handsome on the outside, but I bet his insides look worse than anything we could ever imagine." Stan pulled out the crumpled cigarette pack. He upended it and grimaced when nothing came out. Crushing it in his hand, he tossed it into the corner of the elevator. "Damn," he said under his breath. "But if we can't shoot him, how are we going to stop him?"

The elevator slowed down as it neared the lobby. "Father Mike said the shroud was on its way over. If we're in, we need to be all in. Christian is the anti-Christ. If it's the blood of Christ we need, then bring on the shroud. Whatever we need to do, I'm just tired of seeing that stupid grin." He paused as the doors opened. "And that damn dog."

The girl at the desk didn't look up from her book as they walked past. She blew a bubble until it popped.

"Hoped that worked out well for you."

Danny paused as they headed for the doors. "Do you know who you're..."

She popped another bubble forcefully, smacking her tongue. "Shh. I really wasn't looking for a response. I'm reading."

Stan grabbed his shoulder and pulled him out the door.

Chapter 22

Father Mike bent over, placing the bottle of wine in the tabernacle and closing the doors. He stood up to see Danny and Stan walking up the aisle toward him. The afternoon sun sent streamers of red, blue, and yellow light diagonally across the nave to play briefly across their clothes. From the look of determination set into Stan's face, he deduced that they were all on the same page now.

"Father, we've hit a brick wall."

"In what way?"

Stan leaned one hand against the back of the first row of pews. "Let me start with, I'm on board. All in. Let's get that mother fu..." He stopped and looked up at Father Mike then at the cross behind him. "Oh, sorry."

Father Mike nodded dismissively. "Don't worry about language in front of me."

Stan lip curled briefly before turning back into a frown. "But... If he's the devil, then there's not much we can do to kill him. I'd love to empty a clip or two into him, but I'm afraid that would only make him mad."

"That's probably true. That's why we need the shroud."

"Yes, the shroud. But can we get it, and what do we do with it once we do?"

Father Mike walked around the altar and sat in the front pew, indicating to the two detectives to follow suit.

"I've already heard from Father Vincent. He told me that he's acquired the shroud and will call back when he has flight info and can tell us when he'll be stateside. As to the second part of that question, I don't know for sure."

"What?" Danny slapped the wood beside him, the sharp crack echoing through the church. "You've brought us this far, told us he's indestructible without the shroud, and now you're going to tell us we can't kill him with it either?"

Father Mike shook his head. "I didn't say that. What I said was that I wasn't sure what to do with the shroud once we have it. I know it will kill him. I don't know how."

Stan put his hand on Danny's chest, holding him back as he tried to surge forward. "Wait, let me get this straight. Are you saying we are about to go into combat with the freaking anti-Christ with a weapon that may or may not kill him, depending on if we use it right, which we won't know until we try?"

Father Mike nodded solemnly. "Remember when I said the most important thing was faith? Faith is all we have left. I'm assuming that if we can get Christian in contact with the blood on the shroud, that should do it."

Danny choked back a curse. "Assuming? What is it they always said in catholic school about assuming? It makes an ass out of you and me? In this case it makes a dead person, or worse. It sounds like you're assuming our way into Hell."

"Faith is more than assumption. God will direct us."

Stan laughed skeptically. "Where was His direction when you were making this mess?"

"Stan, I've got to believe that He wants us to be better

people. He wants us to continue. If he doesn't..." Father Mike looked at the floor. "Then nothing we can do will stop this. If he does, then he will help direct our hands."

Stan appeared to mull it over for a second. "Okay, but do you mind if instead of just *contacting* Christian with the shroud, we wrap it around something long and sharp, and stab it all the way through him?" Stan looked up at the cross in the sanctuary. "Sorry if that sounds vindictive, but I would feel a lot better about our chances of success, if Christian's blood met Christ's blood in the open, maybe even pooling on the ground."

Danny nodded in agreement.

"I don't see why not. The quicker it's over, the less suffering there will be."

"Did you just say less suffering? For the devil?"

"I know you might not believe this, but Christian hasn't always been evil. It seemed like it took a while for Lucifer to get a stronghold in the body, and then some more time to build his strength. There must be some small part of humanity down underneath it all, kept at bay by the devil. For *that part,* I pray for less suffering."

A young teenager draped in altar boy vestments came running into the nave.

"Father." He was breathing rapidly as if he had run the whole way. "Phone call for you, from Italy."

"Ah, that must be Vincent now. Hopefully he's calling to say he's on his way. Follow me."

The three men headed to the rectory. While they walked, Stan pulled out a crumpled piece of paper and handed it to Father Mike.

"This was left at a suicide we investigated. The couple described being visited by an angel. It sounds like Christian. What do you think?"

Father Mike read the note, making ticking noises with his tongue.

"Who else would it be?"

"Who else? Father, you've just convinced me that the devil actually exists and that he plans to destroy us. You've blown up my view of what can and does exist. And now you ask me, 'Who else?' If there's an anti-Christ, and a devil, then it only follows that there are other demons and angels as well. I don't think it's crazy to ask if we're being attacked by a legion of demons, and not just Christian. Not that it makes that much difference, I guess."

Father Mike handed the note back to Stan. "I'm sure that Christian has recruited some demons to follow him." His body convulsed as he remembered his vision in Hell. "And maybe some angels, too."

Both detectives looked at him, shocked, mouthing silently, "Angels?"

"Don't forget, Lucifer took almost a third of the angels with him when he was cast from Heaven. But this does have the earmark of Christian. It makes sense."

"How does anything make sense in this whole affair?"

"Because suicide is a one-way ticket to Hell. What better way to hurt God, than to have humans reject him, even though they know they're going to Hell for it? Christian must be loving the irony."

Father Mike gestured to the chairs as he picked up the telephone. "Have a seat," he whispered.

"Father Vincent?"

"I'm at the airport."

"Do you have the shroud?"

"Yes. My flight leaves in twenty minutes. But..."

Father Mike looked at both detectives before he continued. "Vincent, I don't want to make you worry, but we've got to assume he might know what we're doing." Nervous laughter echoed back through the receiver.

"Are you telling me that Christian might know that I have the only weapon that can destroy him? Doesn't that make me a target?"

"It's certainly possible. Take every precaution you can think of. On my end, I'll send two police detectives to pick you up at the airport." Danny and Stan nodded as Father Mike shrugged at them. "Don't forget, he probably won't approach you since you have the shroud."

"If he does, maybe I can end this thing swiftly. That makes me feel a little better. Tell them I should be there in about thirteen hours if we aren't delayed."

"No problem. See you then. And Father, God speed."

Father Mike hung up and turned to the two detectives. "The shroud is officially on the way. Now we have to find a way to get it in contact with Christian's blood."

Stan smiled. "I thought we already decided to wrap it around something sharp."

"Yes, but what are we going to do? Just walk up to him with a sword in hand and ask him to kneel down?"

Danny looked confused. "I still don't totally understand what we're doing here. If Christian was made from the blood on the shroud, then how is that same blood going to destroy him? Isn't that what's running through his veins?"

"The best I can figure is that the blood on the shroud came directly from Jesus. What we did with Christian was make a copy from that DNA. That copy was then tainted by the devil. Don't forget, every cell in your body is replaced as you age, thousands of times. The cells in Christian's blood have been rebuilt since he housed Lucifer, many times over. What flows through his veins now is no longer Christ's blood. If I had to guess, I would say it's sort of like matter versus anti-matter, bring them together, and..." Father Mike demonstrated with his hands as he whispered, "Boom."

Stan shook his head. "So that's the plan? Get the shroud inside the anti-Christ, and he goes bye-bye?"

"Don't worry. It'll work."

Danny stood up and walked to the window, resting his hands on the sill. "And if it doesn't?"

"Have you read the Book of Revelations?"

Stan shook his head. Danny shrugged.

"It doesn't paint a pretty picture. If we fail, there's likely to be no second chance. No secret rebel group trying to overthrow the occupation. If we fail, it's game over."

"The end of the world?"

"What he's done to this point has been merely an introduction, Christian getting his feet wet. This is the devil. There are reams written about him. Take all of the stories of his sadistic torture and pile them together. It doesn't take a religious man to see that it will be very bleak for mankind." Father Mike sat on the corner of his desk and looked down at his hands as he kneaded them. "What he's about to do is to make man's worst nightmares, those things we scare our children with, into reality. We can't imagine the least of what he'll do."

"So what do we do?"

"You two, go do your jobs and get Father Vincent here safely. That's the most important thing at this point. I'll try to come up with the best way to confront Christian once we have the shroud."

"Are you sure you're going to be safe here, by yourself? Do you want one of us to stay with you?"

"What would you do without the shroud, shoot him? This was part of his home for most of his life. I raised him, besides I only need one more day."

"Father, don't forget the other two priests and Sister Mary Elizabeth. This church and his paternal feelings didn't seem to slow him much a few days ago."

Father Mike walked behind his desk, opened a drawer, and pulled out a bottle of whiskey. He waved it at the two detectives, raising his eyebrows in an unvoiced question. They both shook their head. He poured it into a paper cup and downed it, warm. "It's all I've got."

"Alright, Father. Call us if you think of anything else, otherwise, we'll come straight from the airport with Father

Vincent."

Danny and Stan walked out shaking their heads.

Father Mike headed back to the sanctuary. As he walked to the altar, he looked up at the figure of Christ on the wall. His face flushed as the impact of his actions over the last twenty-five years washed over him. Falling to his knees, he broke into tears.

"Forgive me, Lord. All I ever wanted was to do right by this world. I thought I was doing Your will, adding to Your glory. Clearly, we overstepped our bounds. Please, give us the strength to right these wrongs. Don't punish all your children for the misguided actions of a few." He stood up, imploring the crucifix. "I beg you, Jesus. Help us. Help us cast out Satan."

Father Mike turned around as he heard a noise. Everything appeared to be in its place. He heard it again, too low to tell what it was.

"Is anyone there?"

Laughter echoed through the sanctuary, seeming to come from all sides.

"Mikey. Mikey. I had such better hopes for you."

Father Mike searched the sanctuary, looking for a sign of Christian. He turned to the nave, but nothing moved there, either.

"I gave you a choice between the boy you raised and *Him,* and you chose the one who does nothing but curtail your actions and give you guilt?"

"Where are you, Christian? What do you want?"

The laughter redoubled. "What do I want? I was hoping for a little fatherly love, but since I can't get that, I guess you'll have to do."

"What do you mean?"

Father Mike noticed the beams of multicolored light streaming through the stained glass windows begin to move. He backed up, bumping into the altar, as they started to spin counter-clockwise. Trying to retreat behind it, he stumbled on the new wooden threshold. His wrist sent bolts of pain as he fell upon it. The spinning colors disoriented him. He tried to rise, but waves of dizziness rolled over him.

"Come to me, Father Mike." The voice sounded hollow and tinny. He steadied himself by putting a hand on the altar, but couldn't keep his feet under him.

"What are you doing to me?" His voice sounded like it was coming from another room.

"I'm only trying to keep you entertained. Consider me one of Dickenson's ghosts. I'm going to show you the future." His voice grew serious. "I'm going to show you how this ends."

Spots formed in his vision, and he fell back to the ground, stomach convulsing. He closed his eyes to shut out the swirling colors.

"Come to me, Father." Christian's voice no longer echoed from a distance. Father Mike could feel a wavering heat upon his skin. Not wanting to open his eyes and confirm his suspicions, he lay still, curled on the floor. He could hear the crackling of a fire to his left.

"Come now, Mike. It's unseemly for a priest to lie on the floor like that. Get up." Father Mike felt a hand firmly grip his shoulder and yank him to his feet. He opened his eyes to see Christian standing five feet away, smiling. He jerked his head to the side, but no one else was near enough to have lifted him. He recognized Christian's condo around him. The heat that blasted from the roaring fire instantly brought beads of sweat to his forehead."

"I am the ghost of Christmas future." Christian spat, then laughed. "Christmas? You celebrate *His* birthday, although like the humans you are, you celebrate it on a pagan holiday. I'm sure He loves that."

Father Mike tried to back toward the door, but his feet were glued in place. His eyes were the only part of his body free to move. They worked overtime, darting as far as they could to each side. In front of Christian, Danny and Stan were kneeling on the ground. *Shit, he got them before they got... Don't think it. Don't think.* Father

Mike tried to change the direction of his thoughts, but the more he tried, the harder it became. As he watched, he realized that the two detectives remained motionless, not even moving to breathe. *What's the best way to play this?*

"What a powerful being you are, holding us mere mortals paralyzed in your presence."

Christian chuckled. "They're not paralyzed. And for that matter, neither are you." Christian passed his hand through Danny's head. "None of you are actually here. They are projections I'm placing in your mind, to entertain you until my friends arrive at the church."

In my mind? I'm still at the church?

"I gave you a choice. I was hoping you'd give me the courtesy of an answer to my face." He indicated the two prone detectives in front of him. "I see you've made it, but neglected to tell me."

Christian turned and leveled the full fury in his eyes on Father Mike.

"This... is how it ends. Your two paladins in dusty armor prostrate before me."

Where am I?

"Indeed?" Christian smiled. "Where is my stepfather in the end? Where is the man who raised me, who taught me everything I know? What is his rightful place?" He glanced over his shoulder at the wall behind him.

Father Mike felt his body turning. On the far wall, a man hung on a cross, his head bent in exhaustion. Father Mike recognized his priestly garb. He would have shaken his head if he could have. *Lord, give me strength. Somehow, we've got to beat this.*

"I don't want to totally spoil the ending. It'll be a riveting scene, and you'll need something to distract you from the pain once you're here." Christian turned back to him. "Suffice it to say, there will be a lot of groveling, but it will do no good. *He* listens to your sniveling, puts up with your betrayals, not me."

Christian clapped his hands together and two marble statues crushed Stan and Danny between them. Crimson painted the bottom halves of both statues, and pooled on the floor.

Father Mike groaned, struggling to break free. His stomach lurched, and his head threatened to explode. "Oh, don't worry. That's not how they die. I'm much more creative than that. You'll have to wait for the finale to see that."

Father Mike closed his eyes, shutting out the gory scene. Colored flashes played on his lids. Dizziness threatened to overwhelm him. If he hadn't been held in place, he would have fallen to the ground.

"We'll have our happy little family reunion soon." The voice trailed off to a whisper, almost inaudible.

Father Mike felt the bonds holding him loosen and he collapsed, curled on the floor once more. Multicolored lights played on his eyelids as he heard Christian's laughter drifting to the distance. He cautiously opened them to see St. Michael's altar looming in front of him. For a moment, he thought he saw the severed heads of his dead friends again, but they disappeared when he blinked. *Oh, Lord, please let me be able to change this.*

Chapter *23*

Am I worthy, oh Lord? I go into battle against your greatest enemy armed with a cloth that once witnessed your rebirth. For once, all my worldly weapons are worth nothing. I will approach the beast, naked but for your raiment. Carlo knelt at the foot of his bed, eyes closed and hands folded together resting on the mattress. Dozens of weapons from the exotic to the mundane were strewn across the room, emptied from the trunk on the floor. On the bed before him rested the Shroud of Turin, folded so that only the image of Christ's face was visible.

Give me the strength to do your will. The beast was never meant to wear our skin. Your will, Your strength, Your blood will cast him from this plane, never to return, unless foolish men invite him once again. Idiots, the lot of them. What were they thinking? Carlo opened his eyes and gazed reverently on the shroud. Taking care not to accidentally touch it, he pushed himself to his feet. He made the sign of the cross as he turned toward his desk. Smiling, he pulled the worn leather book from the shelf.

Thomas, Stefano, you knew not what had been dropped in

your laps. You lost everything trying to prepare for a calamity that you could not fathom. All you brothers over the centuries who spent your lives devoted to unraveling the mystery so that humanity could be saved... It all comes to this. Carlo carefully opened the book, thumbing past the first handful of pages that detailed the event as it occurred, described in straightforward manner. He stopped where Abbot Thomas had begun his commentary.

The light that took Brother David was terrifying. His cell held no lit candles and the moon was hidden behind clouds, yet there was more light present than on the brightest day. It was a clean light, not yellowed and aged as from a candle. His eyes... they seared with a power behind them, barely held in check. When he spoke, it was his voice, but clearly it was not our friend. The riddles he gave us will undoubtedly take better minds than ours to unravel, but that they must. I fear the import of this prophecy must be greater than even I can imagine.

Golems walking through firefly rain, mankind imprisoned in glass, living in a fog... And these are the unavoidable lesser evils to that which is coming and must be stopped. We must find the source of this evil. He said that whatever brings forth the evil will also be able to exorcize it. In that, there is hope. But how much time do we have? Blasphemy will rule and righteous will be downtrodden. After what the bishop did to our abbey and my fellow brothers, that time is upon us now.

How will we know this evil? He is a beggar and a thief. That describes Bishop Ruiz, but he is certainly no miracle. Why must prophecies always be spoken in riddles? No, we must not question what manna we are given merely because it is not our favorite flavor. We will solve this puzzle, if it takes three generations.

What was much more unsettling, and I can only use that lighthearted of a description after many months have passed, was what followed the light's passing. Some would describe it as shadow, as I did in the previous pages, but that falls short of the actual experience. *It was not so much a shadow cast by the light, as a complete absence of light. Those shadows, as I shall call them, had a life of their own. They moved as snakes upon a hot ground. When they had me in their grasp, I could feel the hatred oozing from their forms. That which took over David was the greatest among them. It must have been a representation of the scourge itself. Its anger was palpable. And it knew... It knew we were being warned, but it only laughed. It railed against God like only the devil might. That is almost enough to turn one's soul. That we may be up against Lucifer himself makes me shudder to my core. That it felt that even forewarned, we were no match for its coming, is enough to make one run crying to his mother, searching for a teat.*

We must find the evil. We must stop the evil. We are human, imperfect by design, but also unpredictable.

Carlo closed the book. *If only you had known about the painted looking glass. How many centuries did it take before that was unraveled? It makes perfect sense now. The shroud is a reflection of our Lord, 'painted' onto linen. Christian would not be laughing now, if he knew we figured it out and had the one weapon that could kill him.*

"I think it's about time to wipe that smile off your face." He opened his briefcase and emptied out the contents. Careful not to damage it, Carlo gently placed the shroud into the case and shut it. He looked over at the journal and sighed. *You know what? I think you and the rest of the brothers deserve to be there at our triumph.* He reopened the briefcase and strapped the book in the top of it.

~~*~*

Father Mike downed the last of his whiskey, staring longingly at the empty bottle. *No more. Just as well, I guess. None to offer to Christian's friends, whoever they might be.* He shuddered. *No use running. I'm sure they can find me wherever I might go.*

He opened one of the earlier journals. *It all seemed so simple then. Clone Jesus, and raise him up right. That sounds so crazy, now. What if it would have worked? One Jesus is good; would we have wanted to repeat the process? What would this world do with a dozen Christs, or a hundred? Would we have been happy with only one? We have more technology now than when we started. Would we have been happy with Jesus as he was, or would we have tried to tweak the DNA, make him even better? Was I really no better than the Nazis, trying to create a super-race? That wasn't our purpose, but is it where we would have ended up? Or, if not us, then someone else?*

He examined a picture of Christian when he was two. *Early on, everything seemed to be going perfectly. He was such a beautiful baby. It was so easy to overlook the little things. How could things have gone so wrong?*

He jumped as the phone beside him rang. Closing the journal, he picked up the phone.

"Hello? This is Father Michael."

"Michael, I'm glad I got you."

"Father Andrew? What are you calling for?" *Calling from the Vatican? That can't be good.* "Is everything okay?"

After a brief pause, Father Andrew continued, "I guess you haven't heard, yet. I know you two were close over the years."

"Haven't heard what?" Father Mike picked up his glass and brought it to his mouth before remembering it was empty.

"Vincent..."

Shit! "Is he okay?" He put the glass down, momentarily forgotten.

"I'm so sorry no one has told you yet. No, he's not okay. He's dead."

Oh, Christ. What happened to the shroud? God damn you, Christian. "Did he... Did he have anything with him?"

"What? No, just his phone. It was quite strange how he died, however. The police suspect foul play, but have no leads."

"I suspect not, that would be pretty quick, unless they saw who did it."

"Michael? I think you misunderstand me. Vincent wasn't killed today."

"*What?*"

"Vincent died three days ago, suffocated by reams of paper."

"Three days?" Father Mike's mind raced. *Three days? Wait, if he's been dead for three days, then who the hell have I been talking to? Who is on that plane Danny and Stan are about to pick up?*

Father Andrew continued as if he didn't hear Father Mike. "They pulled over forty sheets of paper out of his esophagus. He was down in the secret archives. Did you know what he was doing down there?"

"Me? Why would I know?"

"Because one of the pages he was working on had your name across the top. Whoever killed him had some real anger issues. He just about destroyed a whole section of the archives. It'll take years to put it all back together."

"A note?" Father Mike pulled his emails up on his computer. *I wonder if he got that email off before he was killed, or was it sent after?* "He was doing some research for me."

"What are you researching that needed information from the archives?"

"Nothing pressing. I wanted to find out more about..." *Should I tell the truth? Why not? What could it hurt now?* "The shroud."

"You and everyone else." Father Mike could hear the tension drop out of Father Andrew's voice.

"Oh? Why the sudden popularity?"

"I assumed you were interested, like everyone else, following the theft."

"What? What was stolen?"

"The shroud. Isn't that why you were looking into it?"

Father Mike hesitated.

"Yes, of course. This connection isn't that great. I thought I misheard you." Frowning, he reread the note about Christ's blood killing Lucifer. "By the way, did they ever figure out exactly when it was stolen?"

"No. All they know is that it could have been missing for as long as four years. The shroud isn't brought into the light very often. If there wasn't a viewing being planned, they might not have discovered it was missing for quite some time."

"I wonder who would have taken it."

"They don't know, either. Michael? I'm sorry about your friend. It must be quite a shock."

You don't know the half of it. "It is. Thank you for letting me know."

"Wait. I almost forgot about the note. It wasn't until I heard about it that they knew who it was for. Apparently, not many people here know of your friendship, but when I saw 'Father Mike' scrawled across the top, I realized it was meant for you."

"Thank you, Andrew. What did it say?"

"I don't know if you'll thank me when I relay the message. It's pretty cryptic."

Just what we need, another puzzle.

"The word, 'blood' was scribbled at least a dozen times across the top, as if he was deep in thought, followed by 'shroud' with a question mark. At the bottom of the page was what looked to be a couple hastily written lines, 'Birthday. Might still have it.' Does that make any sense to you?"

"Was that it? Just those words?"

"Yes, that was it. If there was anything else, it was lost in the chaos of his murder. You really wouldn't believe the shape the archives were in after his death."

"It doesn't mean anything to me, yet. Maybe something will click after I think about it. Thanks again for calling."

"I wish the news hadn't been bad. Let me know if you figure it out. You know I love a good mystery."

Father Mike hung up. *Shit. Christian must have gotten to him. The phone calls... That must have been him as well. So there's no shroud, no blood, and no way to kill Christian. No wonder he was gloating.*

He looked at the email again, thinking about what Father Anthony had just told him. *What were you talking about? He might still have a birthday? What does that mean, and how does that help us? Father Vincent... Another death on my hands. Oh, crap! The plane!*

Father Mike grabbed for the phone, knocking it to the floor in his haste. He had to get down on his hands and knees to reach the receiver. As he pulled it out, he saw a stray spot of blood on the underside of his desk, missed by the cleaning crew. Something nagged at the back of his brain, but he couldn't coax it forth. *No time to waste. I've got to warn Stan and Danny. Who knows what they're on their way to meet.*

He dialed Stan's cell phone, tapping his foot nervously as he waited for him to pick up.

"Stan, here."

Father Mike could hear traffic noises in the background. "Stan, it's Father Mike. Tell me you haven't gotten to the airport, yet."

"Not yet. We're almost there. I know, we're running late. The traffic on I-10 sucks this time of day. Hold on a sec. *Hey, idiot! The left lane is for passing, not for a god damned siesta! Move it!*" Father Mike heard Danny in the background yelling that for once it wasn't his fault that they were late. Stan growled something incomprehensible back at Danny.

"Stan! Listen to me. Vincent is dead."

"What? Wait. Hold on, Danny. Who's dead?"

"Father Vincent. Apparently, he's been dead for a few days."

"What the fuck are you talking about? Who were you talking to last night?"

"Christian, I'd guess."

"Then who's on the plane that we're headed to meet?"

"I have no idea, but I think it might be best if you aren't there when it lands." He kept staring at the bottom edge of the desk near where he had seen the blood. *Hold on. That might be it. How did we miss that?*

"You think it might... Father, you are the king of understatement. Besides, there's no way we could get there on time anyway." Stan listened for a few more minutes then hung up.

Danny looked at him expectantly. "What's up, partner?"

"Vincent's not going to be meeting us. We're getting off at the next exit. I don't know who's on that plane, but I'm not going to be there to find out."

Stan cut across three lanes of traffic, ignoring the blaring horns, and coasted down to the light at the end of the off ramp. He turned to Danny with a slightly confused look on his face.

"We've got some calls to make."

"What?"

A plane roared overhead, so low that the car shook in its wake.

"What the fuck?" Danny tried to shout over the Doppler-shifted jet engine. The plane skimmed the tree tops headed for the airport. Its wing was tilted at an odd angle as it banked toward the terminal.

"That's not standard approach, is it?"

"No, Danny, it most definitely is not. This is not looking good. Did you notice the tail insignia?"

"Air Italia? Yes."

"Oh, shit! He's not trying to land. He's going to..."

The plane sped straight for the terminal at full speed. The

ground crew raced across the tarmac, waving their arms wildly. As the plane passed over them, sheets of liquid rained down, soaking the workers.

Danny's face flushed with anger. "He's emptying the fuel tanks on them." His face was bathed in orange as the plane barreled into the airport, tearing through walls before erupting in a giant fireball. Even a quarter of a mile away, the explosion was deafening.

"Fuck!"

The flames chased the trail of jettisoned fuel in slow motion, following the ground crews as they scattered. Stan dropped his cell phone as the shock wave hit their car. His foot slipped off the brake and the car inched into the intersection. Oncoming traffic veered crazily as drivers tried to drive while trying to get a better view of what happened.

Danny watched helplessly as a Toyota raced straight at them. He braced himself for impact. Seconds before it could smash into them, a truck in the next lane over, distracted by the crash, rushed past and slammed into it, shoving the Toyota out of their path.

Stan regained control of the car, stopping it before it could move farther into the intersection. Danny opened his door and ran to the Toyota to see if the driver was okay. Reaching in the shattered window, he felt for a pulse. He looked back at Stan and shook his head.

They both turned toward the slowly rising fireball above the airport.

"It seems that being the enemy of the anti-Christ can be bad for your health." He shook his head in disbelief, staring at the chaos in the distance. "Thank God we were running late."

"You think *He* had anything to do with that?"

"Remind me to use that excuse next time I'm late and you want to know what took me so long."

A delayed explosion rocked the airport, causing both of them to duck behind the car. Sirens screamed from all sides.

"Should we go help?"

"Not much we can do. Besides, not to be callous, but we've got more important things to do." He stood up, opening the driver's side door. "That dude is really starting to piss me off."

Chapter *24*

Carlo approached the front doors of McMillan Plaza clutching his briefcase tightly. *The final confrontation. There should be an orchestral movement or something. Walking into his condo seems so anticlimactic somehow.* He opened the doors and tried to look casual as he strolled in. At the desk that had held the two guards on his last visit, a young girl sat glued to her monitor, scrolling past pages of text and pictures. Her face was held enough metal to set off alarms at the airport. *Why do you do that to yourself? I'll never understand.* He walked up to the desk and cleared his throat.

She continued to stare at her computer screen, ignoring him as if he wasn't there.

"Excuse me."

She shushed him with a waving hand. He waited while she typed animatedly on the keyboard. She clicked with her mouse, and then frowned and typed some more, mumbling under her breath, "I hate Timeline."

"Ma'am, I need to see Mr. McMillan."

She looked up abruptly. "Ma'am? Do I look like a ma'am to you? What's wrong with you?" She immediately turned away from him and continued to type, pretending he wasn't there.

Carlo slammed his hand on the counter, inches away from her head. "I really don't give a shit about your rebel attitude, or whatever all those tattoos and piercings are for. I don't care that your parents didn't raise you to treat others with respect. I do care, however that you are completely and utterly wasting my time. You have no idea of the importance of my business, for me and everyone else." At the last comment, she rolled her eyes. "I don't care if you're put out, or if you think I'm some snotty old man. What I need you to do is to inform Mr. McMillan that I would like to talk to him."

She sighed heavily. "Appointment?"

"No, but I think he'll want to see me nonetheless."

She looked him in the eyes as she asked, "Really, think much of yourself?" Clicking her tongue, she punched a button on the intercom. "Name?"

Carlo drummed his fingers and smiled. "Just tell him that the owner of T. and S. Subsidiaries is here to discuss business with him."

She rolled her eyes again and mumbled, "Whatever."

She spoke into the intercom with little emotion. Carlo heard a voice answer her as her eyes opened wide and she looked at him, surprised.

"He said he'd see you. Who are you? No one gets in without an appointment."

"I told you, already." Carlo headed toward the elevator.

Her momentary shock gave way to sarcasm. "We'll see how happy you are after you see him. In my time here, I've noticed that most people are not nearly as cheerful when they leave as when they arrive." Her voice dropped to a whisper. "If they leave." She shook her head, watching him step into the elevator. She realized that she hadn't told him the floor. "Find it yourself, then." She shrugged and turned back to the computer screen, fingers tapping double-time across the keyboard.

The doors opened and Carlo looked down the hall at the security camera. *No need to worry about that this time.* As he neared the door, Carlo studied the carved figure decorating it. At eye level, an angelic Christian stood with arms outstretched. In one arm he held a stack of books, the topmost opened to a page showing scientific symbols. Poised above his other hand, a small star shined almost infinite rays of light, radiating to the edges of the door. *Lucifer. Light-bringer. How does one flip from that to what he is today? God's favorite angel to scourge of the world. It's sad, really. I'd pity him if all our lives weren't balanced in his hand like those books.*

He slowed his breathing and visualized the tree of brothers that stretched behind him back to 1046 A.D. Branches spread in all directions, supporting hundreds of men holding out their hands to lend him support. *It all comes down to this. Abbot Thomas, you would never have imagined this world filled with technology that would have been considered miraculous in your time, and yet we stand on the brink of extinction due to human failing. We brought this on ourselves. We must stop this abomination before he brings Hell to earth, literally.*

Carlo reached out to knock on the door, but hesitated when he noticed the carved smile on Christian's face widen. *Are you watching me?* He purposefully rapped his knuckles on Christian's face as hard as he could. *Can you feel that?* The carved smile slowly faded.

As he dropped his hand, the door drifted open on its own. He half expected to hear the hinges squeal loudly while a string orchestra played ominous music, but it swung open silently.

"Come in, Mr... You know, I didn't get your name." Christian sat back in a leather recliner, with his feet resting on the lip of the fire pit. Three foot flames leaped toward the vent hood attached to the ceiling. Carlo stared at the fire. *Why aren't his shoes burning?*

"Come. Come. Have a seat." Christian's smile looked less natural than the one carved on the door as he patted the chair next to him.

"My name is Carlo Demonte, Mr. McMillan."

Christian stood up and offered his hand. Carlo, distracted by the smoke rising from Christian's shoes, disregarded the outstretched hand. Christian's smile faded.

"Oh, I'm sorry." Carlo gripped his hand and shook vigorously. Christian locked eyes with him, not letting go. Carlo felt Christian's hand begin to undulate. He tried to look down at it, but Christian's gaze held his in an iron grip.

He felt hundreds of insects scurrying up his arm. Christian's eyes turned black, seething with motion. As he watched, his nose started to writhe. It darkened, turning the same color as his eyes. Hairs sticking out the nostril began to move. *Oh my God, those aren't hairs.* Carlo blinked. When he opened his eyes once more, Christian's face was a mass of spiders crawling over themselves. Suddenly released from their hold, Carlo's eyes traveled down the body before him. The mass of spiders that had replaced his head was slowly disappearing down the collar of his shirt. *Stay strong. This is the father of lies.*

Christian's chest rippled with movement. Carlo's attention was drawn down his arm to where their hands met. Instead of Christian's hand gripping his, thousands of spiders raced out of his sleeve and up his own. Carlo tried to pull his hand back, but an unseen force held it in place. He dropped his briefcase and slapped his wrist with his left hand, crushing more than a dozen of them and knocking off even more, but they kept coming.

Christian's body imploded on itself as the insects poured out of him. Carlo felt the bugs scurrying all over his body. Sucking in a breath of air, three spiders crawled down his throat. He choked, trying to cough them out, but more rushed in. *Can't. Breathe. This isn't how this is supposed to end.* Carlo's lungs heaved, trying to get air, but only managing to suck more spiders down his esophagus. *Stop, drop, and roll.* He tried to pull free of the force holding his hand, but it wouldn't release him. His eyes began to blur from lack of oxygen, then they too were covered with spiders. Carlo crumpled to the ground, barely feeling the bodies crushed beneath him. The force holding his hand yanked him back up, holding him steady on his feet.

"Are you okay, Mr. Demonte? It looks like you've seen a ghost."

Carlo opened his eyes to see Christian standing in front of him, still holding his hand. He couldn't see any spiders, or evidence that there had ever been any. *That was all in my mind? I was about to suffocate.* His throat felt raw and swollen. He coughed once and froze as he felt a spiky leg on his tongue. He spit it out into his hand and looked up at Christian's smiling face.

Remembering that he had dropped his briefcase during the attack, he squeezed his other hand and felt the reassuring solidity of its handle. *Thank God. I don't know whether that was a dream or what, but as long as I have the shroud, I will prevail.*

"I'm fine, Mr. McMillan."

"Christian, please, and have a seat. I assume you're here to discuss business. It seems a little rude of you to try to take over my company and then show up unannounced. I hope you aren't seriously contemplating taking control of McMillan Industries. Holding my shares hostage for ransom is bad enough, but you're delusional if you think you can take what's mine."

"I apologize for any offense you may have taken, but I have something here you may be interested in seeing." Carlo lifted the briefcase.

"If it's a bill of sale for my outstanding shares, then I would be interested. I am not opposed to you realizing a small profit out of my failing. I should never have left those shares in public hands once I no longer needed the funds."

"Do you mind?" Carlo indicated the bar.

"Help yourself."

Carlo went behind the bar, placing the briefcase on the counter between them. He poured a glass of bourbon over ice and held it to his nose.

"I can't get over the flavor of this American bourbon. It's almost sweet compared to scotch." He opened the briefcase so that the lid was blocking the contents from Christian's view.

"So, do you have a proposition? I am not fond of having competition for the control of my company."

"What I want to do is stop beating around the bush." He put his hand on the shroud. "I know who you are."

Christian looked at him, confused. "Who I am?"

Carlo picked up the corners of the shroud and lifted it out of the case.

Christian smiled. "Oh, that's who you are. The lone ranger monk, come to make a last stand against the evils of the world. I've been wondering when you'd make your move."

Carlo walked around the edge of the bar, waiting to see Christian back away, instead, he held his ground.

"Is it hot in here?" Christian glanced over at the fire pit, which flared up in response.

"Satan. Lucifer. Christian. Whatever you want to call yourself. You are evil and must be stopped."

"*I'm* evil?" Christian shook his head. "I'm just a figurehead, a scapegoat. When Hitler committed mass genocide, was I there to lead him? When papal leaders sent children to fight their wars for a plot of land, did they use my seal? The popes, the head of the church of God, did that, not me. And you call me evil? I am the excuse men through the ages have used when committing acts of atrocity of their own choosing. Humanity is the abomination. Humanity is evil, not me."

"Father of lies."

Christian laughed. "Do you mind if I sit? I have a feeling this debate is going to get exhausting, and before you interrupted, I was trying to have a relaxing day off."

"Do you know what this is?" Carlo shook the shroud, making it wave like a flag in the wind.

"Really? You hold out one of the most controversial relics of the Christian religion and ask if I know what it is?" Christian, leaned the recliner forward and crossed one leg over his knee. "It is my brother's corporeal remains, all that is left of him on this earth, anyway, and here you are bandying it about as if it is some banner to be your standard. I am not some sparkly vampire to run at the sight of a cross. It just doesn't work that way. And before you go there, bibles and holy water do nothing to me either." He lowered his voice. "Just saying."

"That which brought you into this world will send you away. This is no banner, no flag. This is the blood of Christ." *Why is he not the least bit frightened?*

Christian put his hands on his lap. "Let me start with the fact that I had been around for a long time before that bit of cloth wiped the ass of your *savior.* I existed for an eternity before you humans were even created. Don't think to wave a rag in my face and send me running." Christian's face was smiling, but his voice cut like a dagger.

"You began in Heaven and then were relegated to Hell, but you don't belong here. You should never have been brought here. You will go back to Hell."

"Okay." Christian stood and took a step toward Carlo. "So how do you want to do this? Should I kneel before you as you invoke the name of Jesus?"

Carlo looked at Christian like he was crazy. *He's right. How do I do this? The shroud should destroy him, but how. I guess it's best to start with the simplest way.* Carlo whipped the shroud at Christian's face, jumping at the sound it made as it slapped him. Christian spun around and fell back into his chair, face down. Carlo stood over him, looking for signs of life.

Christian turned around, rubbing the red mark on his face. "Now that wasn't nice at all." His eyes seethed with fury even as his lips curled up slightly in a smile.

Not enough. More contact, maybe?

"Is it my turn now?" Darkness gathered behind Christian, pushing the light to the other side of the room. Carlo could barely make out the picture on the wall behind him. "What did they say in that movie? 'Don't make me angry. You wouldn't like me when I'm angry?'" Christian leaned closer. "By the way, motion pictures are one of the few things you humans came up with that are worth anything, so, kudos on that."

Desperately searching the room for anything that might help him, Carlo noticed the poker sitting in the fire pit a few feet away. It glowed red, nestled in the flaming logs. *Maybe.* Before he could make a move toward it, he heard a rustling behind him. He turned toward the sound to see one of the marble angels standing, wings outstretched, and two feet behind him. The dark veining swam across the stone, giving the whole statue the illusion of motion.

"You..." The statue spread its wings and lifted its right arm wielding a marble sword. *Damn it.* He backed slowly away from the statue, feeling the heat of the fire behind him. *Okay. Okay. Just a little farther.* When he felt the edge of the fire pit push into the back of his leg, he bent down and hazarded a quick glance to locate the poker. Keeping the shroud as far away from the fire as he could, he grabbed the poker with his right hand and swung it at the angel's wrist. Sparks showered to the ground as the head of the poker broke free and flew one way while the statue's hand and sword flew the other. The statue froze, and then toppled to the floor. Carlo turned back to face Christian, holding the headless poker in one hand and the shroud in the other.

"Well played. It appears we are tied. Your turn." Christian's smile never wavered.

"This isn't a game, Christian."

"Not a game? It's *all* fun and games, at least until someone gets hurt, and I think we all know who that is going to be."

"Lives are at stake, not just those you've killed, but the billions of others. We want to live our lives free of your poison."

"Lives? Do you mourn the pawn you toss off the chessboard when taken by the bishop? There are so many of you little rabbits, your worth has been watered down to nothing." Christian picked up the broken head of the angel. "And now, I believe it is your turn. If you want to forfeit, I'll be glad to go again."

Carlo heard movement behind him again. *What now? I need*

to do something fast. He looked from the point of the poker to the shroud. *Maybe, just maybe.* In one fluid motion, he wrapped the shroud around the fractured end of the tool and jabbed it at Christian, like a short sword. Carlo was surprised that Christian didn't react, no jerky dodge, just a grunt as the jagged tip of the poker pierced his side. As he lunged forward, the shroud followed, entering Christian's abdomen.

Christian screeched the minute the shroud touched his wound. Glasses at the bar shattered. Carlo released his grip on the poker and covered his ears. Even shielded, he fell to his knees from the force of the sound. Blood dripped from his nose.

Christian reeled back, the poker jutting from his side. The shroud was rapidly turning red. Christian began vibrating so rapidly, Carlo couldn't focus on him. The shadows that had been gathering behind Christian were pulled closer to his body, revealing the artwork behind him once again. Christian's scream continued, growing in volume as the darkness joined his keening. Carlo felt wetness on his hands as his ears felt like they were going to implode.

The shadows circling Christian merged into a dense cloud, further obscuring Carlo's view of what was happening to him. The rest of the room brightened as the darkness that had pervaded it concentrated on Christian's body. He listed to one side as he flailed in slow motion. The black mass of shapes coalesced into a rapidly moving solid form surrounding him. He continued falling to one side, slowly losing his balance. Carlo jumped as a stone statue behind him shattered into jagged shards, cutting him as they flew past. *Oh my God, can he just die and get it over with? The screaming is going to destroy this whole building, me included..*

Carlo fought his way to his knees while still holding his hands over his ears. He could feel the blood dripping down his forearms from his ears. His chest ached as if something had torn inside him. He struggled to get one foot beneath him. Barely keeping his balance, he used most of his remaining strength to push himself upright.

Christian's fall had begun to slow. *He's fighting it.* Carlo ignored the pain and dropped his hands from his head. Using them for balance he put everything into one roundhouse kick. Spinning, he hardly noticed his surroundings. The condo faded into a haze of gray as he came around to face Christian, balanced on one foot. His other foot hit the cloud of shadows, passing through them with an electrical shock and almost immediately striking Christian in the head. Carlo couldn't stop his turn, overbalancing, and fell to the ground. He hit the floor and rolled onto his back, grimacing as he felt a rib crack.

He turned his head to see Christian falling into the fire pit. The screech momentarily amplified before becoming silent as the flames engulfed his body. The shadows faded as they were consumed, revealing Christian's body once again. Carlo tried to lift himself to his elbows, but the pain overwhelmed him. His vision wavered as he watched Christian's skin darken and begin to char. The fire flared intensely white and burned itself out, leaving nothing left of Christian's body.

Carlo sucked a painful gulp of air and abandoned his attempt at picking himself up, trying instead to roll on his side. After ten minutes of excruciating pain, he managed to pull himself to the table, where, a mere foot above his head sat a phone just out of reach. *If I can just dial 9-1-1...*

Carlo grabbed the foot of the table and heaved, only lifting it three inches. He turned onto his back and using both hands, finally lifted it higher until the phone slid to the edge and dropped to the floor. *Please don't break.* Panting from the effort, he retrieved the phone and held it to his ear.

Thank God. A dial tone.

Chapter **25**

Carlo dialed 9-1-1, rolling onto one side to verify that Christian was truly gone. Not even ashes remained where he had stood. *I can't believe it's over. And I'm alive, if barely. God, please forgive your children their arrogance.* He made a feeble attempt to make the sign of the cross. *We've rid the world of the taint we invited in. We ask only that you forgive us.*

A male voice answered the phone. "Please state the nature of your emergency."

What do I say? I can't say I killed the anti-Christ. There aren't any remains. But how do I explain my current situation? He attacked me and left?

"Hello? This is an official line. If you don't have an emergency, please hang up. You can be arrested for falsely calling this number."

"No, don't go. I'm here. I'm injured."

"Sir, can you please tell me the nature of your injuries?"

"I'm not sure, broken ribs and bruised organs, and my ears

and nose are bleeding."

"Is there anyone else injured?"

Carlo looked once more at the spot where Christian had vaporized. "No, sir."

"Are you at 801 Poydras Street?"

"I believe so."

"Okay, then, I've dispatched an ambulance. Can you tell me what happened?"

This is being recorded. I just saved the world, and anything I say can and will be used against me in a court of law. "I had an... altercation with another man." He surveyed the damage to the room. Two paintings had fallen off the wall, three marble statues were lying on the floor in pieces, broken glass was strewn everywhere, and a haze of smoke hung down three feet from the ceiling. *An altercation... That's putting it mildly.*

"Is the other man still in the area? Is he okay?"

Carlo grunted with effort as he forced himself into a seated position, leaning his back against the coffee table. "No." *No way to explain this.* "I mean yes, he's fine, but no, he's no longer here. After the fight, he left."

"Are you sure he was okay, sir?"

No. I'm pretty sure I sent him to Hell. He's as far from okay as you can get. "Yes. He's okay." Carlo grimaced as a jolt of pain shot through him. "When you get here, you'll have to go to the penthouse. The door's open."

He could hear the operator breathing heavily on the other side of the line. "Sir? Don't you think pierced through the chest with a fire iron and then being set on fire is something less than fine?" The voice deepened, laced with anger. "Isn't it always like your kind to blame me for your aggression."

Carlo dropped the phone as he recognized Christian's voice. The voice continued to ring through the room.

"If I remember correctly, it was you who came here with violence in your heart. I could have destroyed you at any moment had I wanted. You were Hell bent..." Laughter filled the air. "Sorry, the devil is the father of puns. You insisted on bringing violence into *my house,* and then you have the nerve to blame *me?* Who is righteous, here?"

Carlo slumped against the edge of the table, turning his head to find the source of the voice.

Christian walked into the room through the door to the kitchen, stopping at the bar to pick up the glass of bourbon Carlo had poured earlier, miraculously untouched. "Pour my liquor, try to kill me, and then blame me for it." He downed the bourbon in one gulp, slamming the glass on the counter. Shards flew in all directions as the glass shattered in his hand.

"Get up."

"I can't. I seem to have broken something."

Christian ignored the broken glass crunching under his shoes and walked over to Carlo. He reached down and grabbed his hand, pulling him up.

"I said get up."

Carlo felt heat burning down the length of his arm as Christian lifted him to his feet. Pain flared at first, to be replaced by numbness. Carlo poked his side where his rib had broken. Nothing. *Healed by the anti-Christ. At what cost? I didn't ask for it. In fact, I'm being commanded.*

Christian sat down on the recliner where he had been sitting when Carlo first entered the condo. He pointed to the other chair. "Have a seat."

"But how did you..."

"Oh, I was just having you on. Sure that poker smarted. I owe you for that. But it was a minute's work to heal."

"But the shroud should have killed you. The prophecy..."

"The prophecy. Funny thing about that. What did it say again, something about that which brought me into this world will take me out?"

Carlo's eyes widened in surprise. "How did you know about

that?"

Christian chuckled. *"Stopped. You think this can be stopped?* It seems like only yesterday, or maybe an eternity. I guess it depends on how you look at it. You forget that I was there. It was quite painful forcing myself into that vessel, nothing like this one." He rubbed one hand on the back of the other. "This body was built for me."

"You were there?" Carlo sank back into the chair with a look of defeat on his face.

"Who do you think took over your precious *brother* after the prophecy? Of course I was there. I knew all about the shroud."

"Then why didn't it affect you?"

"Because that wasn't the shroud." Christian smiled at Carlo's confusion. "I knew about your silly brotherhood, and thought you might figure out that the shroud was my only weakness, so I stole it first. I made a pretty good copy, don't you think?"

"So there is no shroud?"

"Well, of course not. I destroyed it five years ago. I saw no reason to leave it hanging around."

"And now... that leaves you..."

"Invincible, I would think. I would say immortal, but I was already that before. Now I can remain on this plane for as long as I want in human form. I can do with you as I will."

"I hate to ask, but why did you heal me? Why am I still alive?"

Christian stood up and walked to the bar. He held up the bottle of bourbon with a questioning look in his eye, smiling as Carlo nodded. Sweeping his hand across the bar, he cleared the broken glass. He arranged two glasses side by side and filled them halfway, dropping two ice cubes in each. He handed one to Carlo as he sat down.

"I have a proposition for you."

Carlo brought the glass to his lips and swirled the whiskey over his tongue, swallowing as the alcohol burn lessened. *I tried to kill him and now he's invincible. I'm defeated. We're all defeated. And now he wants something from me?*

"I happen to have had a position open up recently, and you seem to have some financial knowledge. How would you like to work for me?"

Carlo stared at him, dumbfounded. "I just tried to kill you, and if there was any other way, I would try again."

"I know, but since there isn't..."

Carlo gulped another mouthful of bourbon. His eyes narrowed. "You don't want me."

"I most certainly do."

"No, I mean you don't want my business sense. You want me for revenge."

Christian's lips curled up into a smirk. "Go on,"

"You want me as the poster child of your attack on God. 'Look God, I took your champion, your failed champion, your greatest ally, and converted him.' You'd like that, wouldn't you?"

"All that and intelligence, too. So what do you think?"

"What? No offers? I'm not worth even a minor bribe?"

Christian swirled his finger in his drink, sucking the excess off. "Besides your life? Of course, I could offer you eternal life and seventy-seven virgins, but I don't think that would work for you. Am I wrong? Besides I've always been more inclined to go for the whores. They know all the tricks of the trade. I tell you what, name your price. Think big, now. You can have anything you can dream. I can even make you forget your religion if that would make you feel better. I can make you forget everything except your dreams."

Lord please forgive my transgressions. If I die here, please take me in your grace.

"It is your decision, but you must make it now."

"What kind of decision is that? Damnation or death?"

"What damnation? How could you go to Hell if you live forever?"

That would be a form of Hell. Besides, I see through you. I don't know how, but you would find a way to make any wish go horribly wrong.

"I am happy, no, joyous in my convictions. If those are my options, then kill me now and send me to God."

Christian's eyes narrowed and darkened. "Oh, no. You've misunderstood me. Either way, you will serve me." Christian stood and towered over Carlo in his chair.

"Your choice is to be with me or commit suicide. Eternal riches, women, whatever you want, or eternal damnation." Christian held out his arms like the carving on the door, dropping one almost to his side.

"It seems like a pretty easy decision to me. You can't make me commit suicide. It has to be my decision, and I would never do that."

"You don't know what I can and can't do. Trust me, I can make you beg me to let you kill yourself."

Lord, help me. He's right. I can't imagine the things he could do to me. I need to find another way.

Christian held his glass of bourbon to the light, peering through the amber liquid. "Do you see this whiskey?" Christian looked at Carlo's half empty glass. "I could turn it into wine, like my brother did, or... I could turn it into Drano."

"And then I'd die."

"No. I could heal you just enough to keep you alive, but oh, what pain you'd have. How long could you stand it before you *begged* me to let you kill yourself."

Carlo put his glass down, frowning. Searching the room, he couldn't find a thing that would be effective against Christian.

I have only one thing left.

"Our Father who art in Heaven..."

Christian's face screwed up in anger. "Don't you dare call upon Him here. Those words have no power. Can they do this?" Christian waved his hands at the fire pit. Flames shot straight up in a column to the vent hood. Searing with the power of a jet engine exhaust, they formed a solid pier of fire from floor to ceiling. Interlaced between the orange jets, ebony faces rushed to the vent, anger playing across their features. Carlo winced before a calm settled over him.

"Hallowed be thy name..."

Christian clenched his hands as his eyes turned to coal. The flames took more heat out of the air than they added. Carlo began to see frost forming from his breath, and his body began to shiver uncontrollably.

"Thy kingdom come..."

"This does nothing." Christian waved held out his arms, indicating the rest of the room. "See. You get no answer."

Carlo stood up, facing Christian. Christian's wrath was a palpable thing. Pitch-black smoke began to issue from the corners of his eyes, floating upward to mix with the shadows swimming across the ceiling.

"Thy will be done..." *Get madder. Come on. Lose control.*

"Don't." Christian cut each word off like the crack of a gunshot. *"Say. It."* Murky vapors swirled around his arms, as a low rumble shook the room. The shadows on the ceiling began to slither down the walls.

Carlo leaned forward, his nose almost touching Christian's. "On *earth* as it is in Heaven."

"NEVER!" Christian shoved Carlo back. As one, the dark mass of shadows jumped from the wall and surrounded Carlo, pouring into his ears, nose, and mouth. Carlo's body jerked like a puppet on strings as more of the darkness entered him. Just under the surface of his skin, snakelike shapes moved back and forth. Carlo closed his eyes in pain, refusing to scream. More of his skin rippled until Christian couldn't see any that was remained still.

"I have dominion on earth now." Christian looked up. "Unless You want to end this." He glanced back to Carlo, who was looking less human every second as the shadows pulled his skin into shapes they weren't supposed to make. "I thought not."

Carlo's skin began to crack open in several places, leaking an oily substance.

"Give. Us. This. Day. " Carlo grunted out each word as if it was a whole sentence, breathing heavily. "Our. Daily. Bread." More cracks opened, covering the lower half of his body in black viscous liquid.

"*Noooo!*"

The writhing shadows stretched his skin to twice its normal size. Christian could no longer recognize Carlo as the person who had knocked on his door only a few hours ago.

"And. Forgive." Christian held out his hand like a traffic cop and Carlo froze. He struggled to force the air out of his lungs.

"Us."

"*Stop! I command you.*"

Carlo pulled from the center of his being, drawing on a reserve he didn't know he had. What was visible of his face relaxed, looking calm and reserved.

"Our sins."

A clap of thunder rang through the room as the shadows exploded from Carlo's pores. Oil and flesh flew in all directions, coating Christian and his furniture.

"Damn it." He waved the shadows away from him. "Leave me. You weren't supposed to kill him." The fire behind him continued to roar from floor to ceiling.

Christian threw his glass across the room, scattering the remaining shadows. He looked up again, imploring the heavens.

"Another battle. That's okay. Bring them on. Nothing can stop me."

"Only You."

Chapter *26*

Father Mike held his head with one hand and a cell phone with the other. An open bottle of ibuprofen sat on the pew beside him.

"I'm glad you're okay, Stan. Any luck finding him?"

"Actually it wasn't much of a problem, only a matter of a few minute's work. Now that I've converted, I love my magic box." Father Mike heard Danny in the background say, "I told you."

"Your what?"

"Sorry. I've always called Danny's iPhone a magic box. It seemed like he could find out anything at a moment's notice. The name stuck, and now I've got one. If it's out there, I can find it. The good news is he's local."

"Great. See if he can help out, and get back here soon. I have a feeling our timetable is moving up drastically."

"Do you really think he'll be able to give us something that will help?"

"Now that we don't have the shroud to help us, we're going

to have to rely on faith. If there is a way to stop Christian, God will help us find it, and this may be our last resort. Call me when you find out anything."

Father Mike shut the phone and put it in his pocket. *Maybe I should move out of the 90's and get a smart phone. Hell, it might not matter in a few days.*

The church darkened as the sun passed behind a cloud. Shadows chased each other across the floor and pews around him. Father Mike shuddered, remembering the shadows that moved of their own accord. A blast of humid air hit the back of his neck. He turned around to see two dark figures walking in the door. The waning light hid their features.

"Father, so good to see you here." The figure on the left took off his hat. Father Mike squinted to make out more detail. Dressed in priest's black downs, their movements were jerky and awkward looking. *Is someone filming a zombie movie?*

"Fathers?"

"Us? Oh, no. We took these off the last priests we met. They put up a fight, but only for a few minutes."

As they neared him, Father Mike could see pale, almost white skin and eyes of solid black like Christian's. Running to the other side of the altar, he put his hand on the open bible. The pages rattled as he had trouble stilling his fingers.

"You aren't welcome here. In the name of the Lord, I command you to leave this hallowed ground."

Laughter filled the church as the two figures continued to advance. Father Mike swallowed, looking for anything he might be able to use to defend himself.

Moloch turned to his partner. "It is so nice not to have the usual chains binding us."

"Even nicer to have an actual body to wear, don't you think?" They turned back to Father Mike. "Now that Lucifer walks in solid form on this plane, sacred ground holds no sway over us. We can come and go as we please."

Samael stepped back to the holy water font, dipping his

finger. Touching it to his forehead, he smiled, walking back to his partner.

"Even holy water has lost its efficacy. Soon the legions of Hell will roll over this world, consuming all who stand in their way. The world of humans will be thrall to angels and demons both."

Father Mike closed his eyes trying to feel God's presence through the altar beneath his hands. Failing to get any reassurance, he opened his them and faced the dark angels.

"What do you want from me?"

Samael turned to Moloch and smiled broadly. "What do we want? If it were up to me, we would send you screaming from this world. Of course, we'd take our time to make sure you truly comprehended our frustration."

Moloch put a gloved hand on Samael's shoulder. "Alas, it is not up to us."

Father Mike sighed, releasing his clenched hands. *Death is off the table then. That could be a good thing or bad.*

"Christian sent us with explicit instructions, and we will follow them explicitly. He is not happy with all of your *extracurricular* activities. Your new friends are not to his liking at all." The two dark angels stopped at the edge of the sanctuary and looked up at the light fixture where Father Anthony and Father Joseph had hung. Following their line of sight, Father Mike looked up and thought he saw three figures hanging from the light. *The price of failure is unthinkable, but what is the price of success?*

"You were like a father to him. Be warned, his compassion is running thin." Moloch took his hand from Samael's shoulder, looking down at the new wooden threshold to the sanctuary. *They aren't sure.*

Samael lifted one foot and set it down on the other side, smiling as nothing happened. He looked Father Mike in the eye. "He wants you to stop what you're doing and join him. All will be forgiven if you just stand down. He loves you."

Moloch joined him, taking a step toward the altar. "We don't agree with him, but he brooks very little argument."

Father Mike stepped back from the altar. "Why did he send you? Why didn't he come himself?"

Resonating deep in his chest, a sub-audible vibration set Father Mike on edge. For a moment, he thought he saw two giant shadows spread behind Samael like wings.

"He's very busy, what with his little family feud. Besides, he knows how persuasive we can be. Unfortunately, we feel the need for more firmness in this matter than Christian, and while you have to be alive when we leave here, he didn't say we couldn't have a little fun."

Slowly retreating from the oncoming dark angels, Father Mike felt the bottom of the crucifix hanging on the wall press into the small of his back. *Nowhere else to go.*

"I need you to leave and tell Christian to come see me himself."

Samael chuckled. "Not very likely."

Father Mike crossed himself. "Pater noster, qui es in caelis, sanctificetur nomen tuum." He intoned the prayer as a whisper slowly growing in volume. "Adveniat regnum tuum."

"Saying it in Latin won't make it any more potent. God is still not answering." Samael indicated the cross hanging on the wall behind Father Mike. "What do you think, Moloch, shall we? It would have a certain amount of irony."

Father Mike looked back to see the cross stretching up the wall. *No. Oh God, please, no.* With a rush of wind, Moloch rose slowly into the air. *The sound their wings make feels like a threat. It's almost like they make words I can barely understand.*

Samael closed the distance between them in two steps and wrapped his hand around Father Mike's throat. His wings thundered in Father Mike's ears as he was lifted into the air.

"Last chance, Father. Do you accept Christian as your new savior?"

Moloch flew beside Father Mike, holding a rusty hammer inscribed with Hebrew characters, and a handful of four-inch long nails."

"Go to Hell," Father Mike croaked past the tight grip on his throat. His face turned red from the pressure, as he began to lose consciousness.

"Not tonight. Maybe not ever again."

Father Mike's back slammed against the cross. Samael used his other hand to hold his hand still. Father Mike screamed as he saw Moloch approaching holding the nail and hammer.

"Oh, don't scream yet. You'll have nothing left for when the pain starts."

Lightning struck outside, followed instantly by thunder as Moloch's hammer struck, driving the nail through Father Mike's wrist and into the wood. The lightning flash seared indelibly into Father Mike's mind the picture of his blood dripping down the cross.

"I used to think there was something to you humans. Now I don't know what He sees in you. You're pathetic." Moloch nailed his other hand into the cross.

"Frankly, it didn't matter to me whether you had chosen Christian or not. Your kind's time is coming to an end." Moloch waved the hammer in front of Father Mike's face. "This is actually pointless. We've waited so long for this chance and nothing can stop it now, certainly not a few pitiful bugs. But Christian feels like he has a vested interest in you. He thinks that a few well taught lessons might steer you onto the right path."

Moloch brought the hammer down on the end of the nail sticking out of Father Mike's wrist, combining the ringing of metal with a scream of pain. Father Mike struggled to slow his ragged breathing.

"Enough." His lungs refused to let him catch his breath. Hanging on his arms put too much pressure on his chest. He felt hands positioning his feet on top of each other. "Oh God..."

"He won't stop us." Samael tugged at Father Mike's knees, bending them slightly. "He can't. Are you still sticking with Him? This can all stop."

Sweat dripped off his forehead as he shook his head. *He*

sent them because he couldn't do this himself. I hope.
    "Okay, Moloch, Let's make some more music."

~~*~*

Christian looked around his condo, broken debris and blood coated every surface. "Where to start?" He held out his arms, palms up, staring at the large panel window overlooking the Mississippi River. He slowly clenched his fingers, watching them turn white. They shook with effort. As he watched, the glass began to vibrate in resonance to his hands. Without taking his eyes off the window, Christian flicked his fingers outward. The glass shattered away from him. Humid air rushed into the room, clearing out the smoke. From forty-two floors below, he heard horns blaring as the glass rained down on the street.

    "Oops."

He swung his hand toward the gaping opening. Glass and marble shards swept across the floor and over the edge to fall below. He swung his other hand and cleared that side of the room. Satisfied, he listened to the chaos from the street.

    "Again, You can stop this. You know what I want." Christian walked to the ledge, glancing down to see the results of his cleanup before looking up to the heavens. "Still no answer? You disappoint me."

    One voice cut through the crowds below, sending a jolt through his body. From across town, Father Mike's agonized scream hit him harder than he thought it would. "Just make the right decision, then you won't have to suffer."

    Christian watched a bank of dark clouds roll across the city. Lightning flashed from cloud to cloud highlighting their edges. In the afterimage, Christian saw dark angel's shadows burrowing through the angry looking storm. Electric energy filled the room, causing his hair to stand on end. As he looked across town in the direction of St. Michael's Church, the screams built to a high mewling, and then stopped. Shaking his head, he walked back to the bar. Pulling down a bottle of scotch, he opened the top and swigged straight out of the bottle. He hardly noticed the burning liquid as it went down his throat.

"What am I to do with you, Father Mike? My family sold me out. I'm not allowed back *home*." He lifted the bottle again, filling his mouth. "I don't know why I have *any* attachment to you. I've existed for millennia before you were ever born. Your betrayal should bring swift and final retribution." He stared, unseeing out the window. "But I can't bring myself, yet."

Christian looked at the bottle in his hand, having forgotten that he had picked it up. He put it down on the counter, listening for any more sounds from St. Michael's. All he heard were the horns of cars below still trumpeting their displeasure.

"Fuck you people!" He backhanded the bottle across the room. It flew out the opening where the window had once been. "Fuck all of you. You don't deserve what you are given, handed on a silver platter every day. You don't even recognize the gift. You spit on the giver, and now you spit on me." His brows moved closer together as he frowned. "You make it too easy."

Chapter *27*

Danny opened the door to his Mustang and stopped, turning to Stan. "Do you think that's going to be enough?"

"It's going to have to be. It's all we've got. As Father Mike said, the shroud is gone with no sign as to where it went. We've got to try anything, and this may just be crazy enough to work."

Danny looked over at the knife. *It doesn't look like much. I've confiscated much bigger knives off of petty criminals. Somehow, the fate of humanity rests on a four-inch blade.* "He couldn't have made it with something..." Danny watched as Stan twirled the knife with two fingers. "I don't know, more substantial? Like a bazooka?"

Stan opened the glove compartment and removed an evidence bag, slipping the knife carefully into it. Tucking the bag into his belt, he asked, "Have you heard from Father Mike?"

"No. Unfortunately in this case, no news is not necessarily good news. Let's get back to the church. Why don't you give him a call while I'm driving." The engine roared to life as Danny gunned the accelerator, eighty's rock music blared out of the speakers.

"Pantera? Turn that shit down. You had that on the whole way over here. I can only listen to so much hair band music in one day." He dialed St. Michael's. After several rings, he heard a click and muffled laughter.

"Father Mike?"

A blood-curdling scream blasted from the cell phone speaker, sounding like it came from inside the car with them.

He held the phone close to his mouth and screamed, "Father Mike, are you okay?"

From a distance, a voice whispered, "Stan?" Then different voice interrupted, "You must be thing one of the dynamic duo. I'm sorry to say that Father Michael is busy at the moment. He's all tied up."

Another voice spoke over the first. "No, he's just hanging around." Both voices laughed. Stan heard a metallic clang and then the screaming began again. After another click, the line went dead.

"Damn it!"

The tires screeched as Danny accelerated away from the curb. "They're killing him."

"Sounds like it, but who? That wasn't Christian." Stan put the light on the dash and turned on the siren. "We'd better get there as quick as we can. If Father Mike dies, it'll all be up to us. We'll be the last hope."

"I'm not sure I like the sound of that. If we're all that's left, the world is totally fucked."

"Come on, Danny. We can't give up. Father Mike told us to have faith."

"Oh, shit, now you *have* drunk the Kool-Aid." Danny threaded his way through traffic headed for the church.

""Shit, Danny, you're driving like a maniac. How were you ever late to anything?"

"I guess I never had the right motivation."

Stan grabbed the handle above his right shoulder, holding on for his life. He looked out the window. "Hell of a storm brewing out there."

"Yeah, I hope we beat it. I don't want to be driving when it lets loose."

Stan stared at the wall of black clouds approaching. He watched the edges morph slowly as the winds blew. Lightning flashed, etching the shapes in his mind.

"What the? Danny, did you see that?"

"I'm trying to keep my eyes on the road, what with all these crazy drivers." He blared the horn as he whipped the Mustang around another car.

Stan squinted, straining to make out what he thought he had seen. "Shit. There's another."

"Another what?" Danny turned to face Stan briefly before focusing back on the road.

"That cloud is... breaking up."

"That sounds like a good thing."

"No. When the lightning struck, I could see a small part of the cloud break off and float away. No. Not quite float, more like swim."

Danny tapped the brakes and swerved to the middle lane, passing another driver. "A piece of cloud?"

"I don't know. It was dark and fluid."

"Are you sure you're not just seeing things? I know we're in the midst of craziness, but not everything is angels or demons."

"Were you seeing things that morning at your house?"

"But clouds? Come on, kids see horses and butterflies in clouds. It's dark out and we're going..." He looked down at the speedometer. "In excess of... let's just say we're going fast."

"I know what I saw, but I guess it could have been something normal."

"Have you tried calling Father Mike back?"

"Hold on." Stan fumbled with his phone, dropping it as Danny changed lanes unexpectedly. "Can you stay in one lane for more than thirty seconds?"

Danny smiled as Stan dialed.

"Nothing. All I get is static with crackling every time there's lightning."

"As long as the traffic holds up, we'll be there soon."

"Or we'll be dead," Stan muttered.

"I heard that."

"Good, you may have lost your mind, but not your hearing. I have a feeling we're going to need all of our faculties over the next couple hours."

Danny jerked the car to the left as a dark shape flew over the windshield. "Holy shit! What the fuck was that?"

Stan peeled himself off the window. "I didn't get a good look at it while I was being flung across the car. Maybe it was a blown out tire?"

"Sorry, at least we're still alive. But I'm not sure it was solid. I thought for a second that I could see through it."

"Maybe it was a shirt or something."

Stan looked over at the storm as another bolt of lightning crashed to the ground. He lost himself for a moment staring at the churning clouds. *How did I end up here? Freaking Satan hunter?* He jerked back from the window as a black wispy object slammed into it with a solid thump.

Danny glanced over at Stan. "What?"

The thumps walked across the roof before crashing into Danny's window, rocking the car.

"Oh, hell. That's not a shirt."

The dark shadow swirled around the speeding car seeking entry. Danny swerved the car back and forth trying to shake it.

"Toto, we're definitely not in Kansas anymore. Seriously, how did we get caught up in this mess?"

"I was just thinking the same thing."

Another shape crashed into Stan's window. The two shadows

slammed alternately into the opposite sides of the vehicle, rocking the car almost onto two wheels. Danny gripped the wheel tightly, struggling to keep the Mustang under control.

"There are two of the bastards."

"Detective? You should be captain. Captain Obvious. Just drive the damn car."

The shadows circled the car, racing at over ninety miles per hour down the highway. One got sucked into the air intake at the front of the Mustang.

"Oh, crap. Quick, turn off the air conditioning."

"What?"

"*Turn off the air conditioning.* It's trying to get in. That's what they're doing, looking for a way in."

Stan slammed his hand onto a bank of buttons. Hard rock blasted out of the speakers.

"Shit."

Danny took a hand off the wheel and reached for the air controls. Before he could reach them, the other shape began slamming repeatedly into the side of the car. Danny yanked his hand back, trying to steady the car.

Stan hit the dial. "I've got it now. Sorry."

The black wisp flew out of the front grill and across the windshield, disappearing behind the car. The shadow slamming into the side of the car stopped and followed the first.

"They couldn't get in. Do you think they gave up?" Danny jerked the car to the left, passing a Jeep with two teens. The teens stared wide-eyed at the speeding Mustang.

"I hope so." Stan looked helplessly at the console full of buttons. "Danny?"

"Yeah?"

"How do you turn off this damn music?"

"Oh come on. We're only ten minutes out, just enough time to learn something about real music."

"Oh? Well, let's turn this crap off and learn."

"Funny." Danny turned the volume down. "Is that better?"

"Oh, no."

"What? You can barely hear it."

"No. Not that." Stan pointed out his window at the jeep pulling up alongside them. "That."

The two teens had their heads turned sideways, staring at them through eyes of coal as the cars sped down the highway. Neither teen was watching the road ahead, but the car remained on course.

"That can't be good."

"There, but for the grace of God..." Stan mumbled. "It's a good thing you didn't go for the convertible when you bought this thing."

"Shoot 'em."

Stan turned to face Danny. "Do you really want me to open that window? Look at them."

Danny glanced over at the Jeep. The two teens hadn't turned their heads. Both still stared directly at them without blinking.

"That's just creepy."

"Creepy? It's likely to be deadly."

The driver of the Jeep yanked his wheel sharply to the left. Stan braced himself as the vehicle smashed into the side of the Mustang. Metal screeched as the cars ground against each other.

Danny turned the wheel toward the Jeep to keep from being rammed off the road. "Oh, hell no! Now those bastards are dead."

"I think they already are."

Stan turned back to the driver. He hadn't taken his eyes off them. Showing no emotion, he held his hands on the steering wheel tightly, pushing the Jeep against their car. The two cars jimmied back and forth across the three lanes, rapidly approaching a Toyota in Danny's lane.

"Crap! Hold on tight. This is liable to be rough. "

He turned slightly away from the Jeep to disengage and slammed on the brakes. As soon as the Jeep passed them, Danny cut back into the lane behind it, barely missing the Toyota.

"Are you sure I can't do this to some loud rock music?"

"Get us out of this alive, and I'll join you in a little head banging."

Danny glanced over at Stan. "You know I'm going to hold you to that, right?"

The brake lights flared red on the Jeep in front of them. The gap between them closed. He steered to the right, slowly pulling up on the Jeep's right quarter panel. Danny couldn't see the driver, but the passenger had turned around, eyes glued to their car.

"Are you ready?"

"Ready for what?"

"Hold on!"

Danny cut the wheel sharply to the left, catching the Jeep just behind the rear tire well. He cringed as metal met metal. Gritting his teeth, he punched the accelerator while keeping the wheel turned.

The back end of the Jeep began swinging to the left. The driver cut his wheel to steer into the skid, but Danny kept accelerating. Eventually the car turned almost perpendicular to the highway. Danny could see both teens for only a second before the Jeep began to roll. Both were looking him in the eye. *Very creepy.*

The Jeep rolled onto its roof and vaulted into the air, flipping over the top of the Mustang. Danny floored the gas, roaring forward and barely clearing the falling vehicle. He looked in the rear view mirror, ducking as the Jeep erupted in flames.

Stan grabbed Danny's arm. "Look at that."

Danny glanced in the mirror again. "What? Oh..."

Two black shapes swirled through the flames, twitching as they circled. They twisted and whirled before plunging straight down into the center of the wreck. Immediately, the flames collapsed upon themselves and were extinguished.

"Do you think that was the last of them?"

"I hope so."

Danny sighed. "Good." He reached out and cranked the volume up, watching Stan roll his eyes as the speakers shook from the pumping bass. The speedometer topped one hundred miles per hour as they sped to St. Michael's Church.

When they pulled up outside the church, Stan saw an old Ford Escort parked out front with the doors open.

"What do you think is up with that?"

"Come on, Stan. We don't have time for that. Father Mike needs us."

Stan followed Danny as he jogged up the steps, noticing an open Bible on the sidewalk beside the car.

"Danny, before we go rushing in there guns blazing, don't you think we should scope the situation out? After what we've been through in the last couple days, you never know what might be waiting for us inside."

Danny paused at the door. "Okay, a little caution might be warranted, but it's not like we can call for backup. Maybe we shouldn't go through the front door. Do you remember how to get to Father Mike's office from out here?"

"This way."

The two detectives ran around the side of the church to a smaller door set back from the street. Danny tried the handle. *Not locked, thank God.* He drew his weapon, holding it pointed at the floor. Waving at Stan to follow, he moved down the hall toward the office.

The door was cracked open when they got there, no sounds issuing from within. Danny held up his hand, stopping Stan. He bent over and edged his head through the door at hip level. Straightening up, he shook his head and pointed toward the doorway to the church itself, half open. "This way," he mouthed.

Guns held at ready, they walked down the hall. Steps from the door, Danny waved at Stan to stop. He cupped his other hand around his ear and pointed at the opening. Through the doorway, they heard a low moaning.

"He's still alive," Danny whispered.

He crouched and stepped through the opening, entering the nave. Turning to the sanctuary, they saw Father Mike nailed to the cross, his head hanging to one side. In front of him, a priest hung suspended in the air while another crouched on top of the altar. *What the...* Both priests faced away from them, leaving them unnoticed. A shimmering in the air behind the floating priest hinted at wings.

"Now what?" he mouthed to Stan.

Stan shrugged then pointed to Danny and waved is hand to the far side of the church. Danny nodded and made his way across the church, stepping over padded kneelers on the way. From opposite sides of the church, they approached the altar. Danny looked over at Stan, gun trained on the flying priest. *How is this going to work? Christ's blood kills the anti-Christ, but what kills demons? Besides car explosions? All I can do is trust in my training. Or should I have faith in it?* He glanced at Father Mike nailed to the giant cross. *Not that his faith seems to be helping him so much right now.*

Father Mike lifted his head slightly and peered out of swollen eyes at Danny. His lips moved, looking only vaguely like a smile. Danny nodded at him. *I guess his faith in me brought me on board, and brought me here.* Father Mike nodded his head back as if he heard Danny's thoughts.

The priest on the altar turned around. He stared at the two detectives with eyes of obsidian, a smile growing on his pale gray face.

"And who do we have here to pay devotions to us? It's thing one and thing two."

The other priest spun to face them and floated to the ground, his eyes, equally black.

"We're here to send you to your maker. Oh, yeah I guess that part is not going to be possible. We'll have to settle for Hell."

Danny opened fire on the priest nearest to Father Mike while Stan emptied his clip into the priest on the altar. The priests stood their ground for the first couple bullets, until the one on the altar was hit in the head. His head erupted in blood and a black oily substance. As he fell, a long, black shadow wound out of the neck, slithered up the wall, and into an air conditioning vent.

"Go for the head!" Stan yelled.

Stan slammed another clip into his gun and both detectives concentrated their fire on the second priest. Three bullets tore into his body near his shoulder, spinning him around. From his back, the shimmering shapes reappeared and the priest lifted off the ground. As he rose, he turned back around to face them.

"I am Samael, angel of death. You are nothing. You are insects infesting this planet. No matter what you do today, I and my kind will remain."

Danny raised his gun, aiming at his head. *"Go to fucking Hell!"* Pulling the trigger, he watched with satisfaction as Samael's head exploded and the body flipped over backwards to the floor. Stan jumped up onto a pew to dodge the winding shadow that came from the second priest's body. It slinked out the door, disappearing into the night.

Danny and Stan rushed to the cross.

"So guns *do* work."

"Shut up, Danny and help me get Father Mike off of this cross."

Chapter *28*

Christian turned his chair to face the open hole in his condo. The view of the Mississippi River would be spectacular with the rising sun, but that was still many hours away. The pandemonium of the street below had quieted as the business district slowly closed itself down. The chaotic scrambling of the humans cleaning up the mess from his tantrum had ceased, as had the screams of Father Mike. *That's worrisome.*

"I told them he was not to be killed. There will be Hell to pay if anything permanent has happened to him."

His eyes clouded to milky-gray for a moment. "I don't know why I don't rid myself of him right now. He's a human. He isn't truly my father. Why do I care at all?"

He propped his feet up on the end table, smiling. "And why am I talking to myself?"

Lightning struck nearby followed almost immediately by a deafening crash of thunder that echoed through the condo and rattled the few glasses left whole.

"I like the new atmosphere like this. It's apocalyptic-chic. I think I'll leave it open."

Christian grabbed the edge of the fake shroud Carlo had tried use to kill him. Lifting it up, he studied the facial features etched upon it.

"Striking, brother. You were a handsome man, even if I have to say so myself, but you should have waited for Gillette to invent the disposable razor." He rubbed his fingers across the smooth skin of his chin. "I've found that chicks..." He frowned briefly. "Chicks really dig a well kept man." He kissed the cheek of the image rendered on the linen. "Or maybe I should take a cue from my newest employee and get some piercings and tattoos. How scandalous that would have been for you." Christian chuckled as he folded the ancient looking linen. "Can you picture the apoplectic fits church leaders would have had with people worshiping and venerating a tatted and pierced savior?"

"*Humans*. Why do you love them so? No matter how bigoted, no matter what depths they plumb, You and He..." Christian raised his eyes to the ceiling as he stood up, flecks of blue swirling through his cloudy eyes. "You would rather turn your backs on those of us that have been by your side for eons to adore *them*. I don't understand. Please, help me understand. I worshiped You. I loved You. Those *people* you love can't even get that part right."

Christian heaved the shroud out the window. Before it could clear the edge of the condo, he pointed at it and a bolt of lightning struck from outside, vaporizing it in a ball of flames.

"Can we end all this? I'll promise to leave your *playthings* alone." The sky opened and oversized raindrops drove into the room on heavy gusts of wind. "Rain. Of course, You've always been fond of cleansing by rain. Will it be another forty days and forty nights, then?"

Christian walked to the edge of the window, looking down. "You know Your humans often refer to rain as Your tears. I wish they were, but they wouldn't be for me, would they?" He faced the sky. "You never mourned my passing, my banishment."

Thunder echoed across the city. "But I'm still talking to myself, aren't I?" He smiled wryly. "So be it."

Christian turned his back to the downpour. "But know this. I will not stop. *You* must stop me." His smile disappeared. "One way or the other."

He spun around, screaming into the night, *"Do you hear me? STOP ME!"* He backed a step away from the drop off, his suit soaking wet and whispered, "Please."

"Mr. McMillan?"

Christian jumped at the sound, hoping to hear something different than a voice from his intercom. He returned to his chair, falling into it with a resigned thump.

"Yes, Rena?"

"Can I go? You asked me to finish dealing with the authorities. I explained about your accident with the furniture. They weren't happy, but when I assured them you would cover any damages, they decided that no charges needed to be filed. They've left now."

Christian stared into the storm cloud blankly, hardly noticing the lightning flashes. He sat forward, turning to the intercom.

"Rena? How old are you?"

"Old enough." Christian heard her defenses going up even through the tiny speaker.

Smiling, he replied, "I only meant to offer you a drink to thank you for staying late. I don't want to get in trouble with the law yet again by contributing to the delinquency of minors."

Christian waited for her to say something. When she finally spoke, confusion clouded her voice. "In your penthouse?"

"Don't worry, we'll keep the window open." When she didn't respond, he added, "That was a joke. Come on. I'm offering a drink and possibly some conversation. Nothing more. I like to get a feel for the people around me, and you are such a new addition."

"Mr. McMillan..."

"Christian, please."

"Christian, can I be frank?"

"Absolutely."

"Are you asking me as an employee?" She hesitated. "Or as a woman?"

"Neither. I'm asking you as a person, a human being." He frowned as he spoke the last bit.

"In that case..." A pair of twin screams coming from through the window drew Christian's attention, obscuring the rest of what she said.

Christian jumped up, rushing to the opening. He stared at the swelling storm cloud with unease. Clenching his fists tightly, he frowned at the night sky. His focus on the distant screams was so absolute, that he failed to notice that the furniture behind him had begun to vibrate. The fire pit lit with a whoosh, defying the wind whipping through the room.

"Christian? Did you hear me?"

He spoke without turning from the storm. "I'm sorry, Rena. Something has come up. We will finish this conversation another time."

"We will, will we? Do I have anything to say about that?"

He sighed as he turned around. "I must apologize. I didn't mean to presume... anything. I've just received some bad news. Would you *mind* if we continue this tomorrow?"

She laughed lightly through the speaker. "No probs. I was only giving you a hard time. You can seem a little scary sometimes, and I wanted to see if you could take it as well as you give."

Christian shook his head. *Humans.* "Until tomorrow, then." He hit the disconnect button.

"And now, Samael? Moloch? How did you get yourselves banished? I guess it's time to take my family matters into my own hands."

~~*~*

Stan pulled out the last nail while Danny held Father Mike. Father Mike's head tilted to one side, looking down at his own blood mixed with the splatter of the two dead priests.

"I thought guns wouldn't kill them?"

Father Mike lifted his head, struggling to stay on his injured feet. "They won't, and didn't. You didn't kill them." He breathed raggedly, sucking in air then holding it as the pain washed over him. "You only banished them from the bodies they inhabited."

"Banished? So guns can at least banish them?"

"Don't forget, these were lesser angels, only given as much power as Christian allowed them."

"Danny, we need to get Father Mike to the hospital, not interrogate him."

Father Mike stepped gingerly to the altar, wincing as he steadied himself with his hands. He shook his head as he looked over the scene of carnage on the floor of his church. Two decapitated priests lay sprawled in pools of blood where only days earlier another scene of death had been cleaned up.

"No. He's coming. I can feel it. This may be our last chance to stop him. Stan, can you get me something to wrap my hands and feet?"

Stan nodded, heading back to Father Mike's office.

"So why can't we shoot Christian in the head like these angels?"

Father Mike turned to Danny. "Samael and Moloch had to struggle to keep their forms inside the human body. Shooting their heads disrupted their hold and sent them back to Hell."

"So why can't we do that to Christian?"

Danny grabbed Father Mike around the waist as he slumped

and almost fell.

"Are you sure you don't need to go to the hospital?"

"I can't. I must be here." Danny helped Father Mike hobble to the pews and sit down. "And to answer your question, Christian isn't possessing a normal human body. In more ways than one, he is in the perfect vessel. Those two dark angels took over bodies that had housed souls previously. That took some extra power on their part, not unlike trying to squeeze into clothing a couple sizes too small."

Stan strode back into the room carrying towels and a glass of water.

"Here, Father. You need to drink. You've lost a lot of blood." Stan handed two towels to Danny, to wrap around the hand and foot on his side of Father Mike. Father Mike cringed as they tightened them around the puncture wounds.

Danny looked up at Father Mike from his foot. "You said in more ways than one?"

Father Mike opened his eyes, full of pain. "We cloned Jesus. We copied the body that housed God. It was built to hold God. There are no limitations on it like a normal human would have. He has the perfect vessel. Not only that, he did not possess a body that had a soul, pushing it out the way. Our failing... One of our failings was that we cloned a body that had no soul. Lucifer was able to fill it with ease. Shooting him will do nothing more than irritate him. And believe me, you don't want to be around when Christian is angry."

"So, we're back to square one? We need the shroud which is lost?"

"Unfortunately, yes, unless you were able to get..."

Stan jumped up, excited. "Oh yeah. We have this." He pulled out the specimen bag with the knife, handing it to Father Mike. Father Mike turned it over, studying the unimposing blade before handing it back to Stan.

"You should keep it." Father Mike frowned. "I'm sure you can handle a knife much better than I can."

Stan shoved it in his front pocket. "Do you think it'll work?"

"I don't know, but it's our only hope without the shroud. I assume he was able to come up with something for it? Otherwise it's just a pretty knife."

"Not much, but enough for maybe one try."

"Then you'll have to make it count, for everyone's sake." Father Mike studied his bandaged wrists. "Oh, one other thing. Can I borrow your phone? I seem to have lost mine." He shrugged at the mess on the floor.

"Sure, Father. Who are you going to call?"

Stan held his hand up to Danny, shaking his head as Danny whispered, "Ghost Busters."

Father Mike smiled. "I'm glad you still have your sense of humor, Danny." Turning back to Stan, he continued, "There's one more piece to the puzzle. I think we *all* need to be here."

Danny nodded and followed Stan to one of the dead bodies. Stan picked up the left leg while Danny looked at him, horrified.

"What's wrong?"

"I hate dead bodies. They're giving me the creeps."

"*This* gives you the creeps? We've just missed being killed by a kamikaze plane, we've been chased by zombie teenagers trying to run us off the road, and we just blew the heads off two dead priests possessed by dark angels, and *the dead bodies on the floor* give you the creeps?"

"Well, yeah. I can't help what gives me the heebie jeebies. Why do you think I always let you take the morgue runs?"

Stan shook his head. "Whatever, man. Just grab a leg and we'll get these things out of here."

As they reached the door, Danny turned to Stan and asked, "Do you think we should call for backup?"

"Really? Can you picture that call? 'Chief, we've got the anti-Christ on his way over to that church where the priests got murdered. Can you send some major firepower? And oh, you don't happen to have a shroud hanging around, do you?' I'm sure that would go over well. We could watch the end of the world from matching padded cells."

"I just thought I'd ask."

They hurried inside to get the second priest. As they got closer to the altar they saw that Father Mike was holding Stan's phone to his ear awkwardly with his bandaged hand.

"Yes, wake her up. Tell her it's time. She needs to get to the church immediately." He paused, listening. "Yes, she'll know what it's about."

The two detectives looked at him questioningly.

"Who knows? Any distraction may help." Father Mike hesitated, unsure how to continue.

"I need to tell you guys something."

Danny dropped the dead priest's foot. "*Now?* Now you decide to unload something on us?"

"No. It's just that... You need to be prepared. I've seen how this goes. Christian showed me in a vision."

"*Wait?* He knows what we're going to do?" Danny looked nervously to the exits.

Father Mike shushed him with his hands. "No, not exactly. I don't think he knows how it's going to end. He thinks he does, but..."

Stan put his hand on Danny's shoulder to calm him down. "Why the hesitation, Father? What did you see?"

"Do you remember when I told you that you'd need faith?"

Both detectives nodded, looking at each other with concern.

"It's going to get a lot worse before it gets better."

"Can you stop beating around the bush? Just tell us what's going to happen."

Father Mike sighed, slumping back into the pew. "At some point tonight..." He pointed to the blood stained cross behind the altar. "I will be back on that crucifix."

Their eyes darted to his wounds. "And us?"

Father Mike dropped his eyes, studying the floor. "You'll be on your knees in front of him."

Danny threw up his hands. "Shit, Father. That doesn't sound like a happy ending. How long have you known?"

"A couple days."

"And you didn't think we needed to know this?" Danny paced to the altar and back.

Father Mike shook his head. "Everything is not always as it seems. Christian is overconfident. He thinks... He knows that he can't be stopped."

Danny stopped pacing and turned to Father Mike. "And he won't be too far off."

"Danny, let the man talk."

"I'm sorry, go on."

Father Mike lifted his hand to run his fingers through his hair, wincing with pain. "But, that will be his downfall. He won't be looking for us to stop him. He's only coming to gloat, and of course punish us."

"This sounds much too close to a Hail Mary to me." Danny looked up with a smile on his face. "I didn't even try to make that pun. But seriously, you're going to be back on the cross with us on our knees. Then what? I don't see many options from that scenario. How do we use that?"

Father Mike turned to Stan. "Stan, that's where you come in. He'll be close, barely a foot away, gloating over you. That's the best chance for you to make your move. It may be the only chance you'll get to be close enough to use the knife on him."

Stan squinted at Father Mike. "And if it doesn't work? What then?"

Father Mike studied the bloody crucifix. "I'd rather not think about that."

Danny shook his head, looking around the church. "Well, on a lighter note, we only have one more dead body to drag out of here."

Stan smiled in spite of the dark mood he was in. "If that's a lighter note, I'd hate to be around when things start to fall apart. Come on, let's get this damn thing out the door so you don't have to look at it anymore."

Father Mike watched the two detectives drag the second priest down the aisle before looking back to the cross behind the altar. *Please God; lend us Your strength tonight. We need You to guide us. We lay our lives in Your hands. We... I started this with the wrong intentions. I know that now. I shouldn't have tried to guess Your will. And now, as we stand on the doorstep of our doom, I ask You to do Your will. I accept whatever happens.*

He limped to the altar, opening the tabernacle. Pulling out the wine and wafers, he raised his eyes to the heavens, saying the blessings. As the two detectives reentered the church, Father Mike turned his attention to them.

"Communion? It may be our last."

Both Danny and Stan made the sign of the cross as they walked up the aisle toward the altar. "It's been awhile, but I can't think of anything else that would make me feel better right now. There's nothing like the anti-Christ to renew your faith."

The two men prayed as Father Mike finished consecrating the host. As he passed the wine, Father Mike felt a warm strength return to his pained extremities.

"Soon. He'll be here soon."

Lightning crashed with a blinding flash and was followed by a roar that shook the one-hundred-year old building. Before Father Mike could shake off the afterimages, the church was plunged into complete darkness. In the ensuing silence, rain began to pelt the roof.

"Damn electrical system."

Stan lit his lighter, holding it above his head to shine over as large of an area as possible. "It's a good thing I didn't quit yet."

"Power outage, just what we needed. It's not like we have to fight the anti-Christ or anything," Danny grumbled.

Father Mike hobbled to the hallway. "It's okay. We're in a

church. We've got more candles and candle holders than you can count. Stan, follow me with that lighter."

Stan cupped his hand in front of the tenuous flame as he walked to join Father Mike.

"We've got to hurry. I don't want Christian to get here before we're ready."

Danny shook his head. "Before we're ready to kneel before him?"

Stan turned back to face his partner. "Come on, Danny. Like the Father said, Have some faith."

"Yeah, I know. I'd just rather not have too many hands tied behind my back. I've only got two of them."

Chapter *29*

Exhausted, Father Mike plopped down on the pew as Danny and Stan positioned the last two floor candelabras. The whole church seemed to be in motion as the forty-something flames flickered to their own beat. Shadows from the wings of angel statues fluttered across the walls. Father Mike wiped at the sweat rolling down his forehead. *No power. No air conditioning. Perfect setting for a showdown.* He smiled. *Damn. I'm letting Danny's sarcasm take root in me.* He looked at the multicolored saints and angels smiling down on him from the stained glass windows. He could almost see their mouths moving in the dancing light, trying to give him advice. *How to kill him? Or how fast to run away?* He laughed. *Not on these feet. Not tonight.*

Danny approached the pew where Father Mike sat. "Do you want some more water, Father?"

Father Mike shook his head wearily. Danny fidgeted and turned to his partner.

"So, Stan?"

"Yeah?"

"Are you buying this yet?" Danny cracked a small smile.

"I think we're well past the point of buy in. It's balls to the wall time, now." He searched the area. "Where do you think we should do this?"

"I know he's the anti-Christ wearing superman's cape of invincibility, but the cop in me says seek cover anyway. That's the best place I see." He pointed behind the altar in the sanctuary.

Stan nodded affirmation and followed him up the steps. "And you, Father? Where are you going to be?"

"I don't know that it matters much for strategy, but I was front and center at the beginning of this. That needs to be my place now."

"But, Father..."

"It's okay, Stan." He gestured to the cross at the back of the church. "I know where I'll end up. I've made my peace with it. Maybe a show of confidence will throw him off a bit."

Stan shrugged. "Suit yourself. We're gonna hunker down behind a big piece of wood." Stan and Danny crouched down behind the altar, guns in hand resting on top of it. They watched the door expectantly.

"I know these things are no good against him, but I feel better with a little firepower between us." The church echoed with mechanical clacking as they both chambered rounds.

Father Mike frowned, watching the flickering candles. A shadow trailing behind the holy water font detached itself and slithered toward the front door. More shadows halted their random dancing and followed the first. In short time, despite the candles even spacing throughout the church, the front door was cloaked in impenetrable darkness. Stan and Danny crouched lower, leaving only their heads and guns showing above the altar.

"It's time." Father Mike made the sign of the cross.

The front door creaked open, barely visible behind the seething cloud of shadows. Stan and Danny strained to see through them. Slowly the darkness parted, allowing a figure to walk through. Dressed from head to toe in a flowing white robe, Christian emanated a soft glow as he entered the church. Danny gasped when he saw the crown of thorns on his head. He turned to the statue of Jesus and back to Christian, his mouth hanging open.

Christian paid no attention to the two detectives, focusing on Father Mike standing at the head of the aisle.

"Is this what you were going for twenty-five years ago? I've never lived up to your expectations, have I, Dad?"

"I'm not your father." Father Mike tried to stand as tall and straight as the pain would allow.

"Okay, step dad then. Or you might be better labeled as Dr. Frankenstein. How do you calm the beast? Will you play your violin?" As Christian raised his arms, the skin at his wrists ripped open, bleeding down and saturating the sleeves of his robe.

"Here I am, your creation. There you sit in opposition. Would you undo me? You and your Keystone Cops?" He cast his eyes in Danny's direction. "They can't help you now. I am strength and power. You are weak and judgmental. You don't even know how far off you are."

Father Mike held his head high. "You are pure evil. I held out hope for the longest time that there was a shred of a soul hidden in some lost corner of your being. No longer."

"And why is that, I wonder? Could it be that I was *asked* to leave..." Christian pointed up without taking his eyes off Father Mike. "His house? He didn't even show me the courtesy of doing it himself. He used my brothers Michael and Gabriel instead. And why?"

Father Mike frowned. "You wanted to be Him. You wanted to be God."

Christian dropped his hands. His eyes sucked the shadows surrounding him into them as the holy water font beside him cracked and exploded into stone shards. His hand patted his breast. Slowly, his face relaxed, and then he laughed.

"You say that like you were there. Please, enlighten me on what you *people* wrote down many centuries ago about something you did not witness. I believe your kind has a saying about there being two sides to every story. I never wanted to be God, Michael. I wanted to be like God. There's a big difference. For thousands of years, you people have been getting that part wrong. There are a lot of things about me that you've gotten wrong."

"You're a creature of pain and suffering. You are vindictive and thrive on bringing others down to your level. What else is there to know?"

"There isn't much more than that, I guess." Christian's face looked troubled as he pulled off the crown of thorns and tossed it onto the pew beside him. "Do you know what I want most?"

Christian tore off the stained robe, letting it fall into a heap on the floor. He stood before Father Mike in an impeccably tailored black Armani suit.

"I want what everyone wants, Mike. I want to be loved." For the first time since he walked into the church, he made eye contact with Stan and Danny, smiling weakly.

"I want back into Heaven. I want to be like we were before you came along." He walked forward as he spoke, slowly approaching the altar. "In the beginning, I asked over and over again, and I was denied. Do you know how that made me feel? Not only were *you humans* distracting Him from me and the rest of His angels, He chose *you* over *me*. I was his favored..." Shadows began peeling off the wall and circling his ankles.

"I *will* get back into Heaven. Do you want to know how?"

Stan aimed his gun at Christian's head. "Can I just shoot him now and shut him up?"

Father Mike walked to his right, trying to draw Christian's attention from the two detectives behind the altar. "Let him talk."

"God is most proud of the human soul. No matter how far you stray, no matter what atrocities you commit, *you* are His shining stars. Your bards through the years have sung that Satan collects souls to torture them." Christian spat towards a stained glass window depicting a saint. "I haven't collected souls to torment them. I've collected them to use as bargaining chips. The more I gather, the harder it will be for Him to deny me." Shadows continued to wind up his body, spinning around his wrists like bracelets. Christian continued to walk toward Father Mike.

"You can call me evil, but I'm just misunderstood, misrepresented. You can't fathom my nature." He smiled wryly. "Besides, I'll be happy to release all the souls I've collected as soon as He takes me back. All He has to do is let me return home." Christian's arms and legs were obscured by the writhing shapes. He waved his arms, indicating the two detectives and Father Mike.

"When you see Him tonight, please relay what I've told you. The number of souls I've gathered to this point will seem paltry compared to what is to come, and the suffering by those who don't come willingly will be unbearable."

Stan aimed his gun at Christian's head.

"Excuse me, Christian, or Lucifer, or whatever you want to call yourself. That's not going to happen." Stan turned to Father Mike. "I don't care if a bullet won't kill him. It's certainly bound to hurt. And he needs to hurt."

Stan cupped his left hand under his right, steadying his gun. "You're going back to your Hell."

"*Stan!*" Father Mike waved him back.

"*Be quiet!*"" Christian shouted at Father Mike, pointing with both hands. Two black shadows jumped off his wrists and flew at Father Mike, slithering through the air.

Danny stood suddenly, pulling the trigger on his gun. The repeated clicking was not the sound he expected. *Come on.* Working the action, he ejected the misfired cartridge, chambering another. Danny's gun misfired again as he watched the two shadows encircle Father Mike's wrists, lifting him off the ground.

Christian turned his head from Father Mike to Danny. "Those things don't work against me." He twirled his index finger. "But they are quite effective against you."

Danny's hands shook as the gun slowly turned back to point at his head. Sweat dripped from his forehead as the muscles on his arm stood out, but he couldn't stop the gun's progress. Flickering candlelight reflected on the fear in his eyes.

"*Kneel.*" Danny dropped to his knees, his gun still pointed at his head. He grimaced at the pain that shot up his legs from the impact with the floor.

Stan ran to Danny's side.

"*Both of you.*" Stan fell to his knees beside Danny.

Christian glanced at Father Mike, still hanging in the air. "Remember what I showed you? This is how it ends." As he flicked his wrist, Father Mike was thrown against the cross behind him, his arms splayed out to either side. The nails that Danny and Stan had pulled out earlier hovered in the air before him.

"Are you sure? You can still stop this, Mike."

"I've made many mistakes, Christian. I'm done with this one."

Christian nodded and the two five-inch nails rocketed across the space, impaling Father Mike's wrists. The shadows unwound themselves, returning back to orbiting Christian's wrists. Father Mike screamed as his weight pulled on the two piercings.

"I warned you, Mikey, more than once. You can't destroy me. Father Vincent was on the right track, but a couple years too late." He smiled. "Frankly, you were all screwed by a prophecy from almost a thousand years ago. It did nothing more than warn me what I would need to destroy to become invincible. The shroud that made me and could unmake me is no longer among us, and here I am. It's too bad your two friends here weren't there to pick Father Vincent up at the airport as planned." He turned back to face Stan and Danny.

Danny's eyes pleaded for help. Grabbing his hand, Stan added his own strength to pry the gun away from Danny's head, but to no avail.

"This has been way too easy. You know, it's a shame that the children have to pay for the sins of the Father." Christian watched the two struggle unsuccessfully with amusement. "Well, not really, especially since *you are* the sins of the Father." Christian approached the two detectives, stopping just in front of them.

Stan glanced over at his gun by the altar and frowned. *Wait, I've got the knife.* He smiled.

Christian continued, not noticing Stan's smile. "Everything was perfect before you came. *All* of this is your fault. But, the good news is that you've fixed the problem. You brought me here." He turned back to Father Mike, moaning from the cross. "By bringing me into this world, you've made it possible to bring this little impasse of mine to a swift conclusion. So, while my problem was caused by mankind, you..." He pointed a finger at Father Mike. "Are the reason it will end. Unfortunately, I'm going to have to kill all of you since I'm not sure that He'll take you, Father Mike."

Stan let go of Danny's hands. Still smiling.

"Yes. Submit. You can not win. There is simply no way. You are destined to be nothing more than a messenger boy. But, oh, the fun you'll have at the beginning of your journey."

Danny's eyes opened wide as his finger tightened on the trigger. He looked over pleadingly at Stan.

"He can't help you."

Reaching into his pocket, Stan pulled out the knife, concealing it as well as he could in his hand. He looked Christian in the eye and whispered so low even Danny couldn't hear.

"What? You'll have to speak up. *Father* Mike is making too much noise over there."

Stan whispered again, his face showing strain as if he was having trouble speaking. *Come on, damn you. Lean closer.*

As Christian bent down to hear what Stan was saying, Stan lunged with the knife. Light from a nearby candle flashed off the blade and into Christian's face. He pulled back just before the knife could touch him.

"What do we have here?"

A shadow jumped off his arm and wound around Stan's wrist, holding it immobile.

"Spunky, right up until the end, huh? What were you thinking that toy would do to me?" Christian shook his head, ticking his tongue. "And now what do I do with you?"

He smiled as he looked back to Danny, still holding his gun

to his head. "Perfect."

Danny sighed as his arm relaxed, his gun hand falling from his head.

"Stan, you will be the first. Please give my regards..." Christian waved at him, dropping him to his knees. "And my message to your maker."

Swirling black enveloped Danny's arm, twisting it to his right. The gun steadied, aimed at Stan. *No! I won't do this.*

"Pull the trigger, Danny. Go on. It's like scratching an itch. Like an itch, you'll find that scratching only intensifies the feeling."

The undulating shadow began to glow, radiating heat. Danny's arm shook with pain as his sleeve smoldered. Stan stared wide-eyed at Danny.

"Come on. Do it. You will pull the trigger of your own volition. He who lives by the sword dies by the sword." He clinched his fist and the shadow grew brighter, smoke rising from Danny's arm.

I can't. The knife is our only hope. If I shoot Stan... "Stan, do something. I don't know how much longer I can hold out."

Stan smelled scorched skin as he watched the wavering gun. He pleaded for his muscles to move, even if only in his hand so he could toss the knife to Danny, but nothing responded. He remained kneeling before Christian, just as Father Mike had described earlier. *Have faith, he said. He is overconfident... With good reason. And now I am about to die.* He tore his eyes away from the gun and looked at Father Mike, spiked to the cross. *I know I haven't prayed much, but Lord, please help us. We only want to stop this madness.*

A cool numbness spread through his body. Peace flooded his mind.

"*No!*" Danny shouted as his finger convulsed reflexively. The crack of the gun echoed through the church. The knife clattered across the wood floor as Stan fell. It spun to rest behind the altar a few feet past the spreading pool of blood.

"You god-damned mother fucker."

"I'll own the first, but not the second." Christian chuckled. "Do you hate God yet? If He was a just God, then why didn't He stop me? You have no idea how many times I've asked Him to."

Danny stared at Stan's body, seeing no movement, no sign of life.

"Don't worry. Your turn is coming soon."

Sorry, partner. I'll make him pay, somehow. Pain radiated up his arm. *Where's that damn knife?* He searched the floor. *Crap.* He saw it gleaming under the cross where Father Mike hung. He tried to catch his eyes, but Father Mike's head was slumped on his shoulder.

"And now, what to do with *you?*" Christian straightened the lapel on his suit, then wiped at his sleeve. "I think you may have gotten some of Stan on my Armani. Such a shame."

"Keep..." Father Mike's voice was strained, sounding more like a frog. "Faith."

"Keep faith? How? Stan's dead, you're being crucified for the second time tonight, and my damn gun won't work except when *he* wants it to." He pointed at Christian.

"Yes," Christian whispered. "Don't call it giving up; it's giving in. You always seemed like the pragmatic type to me. Tell you what; I'll give you one more chance. Ask *Him* to show Himself. If He listens to you, I'll let you live."

"*Fuck you,*" Danny spat.

Movement on the far wall caught his attention. Father Mike struggled to move his arms. *But they're nailed...*

"Wrong answer." Christian held his hands outstretched in Danny's direction. Two dark wisps snaked from his fingers, extending to Danny's neck. Christian smiled as he pulled them like ropes, watching them coil tightly around his neck.

Fuck. Dropping his gun, Danny grasped frantically at the shadows, finding no purchase. His fingers gouged his neck trying to loosen their hold. Danny's face turned red as he fought for air.

"Remember my message, Danny."

He fell forward onto his hands, the muscles on his neck bulging with effort. Pushing off with his hands, he crawled a step toward Christian. He stopped, lightheaded. A dark wisp whipped from the side and yanked his arms out from under him, toppling him onto his side. Lying on the floor, unable to muster the energy to move, black dots floated across his eyes. *This is it. Wait? What the?*

Through his blurred vision, Danny saw Father Mike pull his left hand off of the nail that had impaled it to the cross. Biting back a yell, Father Mike swung down, hanging on his other hand still attached to the cross. Fresh blood soaked the bandage Danny had applied earlier. *I've got to distract Christian so he doesn't see this. It could be our last chance.* Danny fought with his remaining strength to push himself back onto his knees.

"Well aren't you the stubborn one." Christian backhanded the air in front of Danny, slamming him across the sanctuary into the far wall. Danny's eyes rolled up into his head as he slid to the floor, knocking over a candelabrum.

"And now..." As Christian began to turn back to Father Mike, he heard a noise at the front of the church.

"What now?" He spun toward the door, not seeing Father Mike struggling to free his other hand.

"Mother?"

Mary stood in the open doorway, framed by the light from the streetlamp in front of the church. But for the touch of gray in her hair, she looked exactly like he remembered her as a child. She wore her favorite church dress, a familiar sight over the years at St. Michael's. Her features were softened in the glimmering light cast by the candles.

At first, Christian thought she smiled at him, but it was a trick of the light. A frown furrowed her forehead as she stepped into the church.

"Christian, you've got to stop this."

Christian stood transfixed, his eyes fading as he watched her. He thought he heard a yelp behind him, but ignored it as he stared at his mother.

"Christian, I love you. We can still make this right."

He pushed his hand into his pocket, feeling a timeworn piece of paper, the same page he'd carried every day since he wrote it so many years ago. The light sucked out of his eyes, as they once again became solid obsidian.

"No. You are the same to me as all the rest." He waved his arm around the church without taking his eyes off of her. From the side of the room he had flung Danny, the light brightened. He heard flames from the overturned candles licking up the wall.

"We don't have much time here, Mother. I'd rather not hurt you, but I will if you try to stop me."

"Oh, Christian." She took another step down the aisle, looking past him. "It's not me you're hurting, but yourself."

"Stop right there. I am Lucifer, not a child. I've existed for eons. I don't need you or my so called step father." He turned to point at Father Mike, but nearly knocked him down.

Father Mike stood, slightly hunched over, within arms reach. Christian looked up at the cross, surprised. Blood dripped from the ends of the nails still sticking from in the wood.

"What?" Christian looked confused, milky clouds swirling through his eyes.

"Faith," Father Mike whispered.

"What?"

"It's what separates us from you."

Christian shook his head and then smiled. "It doesn't matter. You can't do anything to me."

"You were never given a chance to doubt God. Your love was automatic, a given. We..." A pop from the burgeoning fire distracted him. "We give our love from faith, never having truly been in his presence. That is what fascinates him about us. It is why he gave us free will, and it's what gives us more power than you. Faith. A simple thing you were never given a chance of having. Faith is why I'm here."

Christian chuckled. "You're here to die. You are born, you

blink, and then you die. I'll be happy to complete that for you. Faith." He spat on the ground. "That's what I think of your faith."

"*Christian!*"

"Sorry, Mary, but if you don't want to see this, then you should leave now. Besides..." He turned to the spreading flames. "You really should get out before *that* gets any bigger."

Father Mike looked over, amazed at how fast the fire had spread. "I guess it's time to finish this."

"Yes. Yes it is." Christian put his hands on either side of Father Mike's head. "*If* he takes you up there, you can tell him all about how your faith overpowered me." Father Mike screamed as the hands tightened.

Christian saw the glint of firelight on the knife out of the corner of his eye before he felt the searing pain of it entering his side. Father Mike's scream was drowned out by the piercing cry Christian emitted.

Dropping his hands from Father Mike's face, he stumbled back, knife still embedded in his side. He looked down in surprise. Turning blindingly white, the blade sucked the whirling shadows into its light.

"What? How did you?" Christian fell to his knees, looking up to Father Mike.

"The prophecy. It said from whence it comes shall the remedy be found. I destroyed the shroud. How?"

Father Mike looked at him sadly. "I don't know anything about the prophecy, but it seems to me that it wasn't wrong."

"But the shroud..."

Father Mike shook his head. "Yes, you came from the shroud, indirectly. More specifically, you came from the blood scrapings we took from the shroud. Thankfully, Gunther is a very curious scientist. He used the minimum necessary to make a clone. The rest he saved to study. He had just enough left to coat the blade of that simple knife."

Father Mike felt the heat radiating from the fire across the church. He heard sirens in the distance.

"Blood of Christ." He made the sign of the cross.

The churning mass of shadows separated into individual wisps, slithering out the front door.

Christian reached down to grab the knife, but it flared even brighter. Black oil began pouring out of the wound like blood.

"No! This is my body," Christian croaked.

The light flowing from the blade faded until it was once again a normal looking knife as the last of the dark liquid poured onto the floor. It pooled beside Christian, churning and bubbling.

"Thy will be done."

The liquid rolled across the floor and down the aisle, leaving a scorched trail where it passed. Mary jumped onto the nearest pew as it passed her, hissing like a snake. After it passed, she rushed to Christian's side, cradling his head in her lap. He struggled for every breath as her tears fell on his face. She brushed the hair away from his face, looking into his bright blue eyes.

"I haven't seen the true blue of those eyes in a long time."

Father Mike knelt beside her, cringing in pain as he steadied himself with his injured hands.

"He's gone, now." Christian fumbled at his side, pulling the knife out. Red blood blossomed on his suit.

"Mother, I'm cold."

Her eyes welled with tears. "I know, baby. I know."

Father Mike grasped his hand loosely with his own. "I'm sorry, son... for everything."

Christian took a deep ragged breath and then slumped back. Father Mike passed his fingers over Christian's eyes, closing them.

"Father Mike?" Danny's voice brought him back to the present. He turned to see Danny pulling himself across the floor with one arm.

"We need to get out of here before this whole place comes down."

Father Mike looked up, noticing that the sanctuary was totally engulfed in flames.

"Mary, can you help Danny? I'm going to bring Christian's body out."

"I think. Can you stand?"

"With help. Thank you." Mary helped Danny up, draping his arm around her shoulder.

Father Mike picked Christian's body off the floor, groaning in pain as the extra weight pressed down on his bandaged feet. Before turning toward the front door, he took one last look at the sanctuary. The flames parted briefly, showing the cross hanging on the back wall before flaring up again. He turned back and saw a firefighter in the doorway helping Mary and Danny down the steps. Limping, he followed.

Chapter *30*

Jason pumped on the Christian's chest while his partner squeezed the air bag. The ambulance's siren screamed through the back of the vehicle.

"Still no pulse?"

"No, and I can't tell why. The knife wound didn't hit any arteries or major organs, and there are no other wounds I can find. There is no medical reason why this man shouldn't be alive and breathing right now."

They bounced in the air as the ambulance raced over a pothole. Jason picked up the defibrillator paddles.

He squirted gel on one of the paddles and rubbed them together. "Charging."

"*Clear!*" He placed both paddles on Christian's torso, releasing the charge. Christian's body arched off the stretcher, then slumped back down. The machine continued with a solid tone.

"Still no pulse." Christian's left hand fell open, dropping a worn page to the floor.

"Charging."

Jason's partner picked the paper off the floor, curious. Faded text lined the page, still readable.

You were there in the beginning
clouds in Your eyes
and stars falling from Your head
I was whole and parts
and more than the sum of both
and You were there

I stood beside You with sunset hair
wearing living rainbow vestments
while I tried on Your gift
waxen wings
and to the sky We rose
with tambourine laughter
all day and all night
We truly were

Them You brought them
both of them insipid on the surface
but beneath boiled failure and grandeur
in a puerile stew
and nothing was the same

You were charmed
even as they betrayed
You were enthralled
even as they warped Your words
and You forgave

Here I stand now
mere parts
not whole
twilight eyes stare through my hands
as I stretch and flex my one possession
the pair of waxen wings

At first I dance the wind to a forlorn dirge
slow sweeps passing inches from the ground
but soon memory takes the lead
and I dance the Grand Waltz
would that Your eyes would stray my way
if I flew higher
then maybe...

Looking down I watch them slaughter yet another
and a tear falls from Your eye
to flood the plains
but you are beguiled

I reach for the sun
and feel wetness on my back
surely You weep for me
but all that remains are empty sockets
where wings once grew
and the rush of air

Would that my tears
could flood the world
for me to drown

Alas, not to be
And so I fall...
And so I fall.

"Clear!"

Christian's body jumped up from the stretcher, falling back after a second. The tone paused, and then beeped.

"Hey, Gino. I've got a pulse. Come on. Put that down and help me out. Let's get this guy stabilized."

The siren echoed off the nearby houses as the ambulance sped toward the hospital. The driver turned back to the two paramedics. "Looks like that storm is finally breaking up."

About the Author

David W Moore III was born in New Orleans, where the rich cultural history helped to flesh out his semi-surreal style. His writings have also been published in *The Cartys Poetry Journal*, *The Medulla Review, Canyon Voices* and the anthology, *22 Naked Bodies Within*. He has two previous books in print, *From the Midst of the Maelstrom* and *Marie Laveau's Hot Pink Hearse.*

He attended St. Paul's High School in Covington, Louisiana and graduated from Tulane University. He married his wife, Amelia in 1991 and has one daughter, Mary Elizabeth. They currently reside in Uptown New Orleans.

Follow David on Facebook as David W Moore III~Author, and on his website:

Http://www.davidwmooreiii.webs.com

David also juxtaposes art with poetry at:

http://www.poet-art.webs.com

Made in the USA
Lexington, KY
05 November 2013